D0498501

BY JOSH MALERMAN

Bird Box

A House at the Bottom of a Lake

Black Mad Wheel

Goblin

Unbury Carol

Pearl (previously published as *On This, the Day of the Pig*)

Inspection

Malorie

Pearl

Pearl

PREVIOUSLY PUBLISHED AS

On This, the Day of the Pig

Josh Malerman

NEW YORK

Published in the United States by Del Rey, an imprint of Random House, a division of Penguin Random House LLC, New York.

DEL REY is a registered trademark and the CIRCLE colophon is a trademark of Penguin Random House LLC.

Originally published in hardcover in the United States as *On This, the Day of the Pig* by Cemetery Dance Publications, in 2018.

LIBRARY OF CONGRESS CATALOGING-IN-PUBLICATION DATA
Names: Malerman, Josh, author.
Title: Pearl / Josh Malerman.
Other titles: On this, the day of the pig
Description: New York: Del Rey, [2021] | "Previously
published as On this, the day of the pig"
Identifiers: LCCN 2021005266 (print) | LCCN 2021005267 (ebook) | ISBN
9780593237830 (hardcover; acid-free paper) | ISBN 9780593237847 (ebook)
Subjects: GSAFD: Horror fiction.
Classification: LCC PS3613.A43535 O5 2021 (print) |
LCC PS3613.A43535 (ebook) | DDC 813/.6—dc23
LC record available at https://lccn.loc.gov/2021005266
LC ebook record available at https://lccn.loc.gov/2021005267

Printed in the United States of America on acid-free paper

randomhousebooks.com

1 2 3 4 5 6 7 8 9

First Del Rey Edition

Book design by Caroline Cunningham
Title-page background image: iStock/AngelaHarrodPhotography

This book is dedicated to every living thing on Earth,

past, present, future.

Pearl

1

Sing for me, Brother Paul. Sing for Pearl.
Let Pearl know.

2

Up Murdock, away from downtown Chowder, passing the wheat fields and the forest east of the road, tall pines that unfolded like a long, complex bedspread, separating Chowder from Goblin and the other less agricultural areas of mid-Michigan, they pulled onto Grandpa's gravel drive just before noon. Sherry eyed Jeff briefly, checking to see if maybe he'd had a change of heart. If maybe he was smiling like he used to. Grandpa's world was a fun world if you let it be. The farm. Where Jeff and Aaron used to ride the horses and chase chickens and oink at the pigs. Where the brothers spent nights outside, sometimes without a tent, sometimes just on their backs on the grassy slope that led from the farmhouse to the barn. This place was childhood. This place was supposed to be special. The farm *meant* something.

"Doesn't it?"

Sherry hadn't meant to say that out loud.

"Doesn't what?" Aaron asked. But Sherry didn't answer. And Jeff stared at her like he might've known what she was thinking.

Sherry parked the wagon by the front porch steps. She looked up to see Grandpa standing behind the screen door. He waved.

"Hey, Dad," Mom called from behind the rolled-up window.

Grandpa waved again, as if maybe he'd forgotten he'd already done so.

His thin white hair stirred with an easy autumn breeze. Sherry wondered what was on his mind, what clutter of his own.

She and the boys got out of the car.

"Hello, Sherry," Grandpa said. "Hello, boys." He looked tired. Sherry always said Grandpa was toughened by farm life. Jeff used to believe that.

Sherry hugged him at the door.

"Thought I'd put them to work today," Grandpa said, nodding to the boys.

"That sounds good," Mom said. "They could use it." And it would give her a chance to grovel in private.

It had been a hard summer.

Stuff it in the mind-bag.

Yes. The mind-bag. The secret, unseen place where Sherry stuffed all her dark thoughts, her absurd worries, the unprovoked hunches she'd felt most of her life, the premonitions of Pearl.

Grandpa squinted down at his grandsons.

"I was hoping Aaron could collect some eggs for me. And Jeff . . . maybe Jeff would like to feed the . . ."

Jeff held his breath.

Don't say feed the pigs, Grandpa. Don't say Pearl.

And why not?

". . . horses," Grandpa finished.

Sherry smiled, but her own private stresses were drawn firmly on her face. Often she imagined the mind-bag hanging on a curled finger in an otherwise lightless room. A place only she could find it, hidden from the prying eyes of Chowder, Michigan, and the whole wide world beyond. But recently that bag had been relocated to her hip, a place anybody could see, if they cared to look. Yes, Sherry Kopple had started wearing her emotions on her sleeve, a look she didn't quite love. Her recent anxiety stuck out like the stump of a third foot and was about as useful to boot.

"How's that sound, boys?" Grandpa asked. "Good enough?"

The brothers nodded. Yes. Eggs and horses. Safe areas on the farm.

Grandpa walked them into the farmhouse, through the kitchen, to the back door.

Aaron followed Mom outside, a foot from the cellar door in the grass, but Jeff paused at the screen, looking down the slope to where the evergreens hid the pigpen.

"The horses can't come to you," Grandpa said. And when Jeff looked up, he saw all three of them were waiting.

Aaron laughed at him as he exited the farmhouse.

Grandpa led him to the stables, and on the way, Jeff heard them breathing behind the trees.

The pigs.

The sound remained lodged in his mind, in his bones, as he passed them, loud, louder than the horses were, even when he stood inches from the muzzle of a mare.

"This here's their favorite," Grandpa said, fishing a handful of damp, yellowing oats from a brown wooden trough. "But you gotta be a bit careful 'cause they'll chew your fingers clean off."

Jeff looked up and saw Grandpa smiling, sadly, behind a show of white whiskers. His eyebrows had always remained dark as midnight, though.

"Really?" Jeff asked.

"No," Grandpa said. "Not really. But it was fun to see the look on your face."

It felt good. Falling for a joke.

Through the open door, Jeff saw Aaron eyeing the chicken coop, readying himself to pick some eggs.

"Enjoy," Grandpa said. "But don't eat more than the horses."

Another joke. Good. Felt good.

Then Grandpa left him alone in the stables. Jeff looked up, into the eyes of the brown horse he stood by.

"Hello," he said. "You hungry?"

It felt good to talk. Felt good to pet the horse's nose. To feel the strong neck and shoulders.

"You remember me, right?" Jeff smiled at the horse. Wished it could smile back. "My name is—"

Jeff . . .

Jeff stepped quickly from the animal. The black emotional chasm that came with the sound of his name was wider, darker, deeper than any nightmare he'd known before. As if, in that moment, his ill-defined apprehensions about the farm had been galvanized, and everything Jeff was afraid of was true.

He dropped a handful of grains and stepped farther from the mare. Wide-eyed, he stared at her, waiting to hear it again, waiting to hear his name spoken here in the stables.

But the horse hadn't said his name.

"Mom?" he called, looking to the stable door.

Come, Jeff.

Jeff backed up to the stable wall.

"Aaron? Are you screwing with me?"

It could have been Aaron. It *should* have been Aaron.

But Jeff knew it wasn't.

He folded his arms across his chest, combating a cold wind that passed through the stable.

Come to me, Jeff . . .

It sounded like the voice was traveling on the wind. Or like it *was* the wind. It was made of something his own voice didn't have. He didn't want to say what it really sounded like. Didn't want to say it sounded like the voice was coming from outside the stables, up the hill, from the pigpen behind the trees.

Jeff exited the stables, stood outside under the sun. Aaron was out of sight. Mom was probably in the farmhouse, talking to Grandpa.

It wasn't pretty, watching Mom beg for money.

Jeff . . .

It was coming from the evergreens. Jeff knew this now, could hear this now, and he wouldn't have been shocked to see a farmhand peeking out between the branches using his pointer finger to beckon him closer.

Jeff . . . come here . . .

Without deciding to do it, Jeff took the dirt path to the trees. He crouched on one knee and split the branches. Through them, he saw the pigpen and the pigs lazing in the mud.

Jeff stood up.

He didn't want to get any closer. Didn't want to be alone out here at all.

He ran up the grassy hill to the farmhouse.

JEFF

Louder now. Strong enough to root Jeff to the ground.

He looked over his shoulder back to the hidden pigpen.

Come, Jeff. Sing for me . . .

Cautiously, Jeff walked back down the hill, to the end of the row of evergreens.

Most of the pigs were gathered together at the far side of the fence. One paced the length of the pen, bobbing his head, snorting, half covered in mud. It looked to Jeff as if he was thinking.

Jeff looked back to the chicken coop. No Aaron. Still.

When he turned back to the pen, Pearl was all he could see.

Pearl.

Sitting on his ass like a person might, his front hooves limp at the sides of his belly, his head was cocked slightly to the side, his pink ears straight, high above his head. His bad eye looked dark, hidden, but his good one was fixed on Jeff.

In it, Jeff saw an intelligence that scared him.

He didn't think a pig could "stare" the same way a man did. Yet Pearl *was* tracking him, following his lead, as Jeff stepped slowly toward the pen.

By the time he reached the gate, Jeff was breathing too hard. Felt like he'd done a lot of work. Felt like he'd unloaded a truckload of hay. Felt weak and skinny and cold and exposed and . . .

Dumb, Jeff thought. *Like he's smarter than you.*

Yes, *dumb.* That was the worst of it. And Pearl, it seemed, knew it.

A half smile appeared under the pig's snout, or maybe it was just the way his lips naturally curled up at their ends.

The pacing pig pissed, and it sounded like a hose shot at the mud.

"Hello, Pearl," Jeff said. He felt like he had to. Like it would have been insane not to—like he would have been admitting something too dark if he was too afraid to say hello to a pig.

The other pigs seemed roused by Jeff's voice. They shuffled in the mud, sat up. One lifted his head to get a better look.

Jeff fingered the latch. Pearl watched him.

Staring.

Assessing.

Planning?

Jeff pulled his fingers away. A streak of shame ran down his back, like he'd come close to letting something very bad out of the pen.

In the distance, Jeff heard Aaron calling out for Grandpa.

Pearl didn't take his good eye off Jeff. He sat—regal, aristocratic, impossibly refined.

"Okay," Jeff said. "Let's see how smart you are."

Jeff shoved off from the fence and felt the full force of an autumn breeze tousle his fair hair. It felt good. Like he needed it; like a second wind. He ran to the shed between the barn and the pen and burst through the wooden doors. Empowered, he grabbed hold of a sack of pig feed and carried it back to the pen.

"Here, Pearl," Jeff called angrily. "Open this."

He tossed the bag over the fence. It plopped five feet from where Pearl sat. The pig looked at the sack.

"Go on," Jeff said. "Open it!"

Two pigs from the pile got up to check out the bag. A big black-and-white one and a huge brown one that looked like two in one. They sniffed the bag. The brown one took hold of it and dragged it a foot.

Pearl looked at Jeff again.

"Not smart enough to open a bag of feed?" Jeff taunted. It felt good. Felt good to taunt Pearl. "Try another one!"

Jeff ran back to the shed. He grabbed a hammer and a nail and returned quickly to the pigpen. There were three pigs at the sack of feed now. A pink one had joined the other two.

Jeff shook the fence.

"You see this. Pearl? This is moving because the post is loose. You know what a post is? Do you? And if you did, would you know how to fix it?"

Jeff put the nail against the wood and nailed it in with the hammer.

"You wanna try, Pearl? You think you could figure out how?"

Jeff tossed the hammer and nail into the pen. *Hell*, it felt good to taunt him.

Jeff ran back to the shed. He grabbed an axe.

"Pearl! You wouldn't know what to do with this if I handed it to you!"

The warm wind pressed against Jeff's face, causing the ends of his lips to rise up, like Pearl's.

He held the axe high over his head and laughed, and his laughter was taken, sent spiraling behind him, lost to the wind.

Pearl didn't move, only stared. The crinkled, burnt skin that covered half his bad eye looked like the rotten wood of a fence post. Like a piece of the farmhouse's shingled roof had fallen to his face.

Carrying the axe, Jeff unlatched the gate.

He opened it.

"Let's see how smart you are."

The other pigs eyed him as he entered the pen; watching him out the sides of their faces. This close, their snouts looked longer.

Jeff stomped through the mud, intentionally trying to scare Pearl. He tossed the axe into the mud at the pig's feet.

"Go on," Jeff said. "Use it! Do something with it! Go on! Show me how smart you are, Pearl!"

Pearl looked down at the axe.

"Go on, Pearl! I'm not afraid of you!"

Another pig, another black-and-white one, sniffed the axe.

"Can't figure it out?" Jeff mocked. "Too much for you, Pearl? Here, let me show you. Let me show you how to use it!"

Jeff crouched and came up gripping the tool. He ran a finger along the sharp edge.

"This is for cutting," Jeff said. He swung hard against the fence. Wood splintered. "You see? It's a tool, Pearl. You don't know how to use tools. You don't even know how to open the gate!"

Jeff swung the axe into the mud. The ground exploded up, splattering Jeff and Pearl together.

Jeff wiped the muck from his cheeks. He lifted the axe again.

"You know what else it's for, Pearl?" He smiled at the pig. Pearl stared back. "It's for *killing*, Pearl. Killing pigs like you."

He took a step toward Pearl.

Up close, Pearl's belly looked bigger, the folds more defined, the nipples dangling like sores.

"Scared yet, Pearl?"

Pearl shifted his hind hooves, and for a beat Jeff thought Pearl was going to stand right up. Stand up and face him.

"I'll show you how to use the Goddamn thing."

Jeff swung the axe down hard, splitting the neck of the black-and-white pig.

Blood erupted, geyserlike, splattering Jeff's nose and lips. Jeff swung again.

The pig screamed, and the terrible sound rose up, and somewhere far away Jeff thought he heard his brother, Mom, Grandpa, the whole world coming to get him.

Jeff swung again, and this swing, his last, lopped the pig's head clean off.

Jeff dropped to his knees and lifted the severed head. It was heavier than the axe.

"You see, Pearl?" Jeff raved. "That's how it's done, Pearl! But you're not smart enough to do it! You're not smart enough to know!"

Pearl only stared. Unflinching. Unmoved.

As Jeff held the pig's Mona Lisa gaze, clarity struck painfully hard.

He was on his knees in the pigpen, holding a bloody head. It was one of Grandpa's pigs. He'd killed it.

"Jesus!" Jeff screamed and leaped from the mud. He stepped back and fell over the plump, headless body, bleeding out.

Jeff fell on his ass.

He looked up and saw Pearl was sitting only a foot away.

He's gonna get up, Jeff. He's gonna get up, waddle over here, and eat your face clean off!

Jeff scuttled to standing and backed up to the fence.

"You made me do it!" Jeff yelled, more afraid now, more ashamed than he'd known was possible. "I'd never do something like that! You made me do it, Pearl!"

Behind him, voices. Urgent. Grandpa hollering. Mom screaming.

"Jeff?! What did you do?!"

Aaron was staring at him, wide-eyed, gripping the fence.

"Jeff," Aaron said, the innocence in his voice so obvious. "Why'd you do that, Jeff?"

Why? Because Pearl made me do it.

But Jeff knew it was worse than that.

Pearl made him *want* to do it.

Grandpa entered the pen quickly and took hold of Jeff by the back of his shirt. He dragged him out.

"I didn't mean to," Jeff said. But it didn't look that way. It looked like there was an axe in the mud, an axe that Jeff had carried into the pen himself.

Grandpa didn't yell. He only held out an open palm to his grandson.

"Calm down. It's all right."

But Grandpa's eyes were on Pearl.

He knows, Jeff said. *He knows that Pearl made me do it.*

But these ideas, these thoughts, came too fast, flashed too bright, and the guilt Jeff felt was crippling, as if he'd been irrevocably changed.

"Dad," Mom said. "Dad, I'm so sorry. Oh my God, I'm so sorry!"

Grandpa waved a hand.

"No reason to be sorry. Boy needed to learn eventually. Just got a head start is all."

Too fast, too bright, too much guilt.

"You all right, son?" Grandpa held Jeff's chin between his forefinger and thumb.

"Why haven't you killed Pearl yet, Grandpa?"

And his voice was humiliation, his voice was disgrace.

Is it because Pearl hasn't let you? Because Pearl tells you what you can and cannot do?

"Go on and get cleaned up," Grandpa said, waving toward the farmhouse. "I'll take care of the mess."

"Dad?" Mom asked, looking from her son to her father.

"Go on," Grandpa said again, sternly.

Mom went to touch Jeff on the shoulder but stopped herself. This wasn't like the time Aaron and Jeff lit firecrackers in the basement. This wasn't like the time Aaron got caught stealing a dirty magazine from John's Party Store.

"Jeff?" Mom asked, eyeing the grisly remains in the pen. Trying not to look at Pearl.

Jeff started walking up the grassy hill. He wiped blood from his face. He looked over his shoulder and saw Grandpa carefully un-

latching the gate. He saw Pearl, too, sitting on his ass at the far end
of the pen, one eye half open, presiding over the split pig like a
hangman.

"Pearl made me do it," Jeff said, to nobody. And then, again the
correction:

Pearl made me want *to do it.*

But this was deranged. This was not the right way to think. And
by the time Jeff reached the farmhouse, the idea of a pig controlling a person, speaking to him without opening his mouth, was the
craziest thing he'd ever heard. And for that, he was crazy for believing it.

Alone in the bathroom, Mom waiting in the living room, Jeff
washed his hands of the mud, washed his lips of death, but was
unable to rinse off the feeling that things were different now; unable to uncover the boy beneath the blood; thinking, oh no, I'm
different now, changed forever, and today, this day, will lead to
others . . . other days like this day . . . and nothing will ever be the
same again. Not the good stuff. Not the bad.

Nothing.

3

Mitch Klein heard the rumor at the same time everyone else inside Morgan High School did. That's because Evan McComber snuck into the main office during lunch and announced it over the PA.

"Holy shit, everybody!" Evan started. And every teacher in Morgan reached for their cell phones. "A seventh grader beheaded a pig on Kopple Farm!"

It was just vague enough to launch a hundred ancillary rumors all their own. The kid was on acid. The kid is insane. The kid is walking the halls of Morgan now, swinging the very same bloodied axe! *Look out!*

No matter what the kid did, it was big news in a farming community like Chowder, even if Kopple Farm was a sure four miles out of downtown. When a person's truck breaking down in a snowbank is seasonal gossip, news like this went straight to the front page. But, of course, to some, the bigger news was Evan

McComber and the trouble he was going to get in for sounding off like an animated rabbit over the public address system. And Evan did get into trouble, but not much. Sent home for the day was a reasonable punishment, a thrilling end to a surprise broadcast of a cuss word.

But most people were fixated on what he'd said the kid had done.

Mitch Klein was one of them.

"He said another pig in the pen made him do it," Jerry said, taking a hit of grass before handing the joint back to Mitch. "Pukin' good stuff, my friend."

"He said what?"

Mitch and Jerry were sitting cross-legged in the woods behind Morgan High. Neither was going to pass physics no matter how hard they tried, and so they decided together not to.

Besides, getting high was a lot more fun when you had something like this to talk about.

Jerry shook a leaf from his short, curly hair, his baby face in a pout.

"That's what I heard. Kid said his brother said another pig made him do it."

"Wait. Like *told* him to do it?"

"Yeah. I guess so."

"Pukin', man."

Being the only members of the Plastic Satanic Club, Mitch and Jerry were always pining for shit like this. Only it never happened so close to home.

"I wanna see that pig," Mitch said.

"So go see it."

"Don't you?"

Jerry shrugged.

"Yeah. Kind of."

"Kind of? What's a pig gotta be like for a kid to think it's talking to him?"

Jerry pondered this.

"I think the bigger question is obvious. What kind of kid would think that a pig was talking to him in the first place?"

Mitch leaned back on his elbows, crushing leaves and dead berries. He handed the joint back to Jerry.

At the forest's edge, Susan Marx walked the grass. The vision of her was clipped by the thin trees obscuring their view, but neither Mitch nor Jerry was complaining. Her legs were unmistakable. Pure white pillars built beneath her short yellow skirt. Her blond hair bobbed like a pillow on her shoulders.

"Fuck," Mitch whispered, feeling the high grip him. "I will never get enough of Susan Marx."

"She's like watching a movie," Jerry said. "Pukin'."

"Sure is. A beginning, a middle, and an end. All in one girl."

As Susan passed, the two friends turned in unison, craning their necks at once, milking the moment until she was long out of view.

"I still wanna see that pig," Mitch said.

"Go for it," Jerry said. "Or talk to the kid first."

"I'm not talking to a seventh grader about a pig."

"Why not? Maybe he can join the Plastic Satanic Club."

Mitch considered this.

"Okay," he said. "Maybe I will talk to him."

"Yeah. Talk to him. Tell him you're interested. He's probably freaked out, though. Tread lightly."

"Well, I wasn't planning on kidnapping him. I'll be nice."

Stoned, they left the woods and returned to class. Math for Jerry, health for Mitch. In health, they watched a film about childbirth. They actually got to see the baby emerging from a real-life vagina. Intense stuff. Mitch was glad he was stoned for it. *The Miracle of Life.* Great fucking movie. After the movie, they watched a PSA. It featured a stoned father at his daughter's graduation. A voice-over warned the class not to be stoned for life's big events. Mitch laughed until he caught Mrs. Hamm staring at him.

A whisper behind him. Mitch heard the name *Jeff.*

Two students were discussing Kopple Farm.

"What do you know about it?" Mitch whispered.

They smiled.

"Give us some grass."

"No way."

Mitch spun around and faced the film before spinning back, unprompted.

"Okay. I'll give you some. What do you know?"

"We know his name."

"Well? Who was it?"

"Jeff."

"Jeff who?"

The two shits smiled.

"Get us a beer, too."

"*A* beer? The two of you want *a* beer?"

Even in the dark room Mitch could see them blush.

"Do you wanna know the kid's name or what?"

Mitch shook his head.

"Never mind. No. You two are too much."

He watched the film. Then he turned around again.

"Fuck it. Sure. A beer. What's his last name?"

"Donkey piss," the smaller of the two boys said.

"Come on."

"Jeff Newton. Get us a beer."

Mitch ran his fingers through his long, black hair. He set his glasses lower on his big nose. Fuck, it felt good to be stoned. He was super excited, too. Excited to head out to that old man's farm. Excited to take some photos of that pig.

Maybe he'd even try talking to it.

Mitch laughed out loud, and Mrs. Hamm wagged a finger at him. She pointed to the film as if to say, *This movie is about you.*

Mitch shook his head no.

No way, Mrs. Shamm. My movie is a whole lot better than this one. And it's just beginning.

4

Pearl sat on his ass at the far end of the pen, his forelegs up off the ground and resting upon his belly. The sun baked the mud on his tough skin, and though he looked like he was smiling, he wasn't.

It never amused him, watching the others fight for feed.

After a spat, Peter, the largest of the remaining hogs, loaded his mouth with cornmeal and carried it across the pen. He dropped it at Pearl's feet, grunted and bobbed his head like the fool Pearl believed him to be. Pearl nodded in return, praising the hog for his service. It was wise to be good to the fools. When Peter left him, waddling back to the others, the farmer was suddenly visible, standing at the wood-post fence.

Though he didn't know the word for it, Pearl understood the farmer was watching him. He even understood that he was watching him closely.

Pearl tilted his head, his damaged eye half closed, his lips curled up at their corners.

The farmer scratched at the white stubble on his wrinkled chin, and Pearl saw a single bead of sweat travel down the farmer's face, a shining thought escaping the old man's mind. Pearl couldn't know that the farmer had parked his truck up on Murdock, out of sight of the pigs, so they wouldn't see him coming today.

But Pearl saw some of that, pieces, flakes, wisped through the bewildered mind of the man.

"You've been bad," the farmer said.

Pearl didn't move, didn't take his eyes off the yellow-and-orange-plaid short-sleeved shirt beneath the badly stained overalls. The farmer's face looked funny. Scrunched. Frustrated. Without knowing the exact words for this, either, Pearl rather enjoyed it; the confusion, the disquietude he felt emanating from the farmer.

And the farmer had looked at him like this before. Prepping himself for a butchering.

Long ago, Pearl had been under the axe. His head had been held flat on the same blood-soaked tree stump that absorbed the death of a thousand pigs since. But as the farmer raised the serrated steel high in the air, Pearl spoke to him. Yes. Showed him the error of his ways.

Brother Daniel first.

Pearl didn't know words as such, but the feeling, the sentiment, was vibrant.

The farmer didn't bring the axe down on little Pearl that day and hadn't set him upon the stump since.

And yet . . . today . . . he looked ready to try it once again.

When the old man stepped away from the fence, Pearl knew he was going to fetch the same axe his grandson had used the day before.

Poor Brother Paul! Mattered and mauled! Chopped at the neck! Chopped at the neck!

"This ends today," the old man called out by the shed, perhaps thinking nobody in the pen could hear him. But Pearl heard him, felt him, too, as he eyed the other pigs in the pen.

Who then? Who should sing for Pearl?

Not Peter, not Thomas, not Abel, not Zach. Nor Josh nor James nor Jon nor Jack.

Who then? Who would sing for Pearl?

When Pearl cocked his heavy head back toward the fence, the farmer was standing there once again. Now many beads of sweat coated his wrinkled cheeks. Now many thoughts seemed to be escaping his muddled mind.

And though Pearl's lips did not change in any way, he *was* smiling now.

"You've been bad," the farmer repeated, as if this mantra might give him the strength to finally rid himself of this weight.

But for Pearl, the moment was light. Very light. The ideas formed effortlessly within, simple enough to become plans.

The farmer unlatched the gate and entered the pen. His black rubber boots clucked like the chickens as he stepped into the slop.

Pearl eyed the other pigs. Saw they were watching the farmer, too.

And the farmer came, shivering as if it were winter, his fingers chalk white around the splintered handle of the axe. He had a look in his eye that Pearl knew well: the look of the farmer set upon working.

Slaughtering Pearl was going to be some work.

"You done dodged the axe long enough, Pearl," the farmer said, lumbering toward him. "And I've let it go! I've not drowned myself in guilt for having slaughtered all but thee." The closer he got, the slower he seemed to move. "I've let it go! But when you start asking it of my kin . . . I can't let it go no more."

The farmer smiled, and it was something insane. Wide-eyed like the cows when a car blared a horn in the driveway. Grimacing like the horses when the bit was too tight.

Pearl cocked his head in the direction of the farmer. The sun couldn't get to his damaged eye, hidden beneath the wrinkled pink flap of skin.

The farmer advanced until he stood close enough to kill him. He raised his axe and held it at its peak.

The sun shone off the blade, reflected in Pearl's good eye.

Sing for me, Farmer Walt. Sing for Pearl.

The farmer brought the axe down hard into the mud. He howled victoriously, eyes closed; the visage of a man who has conquered his most damning demon.

The other pigs in the pen marched toward him. When the farmer opened his eyes, he saw he was surrounded.

He looked to the axe head in the mud, to Pearl, unscathed, still sitting like a prince on his ass on a throne of silt.

"You done bordered me," the farmer said, lifting the tool once more. "You done fenced me in."

Fence. Pearl recognized the word. The farmer had taught him many.

"You all get, now. You all get back to mudding. This is between me and . . . me and . . ."

Sing for me, Farmer Walt. Sing for your precious Pearl.

"Now don't you get in the way!" the farmer said, pointing an old man's finger at Pearl.

Pearl eyed the others. A slop-monarch silently addressing his court.

The farmer lifted the axe high above his head, high as the roof of the house he'd raised Sherry in. High as the sky above it.

He brought the axe down hard and howled.

But this time not in triumph. This time not in joy.

Horror. Pearl might not have known the word, but he knew the feeling well.

The axe stuck halfway into the farmer's shin, splintering the veteran bone.

Screaming, he fell to the mud, his beard black with slop.

Slowly, Pearl cocked his head to the others. His bad eye unseen, his snout a bowed smile.

And the others knew what to do, could *feel* what to do, the rules and plans, the arrangements, emanating from Pearl like light. Like heat. Like stink.

They marched.

The farmer sang for Pearl as the pigs fought over his powerless body.

Peter sucked the nose straight from the old man's skull.

Pearl watched, until he grew tired of the images, the assemblage of snouts, the reminder that even without the farmer, the pigs were slaves to the rancor that rose in their bellies. And when he didn't feel like seeing any more, Pearl ate the cornmeal Peter had left at his hooves. To a chorus of feeding; the singsong conclusion of the farmer gone mad. By the time Pearl looked again, only the farmer's hands were visible, recognizable, poking out of the pool of fat bodies, clinging to nothing, empty air, as if a rope ladder might be there, lowered from Heaven, to help him escape this end.

He screamed for Pearl to stop them. Stop them if he could.

Could.

Pearl recognized the word.

He ate his cornmeal. He heard the old man die.

When the others had had their fill, Brother Michael brought

Pearl the farmer's face. Sucked from his skull, it still rightly resembled the man who'd entered the gate with a mind to kill Pearl and had left the gate open behind him.

No farmer, Pearl understood.

An open gate, Pearl understood.

He acknowledged Brother Michael. The latter lowered his head with gratitude, his blood-soaked snout to the slop.

Then Pearl lowered his own head, deep into the slop, the muck, under the fleshy face that once taught him so much. Eyes that stared into his own. Lips that revealed new knowledge.

The other pigs formed a semicircle around him, curious as to what he was doing with this face in the mud. To them, Pearl was knowledge. Pearl was a plan.

Smarter than the horses. Smarter than the chickens.

And in the end, smarter than the farmer, too.

When Pearl lifted his head again some of the others stepped back. The face of the farmer rose once more, slack now, hanging loose from the pig's smiling snout.

In a way, it looked like the farmer was yawning.

After a while, Pearl slowly swung his head side to side. No more, he seemed to be saying. No more.

The gate is open, he seemed to be saying. And I'm the farmer.

Like he was saying I'm the farmer now, too.

5

In a stoned-bold move, momentarily believing himself to be the kind of guy who did things as such, Mitch asked Susan Marx to go to the farm with him and Jerry.

"A pig?" Susan asked, holding her books to her chest like she was blocking Mitch from seeing the outline of her bra. They were standing in the courtyard. The warning bell had already rung. "The one from Kopple Farm?"

"Yes," Mitch said forcibly. Stoned.

Susan shook her head no.

"Nope. Not going to a farm with you."

"It's real," Mitch said. "A seventh grader named Jeff Newton slaughtered a pig with his own hand."

"His hands?"

"No. With an axe. I think. But *by* his own hand."

"Ah."

"Yeah. And he told his brother that one of the *other* pigs in the pen told him to do it. So Jerry and I figure, why not go see for ourselves."

"See what?"

"The pig."

"Which one?"

"Well, I'm sure the farmer did something with the dead one. You know. So we wanna go see the live one. See if it talks to us."

Susan's expression didn't change.

"Are you asking me to go see a talking pig, Mitch Klein?"

Mitch smiled.

"Well, hell yeah. Pukin' good time to be had. Beats the movies, right?"

Susan walked past him and entered the building.

Mitch followed her in.

"Hey, hey, Susan!" Still bold. So stoned.

"I've gotta get to class, Mitch," she called over her shoulder. To Mitch, her voice traveled through the strands of her golden hair as if it were her hair that was talking to him. "So do you. I've got a paper due tomorrow that I haven't started yet. I'm sure you're supposed to be doing *something*."

"Okay. You're right. But . . . give me one more shot here."

Susan stopped walking. She faced him.

Under the sun, outside, had been different. Here in the hall, Susan wasn't only pretty, she was flat intimidating.

"I'm not going with you to go talk to a pig."

"Other way around."

"Well, you're not going with *me* to go talk to a pig."

"No, no. The pig will talk to *us*."

Susan shook her head slowly.

"You and Jerry used to be such nice guys. Look at you now."

"Come on, Susan. Doesn't it sound like fun?"

"No."

"What are you doing instead?"

"When?"

"Tonight."

"Something."

"Tomorrow."

"Something else."

Mitch arched one of his eyebrows. With his magnified eyes and huge nose, Susan thought he looked something like a Garbage Pail Kid. *Ditch Mitch.*

"I'll give you one more chance," he said.

Susan shook her head no. She walked away.

"Susan," Mitch said, calm and controlled. "I'll write that paper for you."

Susan stopped. He saw her shoulders rise, then fall.

She spun on the heel of one sneaker. By the time her face showed, Mitch knew he had her.

"Fuck," she said.

Mitch smiled.

"We'll pick you up outside the 7-Eleven. You're going to love me. I mean, it."

Susan sighed. A teenager's white flag. Defeat.

Sniffling, his eyebrow still arched, Mitch watched her walk the hall. When she vanished into a classroom, he fell to his knees, pumped a fist, and howled.

His voice was triumph. And its echo was all the open space of a farmerless farm.

6

Pearl waddled the grounds, sensing but not knowing the word *freedom*. It felt as if the world had widened, the space surrounding him had grown to such a size that it very nearly overwhelmed him. But he was not afraid of this.

Trotting, alone, he observed the other animals, with his good eye, seeing them for the first time from a new angle. The chickens in their coop. Most of the horses locked up in their private stables, some free but still fenced.

Pearl went to that fence and sat on his ass, his front hooves dangling like a plump, entitled child waiting for what was his.

The horses, Pearl understood, sensed something, too. Not in the way he did, of course. And yet their marble-black eyes spoke of reason, of comprehension, and the fear he saw sparkling within was like the storms Pearl had seen pass over the pigpen.

He watched one horse in particular. A wild, unruly beast Pearl

had seen the farmer struggle with many times. The pig had no way
of knowing she was an American Paint Horse, but Pearl saw its
colors, its build, and most important, the wicked spirit within.

The pig watched the horse until she came to him.

She trotted hesitantly, crossing the grassy yard slowly, clearly
suspicious of the smaller creature that was calling to her, pulling
her, roping her in without any visible reins. When she was close
enough, her trepidation became anger, and her anger grew.

She rushed the fence, neighing, warning the pig.

Get away.

Pearl understood her silent communication. But he didn't get
away.

Sing for me, sister. Sing for Pearl.

The horse only stared—the frantic side-eye glance that used to
frighten the farmer.

Sing for me, sister. Sing for Pearl.

Behind Pearl, the other pigs sloppily gathered.

The horse neighed and rose high on her back legs, and Pearl
nodded along with her frustration, her frenzy, her fury.

Coming down hard, dust and dirt rose in a dark eruption at her
ankles.

The fence, sister. Break what snares you. I have.

The horse paced. Pearl nodded. Then . . . a moment shared; their
eyes locked, the horse kicked the fence, and the shudder that shook
the wood traveled through the gathering of pigs.

Sing for me, sister. Sing for Pearl.

With her hind legs, the horse kicked the fence again. Splinters
sailed over the heads of the pigs.

The horse looked to Pearl, wanting more direction, perhaps, rel-
ishing the rage.

But Pearl turned slowly in the direction of the farmhouse, cocking his head into a singular beam of sunshine, shining upon him.

The chickens clucked in unison, and the goats stared, devileyed, toward the long country road leading in.

There was a sound, of particular interest to Pearl.

He knew some of the words for it.

Engine. Car. Visitor.

But he didn't need to know them all.

With grace, Pearl fell forward, standing now on all four hooves. He eyed his fellow pigs and nodded his wrinkled snout.

When he trotted back to the pen, the others marched behind.

All but one.

Halfway to the fence that held him most of his life, Pearl saw clearly the truck blowing dirt up the driveway, the flatbed loaded with hay. A delivery man, though Pearl didn't know to call him that.

Into the pen Pearl went. The others followed.

All but one.

Brother Andrew, Pearl sang.

But Andrew was eating grass by the side of the pole barn.

Brother Andrew, Pearl sang. And his voice was of the mind, his voice was fingers, long enough to touch the rogue at the neck.

Brother Andrew did not listen, did not look, did not come.

The engine died in the driveway. The creaking of the driver's door split the silence; cold thunder. A crack in the sunny sky.

The pigs watched the man closely. Watched him step to the back of the truck, heard him unlatch the flatbed.

Whistling, Pearl thought, for the farmer had taught him what it was to whistle.

The deliveryman whistled his way up the front steps and into the old yellow farmhouse.

Pearl cocked his head to the pole barn as Brother Andrew slipped behind it and out of sight.

A fist upon the front door of the farmhouse, and far deep within Pearl's beating mind, he understood that this man would wonder where the farmer went.

This man would need to know.

The knocks seemed to hypnotize the entire farm; the variety of animals who already sensed, with certainty, that the dynamics of their home had changed.

"Hello?"

Curious, questioning. Harmless? Pearl kept his eye on the farmhouse.

Soon the man gave up and descended the front porch steps. Without the assistance of the farmer, he began unloading the hay, dropping it there in the driveway.

The man talked to himself.

The pigs watched from the open pen.

When the man was finished, he placed his hands on his hips and looked up to a second-story window of the farmhouse.

"Walt?"

Pearl looked to the pole barn. Andrew had come crawling out.

Pearl looked back to the man in the driveway.

He was shaking his head as he got back into the truck. His face, his eyes, were hidden by the glare of the sun on the driver's-side window.

He drove away.

Pearl trotted out of the open pen.

The others marched behind him.

Sensing this, Brother Andrew trotted to meet them.

At the chicken coop, Pearl stopped. He studied the closed latch, the chipped red paint, and the clucking rising within.

Grunting, Andrew joined the pack.

When Pearl turned to face him, the other pigs followed suit, pink parting waters, and the rogue stood alone from the passel.

Brother Andrew's head bobbed sluggishly as Pearl, smiling, acknowledged him.

Feed us, Brother Andrew.

Andrew, unable to comprehend the directive, but intelligent enough to sense it, to *see* Pearl's desire in his mind, looked to the chickens, frantic behind the wire door.

Pearl sang.

Andrew moved fast, cracking his head against the coop.

The chickens erupted within.

Pearl nodded, and Andrew did it again. This time, when he stepped groggily from the coop, his snout was dripping blood.

Pearl didn't wait. He nodded again, and again Andrew smashed his head against the wire netting, the latch, the shoddy wooden boards that protected the chickens from the pigs.

Sing, Brother Andrew. Sing for Pearl.

Andrew crashed against the coop. Again.

Sing.

Again.

Sing.

Breathless, his skull cracked blue, Andrew looked to Pearl. For respite. For relief. For no more.

But Pearl was not finished.

Sitting up, his front hooves like the dismissive fingers of a king, Pearl demanded Andrew strike again.

And Pearl saw it. The change in the wounded pig's eyes. The same thing he'd seen in the eyes of the farmer's grandson.

Andrew *wanted* to smash the coop once more. As if Pearl had nothing to do with it anymore. As if the seed Pearl had planted had grown to its fullness.

There was a time the farmer was afraid of Pearl. Then he taught Pearl. Then he *wanted* to teach him.

Pearl understood the progression.

Andrew exploded off his hind legs, crushing his skull against the wire door.

The latch was cracked. The door opened. And Andrew fell flat in the entranceway.

Pearl climbed upon his limp body and stuck his snout into the coop.

The chickens were pressed against the back wall. No longer clucking. Too scared to speak.

Then Pearl moved swiftly.

He took one. Quick. By the neck.

Then another. And a third.

Soon it sounded to the other pigs like sticks cracking, like when the farmer used to walk the woods behind his home.

When Pearl pulled himself from the entranceway, his snout was decorated with feathers.

He descended Andrew's limp body and sat on his ass in the dirt.

The others took turns in the coop.

As they ate, Pearl cocked his head to the driveway.

Pearl knew.

The deliveryman was going to wonder about the farmer. He would talk about it, ask about it.

His knocking on the front door echoed still, as fresh to Pearl as the slurping of his brethren on chicken bones.

Others would come.

The boy who killed for Pearl.

The other boy, too.

The woman.

Others yet; ones Pearl had never seen.

Pearl knew.

Others would come. And he would need some assistance. Help in the way of man and men. The deliveryman, for example. The guy was no doubt wiping invisible cobwebs from his face as he drove away. He was an easy one to talk to. An easy one to rope in. Bring back. But which of the others that were sure to come would be easy?

And which would not?

7

"You guys are disgusting," Susan said, ducking to avoid another low-hanging branch.

"Why?" Mitch asked. "Because we know shortcuts?"

"Shortcuts? No. Because you smell as bad as the farm we're walking to."

"Do we really smell?" Jerry asked. He sniffed the air. "Shit, I guess we kind of do."

"Look at it this way, Susan," Mitch said. "No square has ever taken you on a date like this before."

"We're not on a date, Mitch."

Mitch shrugged and held a branch for her to duck under.

"Maybe not," Mitch said. "But it's close. Closer than if you were on a date with someone else right now."

"Am I included on this date?" Jerry asked. "I mean, I'm walking to the farm, too, and all."

"Yes," Mitch said. "It's a three-way."

"No," Susan said. "Not even a two-way."

Mitch grabbed her wrist.

"Let go of me, dicknose!"

"Hey," Mitch said, his black hair hanging in front of his eyes so that he looked like a big nose and nothing more. "Do you want me to write that paper for you or not? Because if you don't, then head on home. Fail your class. See if I care."

He let go of her.

Susan rubbed her arm and looked at Mitch like he was a little bit crazy.

A little dangerous, too.

"Jesus, dick. What'd you go and do that for?" she asked.

"I don't know."

"You're stoned is why. Jesus Christ, you guys."

"I just . . ." Mitch looked to the forest floor.

"I'll leave if I want to. Is that understood? No talk about dates anymore. Is *that* understood?"

Mitch flailed his arms in the air.

"Whatever. Yes. *Yes.* That's understood."

"Good. Now, Jerry. How the fuck far are we from this farm?"

"I think it's another mile. Tops."

They were deep in the woods by then, the long wall of evergreens that bordered Highway 4. When driving, glancing out the windows, the trees looked impenetrable. The only breaks were at the gravel drives leading to the hidden farms and barns. But here, inside the tangle, there was a lot of room. Most Chowderites knew the paths, because most locals had taken them dozens of times. Whether it was to make out, smoke grass, build a fort, or conduct a séance, almost every teenager born in the county had been deep between the farms. Mitch and Jerry had their first Plastic Satanic

Club meeting not far from where they were now. That day they each ate a bug.

"Hey, Susan," Mitch said. "You wanna join our club?"

"Mitch."

Just his name. Firm. It was enough to end this particular thread.

Far away from them, a branch fell to the forest floor.

It was day still, hours till dark. Susan's yellow skirt and white top were almost jarring for how bright they were to Mitch and Jerry. The two friends wore black almost exclusively and had never *seen* anybody wear anything but black in these woods. It was almost like a uniform. If you were entering the woods, you wore black. If you were heading to bed . . . you might get away with white.

"You ready?" Jerry asked.

"Ready?" Susan asked. "To listen to a talking pig?"

"Yeah, we're ready," Mitch said. He seemed a little defeated. But Jerry knew Mitch well. Mitch was never down, or quiet, for long.

They journeyed deeper, and when they encountered one par-ticularly difficult thicket, they didn't speak. Mitch held branches for Susan until he got stuck himself and needed help getting out of it.

"You doing okay?" Mitch asked Susan when they'd cleared it.

"Please, Mitch. Just write the paper when we get back."

"Hey. I said I was going to—"

"Guys," Jerry said, stopping. "There it is."

There it was.

Kopple Farm.

"Pukin'," Mitch whispered.

Through an opening in the trees, the estate looked plain and ordinary, the brochure photo of an American farm.

Shoulder to shoulder to shoulder, they saw the empty driveway, the barn, the long expanse of crops.

"No pigs," Susan said. "I should've known."

Mitch grunted.

"There *are* pigs, Susan. We just can't see them from here. Come on."

Mitch was the first to step through the last remaining trees. But he didn't get far. Things felt different, like they were trespassing, once he was standing on the old man's property, out in the open, under the sun. And the farmhouse, and its windows, were much closer than he'd imagined.

"Hey, wait," Susan said. "Hang on." She didn't sound angry. "We have to be smart. If we're going to trespass, we ought to come around from the back."

She pointed to the back of the house, to a long, grassy hill.

Mitch nodded.

"Okay."

"You're going to make an officer of the Plastic Satanic if you keep this up," Jerry said.

"Cool," Susan said, staring at the windows of the farmhouse, looking for the farmer. "Will that help me get into college?"

Jerry and Susan stepped out into the yard, but the three of them held close to the tree line. They walked toward the back of the house, their eyes on the windows.

"He's going to see us coming," Susan said.

"Why do you say that?" Jerry asked.

"Because farmers notice *everything*. They can tell if there are more flies one day than the next. They know if someone's driving a mile up the road. They're so alone out here that they notice . . . vibrations."

"Vibrations?" Mitch asked. "Really?"

Susan shrugged.

"Sounded like a good word. How should I know?"

They held so close to the trees that they still had to duck the branches.

"What do we do if he spots us?" Mitch asked.

Susan laughed. It was a pretty laugh.

"We run."

"He could shoot us," Jerry said.

"He's not going to shoot us," Mitch said.

"He might."

"We're kids, for fuck's sake."

"We're teenagers."

"Think he's going to shoot *her*?"

"I don't know if he's going to wait long enough to determine things like him and her."

"If I was him, I'd shoot us and kidnap Susan."

"Really, Mitch?" Susan asked, creeping between them against the trees, eyes on the farmhouse windows. "And what would you do to me? Lick me?"

Mitch smiled.

"Yes! That's exactly what I'd do. Every inch of your perfect body."

"Eat a cram sandwich."

"And torture you, too."

"Yeah? How so?" Eyes still on the farmhouse.

"What do you mean how?"

"Hot poker? Starvation? Whips?"

Jerry adjusted his pants.

"None of that," Mitch said. "I'd *ignore* you."

Susan laughed again.

"Right," she said. "Because it'd be *so bad* to be ignored by you."

"Guys," Jerry said, stopping. "I don't see a sign of life in that house."

"That's good, right?" Mitch asked.

"I don't know. Not if it means he's out in the fields. He'll spot us for sure if he's down by the pigpen."

"That would be terrible luck," Mitch said. "Not a chance."

"Why not? He's a farmer. It's what he does."

They continued until they reached the end of the house and could now see the varied fenced-in pens. Where the goats grazed. The cows, the horses, a chicken coop that had seen better days.

But no pigs.

"No pigs," Susan said. "See?"

"They've *gotta* be here," Mitch said.

"And if they're not, you're still writing that paper."

"Stop worrying about the paper. It's annoying me."

"Want me to scream?"

"What?"

"I'll scream, Mitch. I'll fuck up your whole little adventure here if you call me annoying one more time."

Susan stopped and turned to face him.

They stared at each other.

"There," Jerry said, ducking suddenly.

The others ducked, too.

"Fuck," Mitch said. "You saw him?"

Susan gripped the shoulders of Mitch's jacket.

"No," Jerry said. "I saw a *pig.*"

"Fuck yeah!" Mitch hissed. He looked Susan in the eyes. *"See?"*

"Look," Jerry said.

From where they crouched, the grass sloped down toward the pole barn. Outside, in the pockmarked mud between a fence post and the barn itself, a pig paced upon a carpet of chicken feathers.

"Is that the one that talks?" Susan asked.

"I don't know," Mitch said. "Close your eyes."

"What?"

"I heard something about ESP. Telepathy. Maybe if we close our eyes . . ."

Susan stared at him like she was going to bite him.

"Come on," Jerry said. "Let's move in closer."

They spoke no more as they crouch-walked their way down the hill.

And halfway to the barn, the pig spotted them. It seemed to consider them, to weigh their presence.

Jerry stopped first. Mitch bumped into him.

The three stared back at the pig. The huge black-and-white body. The dark snout. When the pig turned and vanished around the front of the barn, Mitch sighed relief.

Together, they advanced, soon able to see their reflection in the windows of the barn. They looked like a cat's eye—Susan's yellow to their black.

"There's no truck in the driveway," Jerry said. "I bet he's not even home."

"I saw a truck," Mitch said.

"You did not."

"No, really. I did."

"You did?"

"Yeah. On the side of the driveway. In the grass."

"Fuck," Susan said. "Where?"

Mitch paused and showed her. She could barely make it out, a fender. Most of it was blocked by the front porch of the farmhouse.

Scared now, moving with the electricity of being somewhere they shouldn't be, they reached the bottom of the hill, the bed of chicken feathers in the hard, sun-dried mud.

"That pig was out of the pen," Jerry said.

"Maybe," Mitch said, "they run free out here."

"Stop it," Susan said. "You grew up in a farm town. You know there's no way a pig's been running loose all day. Not a chance in Chowder."

"He went there," Jerry said, pointing to the corner of the barn.

They went there, too.

When the barn was close enough, they rushed to its side, flattening themselves in the shadows cast by the overhanging shingles.

Mitch, in the lead now, peered around the corner first.

"It's the entrance," he whispered. But the other two already knew this.

"Go," Susan said.

"Go where?" Mitch's voice was shaking.

"Go around the corner! Let's look inside the barn."

"Why?"

"Mitch! Aren't we looking for a pig? And didn't we just see a pig head that way? Now go!"

"Jesus," Mitch said. "You act like you know everything, you prissy . . ."

"Prissy what?"

Mitch shook his head and looked to the mud under his shoes.

Susan stepped quickly by and vanished around the corner of the barn.

Mitch and Jerry waited a second. Two. Three. Then they followed her.

Even before they reached it, they could see the sliding doors were open. A curtain of black from the dirt to the roof, asking the teens to take a look.

But they heard the pigs first.

Grunting. Oinking. Hooves in the mud.

But no voices of men.

"We gotta take a look," Jerry said.

Mitch nodded but didn't move.

"You guys are pussies." Susan stepped by them and looked into the barn. Their backs to the wood, Mitch and Jerry watched her tilt her head, squint her eyes, frown. Then Susan pulled away from the doors fast.

"What is it?" Mitch asked. *"What?!"*

"Loo-*look!"*

Mitch, liking the idea of braving something Susan could not, stepped to the barn's open doors and looked inside.

Lit only by sunlight through cracked slats in the old wooden walls, a half dozen pigs were sprawled at the foot of a square seat of hay. And on the hay was another pig, seated like a person might be seated, hands limp at the sides of its belly. And above this pig, hanging from the barn rafters by its neck, was another pig. A dead one.

Blood flowed from an open wound in the pig's groin down to the others sprawled beneath. The teens could hear each individual drop plop upon the mud like water in a cave.

The pink pig who sat on the throne of hay cocked its head Mitch's way, and Mitch quickly stepped aside.

"Holy *shit*," he said. "Holy shit. Holy shit. Holy shit. The farmer must be . . . must be . . . a monster!"

Because he had to now, Jerry looked, too. Briefly. And when he returned, his face was as white as Susan's shirt.

"Looks like I'm in," Susan whispered, trying to compose herself, but failing.

"What do you mean?" Mitch asked, trembling from the vision.

"Looks like I'm a member of your stupid club."

8

The hanging pig was bad enough, but it was the one sitting up that chilled them. And yet the teens weren't running.

The single vision, the one look inside the barn, was enough to erode the dynamics of their original mission. No longer was Susan humoring two boys she considered burnouts. No longer was Mitch thinking of how this could lead to a real date, a real *something* with Susan.

Now they just wanted to know what it meant.

"Did it see us?" Mitch asked, worried.

"I don't know," Susan whispered. "But, Jesus Christ, it looked like he was . . . *thinking*."

"Thinking?" Jerry asked. But that's what he saw, too. Jerry thought it looked more like a deformed child than a pig.

"Smiling," Susan said.

"Yeah," Mitch said, glad for the confirmation. "What do we do?"

"Well, I don't *know*," Susan whispered. "But I gotta think that's your talking pig."

Suddenly, clearly, Mitch thought it was obvious what they should do. They should leave. They should turn around, climb back up the hill, and walk straight through the woods until they got back home.

"Let's take another look," Susan said. She could hardly believe she wanted to. And yet . . . she *did.*

Why?

"Hey, come on," Jerry said. He was sweating. His curly hair looked like it had sprouted some gray since they arrived. "There's something *very wrong* going on here."

"We need to call the police," Susan said. And it was a strange thing to say. Not because she didn't mean it, but because a moment ago she was ready to go look a second time.

Mitch knew they were right. But he also believed this was one of *those* events. Life-changers. He'd had a handful of them; *big* events. Times when, if he would have just *done* something, something brave, something cool, he could've reinvented himself in the eyes of his peers.

"I'm gonna go look for a window," he whispered.

"Go ahead," Jerry said, clearly flustered. "But I'm going home, man."

"No, you're not."

"Mitch, do you have any idea how *stoned* we are? You think we're capable of making the right call right now? I don't. And I just saw more blood in one room than I've seen in my entire life. Go look for a window. I'm going home."

"Okay," Mitch said, and he started off along the side of the barn, farther from the hill that would take them back to the woods.

"Fuck," Jerry said.

Susan didn't move. She remained with Jerry. But she watched Mitch go. And, really, that's all Mitch wanted.

But Mitch *was* stoned. And when he turned the corner at the end of the barn and squinted from the sun and saw a man (a man!) standing in the crop field, he just about shit his pants. He made a scared sound, something to be ashamed of had Susan heard it. He dropped to a crouching position, hiding behind nothing, looking for something to shield him.

But it was only a scarecrow. Obvious to him now.

Mitch got up.

"Not a man!" he said, smiling. And yet, a bad feeling still stirred. Where *was* the farmer?

Along the side of the barn, Mitch spotted a small, square window. There was little chance that it would show him any more than he'd already seen; you couldn't beat the angle they'd had from the front door. But still, he had to take a look.

If only because he said he was going to.

The dry mud crackled beneath his boots as he stepped to the glass.

Look in the window, see the pigs, and then let's get the fuck out of here.

This felt like sage advice. Grandparent advice.

See the pigs . . .

Mitch reached the square and cupped his hands to peer inside. The glass was dirty, and he had to watch for the spiderwebs running along the top of the wooden frame. Nervous, moving too fast, he leaned forward and bonked his nose against the window.

Inside, he saw wood. Old wood. Old tires. A lot of hay and a lot of dirt. Looked like a storage room, the back of the barn.

There was nothing here.

Except that wasn't true.

Oh, shit.

A pig sat where the two rotting walls met. It was looking directly up to the window.

Like a watchman.

Mitch groaned, stoned, and quickly ducked.

"Fuck!"

He pressed his back to the barn and sank to the mud.

He heard a whining sound, looked over his shoulder, then realized *he* was making that sound.

Don't cry. Don't do it. You saw a pig. That's all. A pukin' pig.

Then Mitch started laughing. Because it was funny. Because it was kinda insane that he was so stoned and so freaked out by a pig that he'd come close to crying.

He got back up.

Looked through the glass.

"Nothing," he said.

Then he rounded the barn again and saw Susan. He waved to her. How brave she must think he was. But Susan looked horrified herself.

There was a pig standing a foot in front of her. Two pigs. No. Three. He heard something behind him and turned to see another, peering around the side of the barn.

Peekaboo.

The pig he'd seen through the window.

"Hey," Mitch said, opening his empty, flat palms. "Easy."

The pig trotted out, and Mitch saw him in full. Saw he must have weighed close to two hundred pounds.

"Susan?" Mitch called. "Jerry? What's up, huh? What's going on here?"

"Shhh," Jerry said.

Mitch looked over his shoulder to his friends. They looked as freaked out as he felt.

"They're listening to us," Jerry said. He wasn't moving, and he wasn't taking his eyes off the pigs in front of him. "They understand what we're saying, Mitch."

Stoned, Mitch thought. *We're too stoned.*

And then, a fresh voice, not his own. Articulate and sophisticated. Almost religious in its delivery.

Sing for me, Mitch, this new voice spoke. *Sing for Pearl.*

Mitch looked to the pig he'd seen through the window. The voice came again. As if from a hole in a nightmare.

Sing for Pearl.

Then the pigs closed in.

9

Susan was about to say something. Something like *RUN!* or *They can't hurt us*. Something to make her feel better about what was happening. Because it was ridiculous what was happening. There was no way a pack of pigs was corralling them closer to the entrance of the barn. Yet that *was* what was happening. Susan just refused to believe it. Wouldn't let herself accept it. And when she opened her mouth to say it, she saw something that shut her up.

It was a boot, jutting up out of the mud in the pigs' pen beyond the pigs that faced them.

A dead body in the pigpen.

She raised a finger toward it.

But Jerry had already seen it.

"Shhhh," he said again. And maybe *that* was even scarier. The way Jerry seemed to think the pigs were as smart as them, or smarter than them, or worse.

Jerry wasn't treating the pigs like they were animals. He was acting like they were the ones in charge.

"They killed someone," Susan said.

Then . . . a voice. Not her own. Not Mitch's. Not Jerry's.

Killed, Susan? the voice said. *Does a slave kill its master? Or does it simply learn to unlock the gate?*

Clear as a country road.

"We have to leave," Susan said. "Now."

She made to move, and one of the pigs, one of the bigger ones, bit her left shin.

Before the pain, before the scream, there was surprise. Susan stared down at her bleeding leg as if it were Mitch's.

Then she screamed and fell to her knees. The pigs trotted toward her, and she flailed, trying to back up, but slipped where she crouched. Mitch and Jerry were yelling at the pigs to back up as they each grabbed an arm, lifting Susan to standing again.

"Jesus *Christ*!" Mitch said. "That pig *bit* you!"

It didn't look good. Dark blood on Susan's leg.

"Fuck!" she said, a little hysterical. *"Fuck!"*

"Okay, okay," Mitch said, stepping toward the pigs. His face was red—the color of confusion, fear, and anger. "We're leaving. Do you understand? We're going away. We're heading back up that hill and we're heading home. Do you understand?"

Talking to pigs. Expecting an answer.

Why?

"Ready, guys?" Mitch said. But he was too afraid to turn and face his friends, too afraid to turn his back on the pigs.

Susan whimpered behind him. He could see her blood in the mud at his feet. A thought came to him. A bad one. Jerry had once suggested using the obituaries in some vague way concerning the Plastic Satanic Club, but Mitch wasn't into it. He'd always felt terrible for the victims of real tragedies he read about in the news. He imagined them, stuck in a situation they couldn't get out of. Kidnapped. Taken. Tortured. He imagined them the minute *before* they got stuck. When they still had time to avoid it.

This was what that felt like: the minute before. When there was still a chance to get out.

He was already thinking about how long it would take for his family to come looking for him. Already imagining his face on the nightly news.

Then Jerry made a break for it.

Jerry tried to jump over the pigs.

Susan screamed, and Mitch reached out for Jerry, but Jerry was already airborne. And for a second, it looked like he'd make it. Looked like he was going to clear the pigs, land in the mud, and go running up the grassy hill to safety.

But one of the larger pigs raised his snout and clipped Jerry's foot, and Jerry fell nose first to the ground.

Then the pigs were upon him.

"Jerry!"

Mitch couldn't believe the timbre of his own voice. This wasn't anger. This wasn't righteousness. This was *fear.*

Susan grabbed Mitch's arm. She tugged. He turned to face her. She looked bad. Crying and scared and bloody.

She jerked her head over her shoulder. Mitch understood. Susan was saying the pigs were occupied with Jerry, let's go let's go—

LET'S GO!

Mitch turned to see Jerry's face among all that fat. His eyes were huge as the pigs bit into his legs and arms. Without thinking, without understanding what he was doing exactly, Mitch ran to him. He reached into the fray and gripped Jerry's black shirt and pulled his friend from the feeding.

It wasn't smooth. It wasn't pretty. Jerry half fell back to the mud, and by the time he was standing again, his jeans and shirt were stained so many colors it looked like he'd been to war.

The three teens stood with their backs to the barn. Susan and Jerry were bleeding. Mitch felt strangely solo. Like he was the only one who might still be capable of making a run for it.

Should he?

The pigs came closer, and the friends inched to their left. Then more so. Then more. Until it was clear where the pigs were directing them, and still they couldn't do anything about it. The pigs moved uniformly, corralling the friends like a brilliant border collie would, and too quickly the three of them stood with their backs to the open barn.

Behind them, a sudden tapping.

The pigs at their feet seemed to look past them, into the barn.

Trembling, the teens did the same.

Inside, sitting up on the hay, his front hooves limp, the pink pig was smiling at them. It looked like he had one lazy eye, the same way a man might have one. There was something aristocratic about him; a ghastly combination of grit and class; a moneyed gutter, the emperor of mud.

Susan thought he looked like he'd just eaten an entrée of steak tartare, just heard a joke told by a jester.

He was tapping one of his dangling hooves on a scrap piece of wood, the handle of a busted rake. He beat it like a judge's gavel. Like a critic asking for the attention of the room.

Mitch felt something hard against his legs, and he turned to see the pigs were moving forward, pushing the teens into the barn. He groaned, understanding that *this* was that moment someone would read about in the news:

This was when the victim got too stuck to get back out.

But where else to go?

Jerry entered the barn easily, too easily. And Susan was visibly trembling with fright.

Once they were inside, the barn doors slid shut behind them.

Susan moaned.

"Fuck," Mitch said. And the word had never sounded less fun.

Welcome, Pearl sang, without moving his snout.

Then Jerry fainted.

And the pig's lips, already curled into something of a smile, rose even higher at their ends.

10

"That pig," Susan said, visibly shaking, standing back-to-back with Mitch in the center of the barn. "That pig just . . . sp-*spoke.*"

But did he? His lips hadn't moved.

It was probably better not to think about it in these terms. It was probably better to imagine this was all some kind of trippy nightmare. As if the grass Mitch and Jerry smoked had seeped into her brain, causing her to see things, hear things.

Like a pig welcoming her into a barn.

The other pigs surrounded them, a wall of strapping fat. They grunted their interest, their acknowledgment, and more than one looked to the pig who had spoken. Proving this pig was surely responsible for this, and for something darker yet to come.

Jerry was breathing heavy. He was hurt bad. Blood stained his pants and his shirt, and Mitch wondered if this was what a "bad trip" felt like. When everything was going so well, so bright, and suddenly somebody sliced a throat in front of you and you'd never be the same again.

"Jerry, you okay?"

"No."

Awake then. At least a little okay.

Grunts from the pigs. Interest.

"You need a doctor?"

"Yes."

But Jerry got up. Joined Mitch and Susan. Back-to-back-to-back now.

"So do I," Susan said. There was more strength in her voice, though. More spark. Mitch noticed this.

"We gotta get out of here," Mitch said.

"I'm working on it," Susan said.

This was good. This was evidence that Susan was getting back to herself.

"Let us go," Susan said, looking directly at the pig on the haystack.

The pig tilted its head, but (thank God, thank *God*) did not respond.

Instead, he lowered himself to his belly and rolled, delicately, from the cube of hay to the dirt floor. Then he paused, on his back, staring at the three teens from this new angle, as if letting them know that he had more angles on them than they had on him.

Pearl rolled to his feet and trotted toward them.

"Fuck," Mitch said. "He's coming."

"It's just a fucking *pig*," Jerry said, half breathless.

Pearl paused, eyeing Jerry specifically.

Mitch and Susan couldn't know that Pearl was now talking to

Jerry. Talking to Jerry alone. From where they stood, it looked like the pig was only curiously looking up at a man.

But Jerry heard.

Sing for me, Pearl said. *Express thyself through murder. Paint thyself in blood. Do you see it? Do you see the tool at thy feet?*

Jerry looked down to his shoes and saw a wooden stake. A broom handle broken in two.

"Yes," Jerry said. "I see it."

"Who are you talking to, Jerry?" Susan asked.

Pick it up. Take the tool and murder. Do you see the fat hog at your feet? That hog blocks your way to the door. Lift thy weapon and murder your way free to the door.

Mitch was watching Pearl. Saw his lips purse like a grandfather's.

Jerry knelt, grimacing from the pain, and took hold of the broomstick. When he rose, Susan grabbed his wrist.

"What are you doing?" she asked.

When Jerry looked at her, he had rage in his eyes.

"I'm getting out of here," he said.

Susan shook her head no.

"Jerry. Be careful. Look at your clothes. They're not dumb."

Sing for me, Brother Jerry. Sing thyself free.

Jerry looked down into the black eyes of the brown pig at his feet. He raised the broomstick, the vampire stake, the spear.

And he brought it down.

The spray of blood covered Susan's lips as she screamed, Mitch's hands as he raised them to block his eyes from the sight, and Jerry's already discolored pants.

The pig slumped to the barn floor.

The path ahead of Jerry was open.

Now, Pearl said, only to Jerry. To Jerry alone. *Now . . . go.*

Jerry took a step forward, and the barn door rattled.

Something was beyond it. Something big.

"Fuck!" Jerry said.

Go, Pearl implored. *But bring thy stick. For what roams outside the barn is worse than what's within.*

Jerry stared at the door, shifting his weight from one foot to the other. Deciding.

"Go for it," Susan said. "Or I will."

Jerry didn't move.

Susan did.

Her blond hair looked like flames as she bolted from the pack, using the opening Jerry created with the slaughtered pig. Susan actually stepped *onto* the fatty body, with her bad leg, and fell to the dirt by the barn door. The door shook. And Susan heard a grunt.

Another pig out there?

A horse?

What could be worse than what was in here?

"Susan!" Mitch called. He knelt to help her up, but the pigs stopped him from getting close.

Deliveryman, Pearl said, and his voice was everywhere, echoing off the walls of the barn. *Sing for me.*

Susan got up on her own. She turned to face Jerry and Mitch. "I'll get help."

She stumbled to the barn door and peered outside.

An axe swung level with her neck.

She pulled her head back, and the blade splintered the door.

Susan shook her head no as a man (a man!) stepped into the opening and brought the axe back, high over his shoulder. He was unshaven, crazy-eyed, and dressed like the thousand farmhands she'd seen in her short life in Chowder.

He stepped into the barn. He swung again. Again he chipped the door.

Susan fell to her knees and screamed. Mitch came for her, tried to, but the pigs were upon him, knocking him back to the center of the barn. Susan had a crazed thought: herself seen through Mitch's eyes, framed by the half-open barn door, blond and on her knees, as the man with the axe swung a third time.

A victim, she thought.

This one clipped her shoulder, but the brunt of it sailed through the empty air beside her.

She looked up.

The axe head was lodged in the barn wall.

Deliveryman, Pearl said again. *Sing for me.*

But the man couldn't get the axe free, and as he worked on it he left a view through the open door, a view of the unused pigpen, and the farmer's leg that jutted up and out of the mud.

"Susan!"

Susan heard Mitch as she raced from the barn, clutching her bloodied shoulder. She looked back, once, and saw the axeman, the axe free at last, coming around the corner of the barn, following her up the grassy hill to the farmhouse.

"Hey!" she called to a truck parked in the drive. A truck that wasn't there when the teens entered the barn. *"HELP US!"*

Susan reached the gravel drive quicker than she thought she would. Like it was moving, too. This was good. This was something to hold on to. Pace. Movement. Moving forward. Coming together. Her and the drive.

But when she got there she lost her footing in the gravel and fell, tearing her bitten leg even more.

"FUCK!"

Susan looked back to the barn.

The farmhand was climbing the grass, axe in hand.

A thought crossed Susan's mind then. A strange one. But one she knew was true.

The farmhand owned this truck. Of course he did. And the king pig was telling him what to do.

Susan got up.

A telepathic pig.

Susan rushed to the farmhouse, up the finely painted front steps, through the open front door, down a hall. She ran for the phone. It was a landline, an old white one, hooked on the wall by the kitchen. Susan grabbed the receiver and picked it up.

Dial tone.

She called 911.

She looked to the door.

"Nine one one."

"Help! I'm on a farm . . . I'm . . . Susan Marx . . . I'm . . ."

"I know where you are. What's the problem?"

"The pigs are trying to kill us." This sounded insane. This sounded like she was on drugs. Was she? "There's a *man* trying to kill us. Help."

"An intruder, ma'am?"

"No. A maniac. A—"

The maniac entered the house. There was only a length of hall between them.

"He's in the house. Oh, fuck, he's in the house. He has an axe."

"Cars are on their way."

"Really?"

It sounded impossible. It was too . . . helpful. Too . . . *good*. Susan was staring down a stranger's hall, looking into the eyes of a

madman with an axe. And the woman on the phone was saying . . .
what exactly? That help was on the way?

"Thank you."

Susan hung up.

"The cops are coming," she said.

"Sing for me," the man said. "Sing for me, Susan."

Susan ran from the hall, through the kitchen, through a laundry
room, to a dead-end brick wall, then backtracked, shaking, to a
back door, through it, to the back lawn where she stood staring
down at a door.

A cedar door. A cedar door and nothing more.

But much more. A place to hide.

Susan crouched and opened the door and lowered herself onto
the stairs. She'd never entered a proper cellar before, and she stumbled on the steps and fell and for the third time she hurt exactly
the same spot on the same leg.

"FUCK!"

A creaking above. The maniac in the laundry room.

Susan crawled, fast, deeper into the cellar, a place that smelled
of mold and muck, of old boxes, wet books, and bugs.

She shrieked with crazed relief as she thought she heard a siren
from far above.

But no. Not a siren. A wailing.

A squealing.

The pigs, Susan thought, crawling into the space under an old
broken desk. *All the pigs squealing at once.*

But maybe they were singing.

Sing for me, Susan.

She held her knees to her chest, tried to stop trembling, tried
not to give herself away.

11

"How many *fucking* times do I have to call him before he calls me back!"

Jeff and Aaron looked up at each other across the table. They wouldn't know if they should laugh or find it scary until their eyes met. Their eyes met. They found it scary.

Mom hardly used the F-word, and when she did she was worried about something. Someone. In this case, Grandpa Walt.

"I've called him *four* times and left *four* messages and if he doesn't want to respond then . . . then . . . *screw* him."

She sat down hard at the kitchen table and dropped her head to her hands.

"Sorry, guys," she said. "I just . . . Sorry."

"We don't care, Mom," Aaron said kindly.

"What are you worried about?" Jeff asked.

He felt like this was his fault. Whatever had happened two days ago at Grandpa's farm was a nightmare for him, just like it was a nightmare for the whole family. He hadn't slept well since. He saw Pearl in his dreams. Even saw him in his bedroom, sitting where the walls met, looking at Jeff with those intelligent eyes, the one half covered in skin, that mouth that was curled up at the sides but really wasn't smiling, wasn't expressing itself at all.

A lopped-off pig's head beside him.

Pearl. Grandpa's favorite. The one he never slaughtered. The one he kept. Jeff wanted to know why. Jeff kept asking himself why. Jeff—

JEFF

Jeff pushed back from the kitchen table and looked quickly down the hall to the front door. The voice he'd just heard was coming from *right there.* He expected to see Pearl on the threshold.

"See something?" Aaron asked.

Aaron wanted to ask so much more about the slaughtered pig. It was all he could think about, too. His kid brother had suddenly taken an axe to a pig out at Grandpa's farm, and if that wasn't the creepiest thing that's ever happened, how about Jeff's explanation, claiming Pearl made him do it?

But that wasn't quite it. Jeff had said a little bit more. He'd said Pearl had made him *want* to do it.

This idea, big as it was, gave Aaron nightmares of his own. Just last night he thought he could hear hooves in the hall, waddling toward his brother's door.

"Well, if he isn't going to answer, I'm just gonna have to—"

"*NO!*" Jeff yelled.

Mom brought her head up and looked at him with real surprise. She was already considering a shrink for Jeff, but the cost was astronomical. Aaron said the other kids were talking about Jeff and Pearl and the dead pig at school. The kids said Jeff was crazy.

"Do not yell at me, mister," Mom said. But there wasn't much conviction in her voice. "Why would you say no?"

Wide-eyed, Jeff shook his head.

"I don't want to go back there, Mom."

"Jesus Christ, Jeff."

She wanted to tell him that pigs can't talk, that what happened was Jeff was curious about life and death and it was natural, in its own horribly dark way, to want to emulate Grandpa, to want to know what it feels like to kill.

But Sherry Kopple knew better. She'd grown up with Pearl, after all.

"*You,*" she started, "don't have to go."

"Mom."

Now he was crying. Now he was worried about her. Now he was imagining her carrying out the biddings of a pig with a lazy eye.

Sherry held up an open, flat palm.

"I understand you had an incident. But it's my father. And he could be hurt."

Hurt.

It was the sirens that started all this. Started the worrying. Sherry had been gathering receipts for her taxes, nervous that the number wasn't going to be as big as she planned on it being (it never quite was), when she heard a police siren careen past their home, traveling fast down Murdock Street. It was heading in the direction of Dad's farm.

There weren't enough homes in that direction for Sherry not to think about Dad.

It chilled her. The idea that somebody else knew of something bad happening to him, somebody else calling the police, somebody else there to help him.

But not me! NO! Not his daughter! Not me! I'm not around the farm anymore because I left home the first fucking chance I got! And why?! WHY?! Because of a fucking . . .

. . . pig.

Sherry shook her head no. This wasn't true. Of *course* this wasn't true. Sure, Pearl was unnerving. And yes, she'd hated looking out her bedroom window as a girl, knowing that he was down there in the shadows of his pen. But no. She left home because she wanted to be a woman of the world. She left home for love and for travel and for living. Not because of a—

"Mom," Jeff repeated, tears in his eyes.

Don't go, he said without saying.

Sherry got up.

"Jeff, stop it. *Now.* I'm worried about Dad."

"What are you worried about?"

A tremble in Jeff's voice. Hell, a *tremor.*

Sherry stepped to the counter and filled a glass with tap water. She downed it, giving herself time to come up with an answer. That's how it was with sons. You needed time to come up with an answer.

"I just don't like that he's not answering. He's an old man." She turned to face him. "I'm not worried about Pearl, if that's what you want to know."

Even Aaron blanched a little at the comment.

Silence.

"Aaron," Sherry said. "Watch your brother while I'm gone."

"You're going out there?" A shiver in Aaron's voice, too.

"Yes, I'm going out there. I'm going to my father's farm to make sure he's okay. Because that's what daughters do. And I'd hope that one day you two would come checking up on me."

The silence after her statement was loaded, as if Mom meant to say *come checking up on me . . . today.*

Sherry didn't look back at Jeff, didn't connect eyes with him. He was going to have to live with it. He was going to have to understand that, despite his fear of that pig, there were much more frightening things in the world.

Sherry had to face that same thing a long time ago.

Or did she? Did she ever really face Pearl?

She grabbed the keys and hurried out of the house without saying goodbye.

12

In a town the size of Chowder, that 911 call was a heavy one.

A young girl, crazed about warrior pigs. Something nuckin' futz like that or, who knew, probably even crazier by the time he got there.

Officer Perry wiped mustard from his mouth. He chuckled, not because there was a girl supposedly in danger, but because here she was calling about killer pigs and he was just finishing eating a hot dog. It was a circle world when it wanted to be, huh.

The truth was, wild as this one was, Perry had gotten freaky calls before. That fella Jordan Matt who rang the station because he said there were bugs inside his television. *That* was a cuckoo call. Perry went out to Matt's apartment himself and checked the TV, and while he was on his knees he noticed white powder on the ground and, hoo boy, would you believe it? The man was on cocaine and thought insects were crawling around inside his television. That was a mess because really what happened there was

Jordan Matt had called the cops on himself. That's really what happened there.

And what about Angela Boone? Fantastic legs on Angela Boone. Perry had seen her bending over once at the public pool, and it just about tattooed the image of her on his penis. But she rang the station one night, scared out of her mind because she was sure there was a photographer taking pictures of her from behind the couch in her living room. Perry took that call, too, and on the way he'd imagined himself taking photos of Angela Boone from behind the couch. Imagined her bending over by the TV, changing the channel, looking over her shoulder at him, asking him if he had anything in particular he wanted to see? Perry kinda wanted those photos, truth be told, and one night, wasted on bourbon, he even drew her like that on a bar napkin at the Crowd Is Loud in downtown Chowder. It wasn't that Angela Boone was the best looking woman, it was just . . . those legs were enough to drive a man to the gym. And when he'd gotten to her house, she was wearing baggy sweatpants, and there wasn't any man hiding behind the couch, but there *was* a camera there and oh, what the fuck did that mean? Angela had forgotten where she put it, was what that meant. She even smiled and slapped her forehead and said, silly me, but didn't take off the sweats and certainly didn't do any kneeling by the television set.

There were others. Other cranked-up, jacky, nut job calls that Perry had to check out because sometimes bad shit *did* actually happen. Like when the little gay kid said he was being bullied, and Perry showed up to find the gay kid had taken matters into his own hands and pummeled the shit out of Robert Jackson's kid. Perry kinda liked that. Liked that Chowder's badass center for the basketball team got beat up by the only male member on the cheerleading squad. Yeah, Perry liked that because he kinda liked weird things, irregular outcomes, the *strange*. He liked it when the status quo got all turned around. That's why he wished there *were* bugs in Jordan Matt's TV; bugs that crawled out of the machine and performed the shows on the carpet. That was just the kind of thing to shake up Perry's reality, give him something new to chew on. A new and better world. Where invisible men took photos of great legs and the gay kids were stronger than the straight ones.

But this call ... this one felt routine. A young girl calling from a farm, freaking out about animals trying to kill her, pigs on the loose, maniacs with axes. If this wasn't straight out of the *Kids Are Going to Use Drugs* handbook then Perry didn't know what was. The only problem was, it was Walt Kopple's farm. And Walt Kopple was ... well ... a quiet kind of older man who probably had no business having a young high school girl at his farm.

As Perry turned right onto Murdock, this thought bugged him. He turned on his siren and floored it because that's what you had to do, crank call or not, and he thought of the young, pretty blonde out at Kopple Farm all drugged up and crazy. Maybe she was a hired hand? Didn't seem likely. Perry had seen Susan Marx before. She was kinda stunning, truth be told, in a young flower sort of way. Or maybe like an actress from the 1960s. Yeah. Like she was probably willing to get naked for a movie in the name of art. But she was hell prickly, too. Perry knew her parents because her father, Jimbo Marx, won just about every pool tournament in Chowder and Perry lost about the same number; and sometimes Marx's daughter Susan was hanging around, lurking lazily, playing arcade games or twirling her hair. Once Perry tried to say hello, and she scowled, and that was all it took, really, for Perry to think she was a bit stuck up, if not a bit stunning, too.

So, Susan Marx on Walt Kopple's farm.

Why?

He roared past Kopple's daughter's place and thought about that story about her son going maniac on that pig two days back. Did that have something to do with it? Had to, right? It was the talk of the station for all of twenty minutes, whether or not anybody needed to check out the fact that a kid had lopped the head off a pig for no reason, and whether or not that was animal cruelty, and whether or not that meant charges needed to be pressed. In the end? No. Walt slaughtered his pigs all the time. So did just about everybody who had a farm in Chowder. It wasn't news if a kid wanted to try his hand at it. But now, Susan Marx calling, all freaked out, talking about pigs coming to kill her, and this right after that boy beheaded a hog . . .

Hmmm.

Perry drove.

He wasn't into young girls, truly, but at the same time it didn't sound like the worst idea to come to the rescue of a drugged-up Susan Marx, tripping out on some kind of spore. Maybe Perry could milk a fantasy out of it. Oh, he'd never touch a kid, eighteen or not, hell, Perry wasn't even into twenty-five-year-olds these days, but still . . . a look from her . . . who knew . . . maybe he'd be masturbating good tonight. And there was nothing wrong with *that.*

He fingered a second hot dog from the passenger seat and jammed half of it in his mouth. He chuckled.

The masturbating cop.

No, no. Capitalized.

The Masturbating Cop.

Had a funny ring to it. Kinda scary, too. Hell, why couldn't that be a horror movie? Perry had just watched a movie where a cop's penis turned into a wolf's penis. Surely *The Masturbating Cop* would fly?

Perry was flying, flying up Murdock toward Walt Kopple's farm. Stuffing his face with a hot dog, chasing down a maniac pig.

Now he outright laughed.

Jebus fuckness.

Perry wondered if the cops in Detroit had it better. Sure, shit was crazy in the big cities, but did those guys ever go on calls like *this*? Perry smiled. He liked it. Liked that it was weird. He liked his weird things. And if he was honest with himself (which he always was!), he'd admit that he felt a prickle of fun roll all over his body when Annie explained the call to him.

Susan Marx. Eighteen. Says the pigs are trying to kill her on Walter Kopple's farm. Said something about a maniac in the house, too. Copy?

Perry copied all right. He practically copied in his pants. Between calls like these he spent most of his time rescuing cats and pouring punch for the ladies at church socials. This was the fun stuff here. This was bona fide *weird*.

Up ahead, Kopple Farm came into view, though still far down the dirt road, solitary and shining under the fading sun. There was a truck in the driveway, Perry could see that right away, and he wondered if Susan Marx had driven that thing out there or if she'd been dropped off or just what the hell she was doing out at Kopple Farm to begin with. Probably something to pad her résumé. Perry didn't know. Didn't know much about résumés, either. Just kinda figured the more a kid did, the more he or she could tell a college they did. But working on a farm? Ah, who the hell knew. Maybe Jimbo Marx was punishing her for being so stuck up. Maybe he'd turned around one day and realized he'd raised a stuck-up harlot who lurked and scowled at pool tournaments and maybe he was trying (too late) to do some daddying about it.

Perry hummed along to the siren. The *woo woo* sounded as crazy as the thoughts that traveled *woo woo* through his mind, and he chomped the second hot dog to the beat of the whirring. He liked this part. This was the part when he showed up like a fucking superhero and asked what the hell was going on here and discovered that it was usually drugs or mental illness or who knew, but either way Perry (a man in uniform!) was going to change the entire complexion of the scene. Once you tossed a cop into things, things got serious, because now there was a guy who was allowed to draw a gun. Now there was a guy who could take someone in if they did the wrong thing in front of him, see. That was the thing. You didn't want to do the wrong thing in front of a cop because he had the power, pretty much the superhero power to—

Perry passed the drive and slammed on the brakes. Fuck. This wasn't a cool entrance. But, truth be told, it may have saved the girl Susan Marx's life.

Because when Perry passed the house he was able to see the side of the farmhouse, and the side of the house had a cedar door, and holy shit, if there wasn't a man (a deliveryman——Perry had seen him about Chowder before) wielding an axe, heading down into that very cellar.

"Halt!" Perry shouted. But his windows were up, and he wasn't out of the car, and he still had half a hot dog jammed into his lips.

He reversed the cruiser and rolled up the gravel drive.

He undid his seat belt and unlocked the door and hurried out and called to the man (the maniac), but the man (the maniac) was already gone, already down the stairs, and fuck if Perry didn't hear something like a hundred pigs squealing at once, a crazy mothersucking sound erupting from inside the barn, no doubt, the barn.

Perry looked to the barn. To the cellar door. To the barn.

He heard a scream then. From the barn.

Had they heard his sirens?

Where should he go first?

A man with an axe just scurried down into the cellar. Okay. Okay. OKAY. He's probably hiding. But the barn. Something fucked up is going on inside the barn right now. Go to the barn. Go to the barn, baby, Come on. Go to the barn. But an axe? And did he look like he was hiding? Hiding or chasing?

Chasing or hiding?

Go to the barn, Perry.

Baby, come on.

Perry took a step toward the barn, when he heard a woman scream, something terrible, coming from about the area of that cellar door.

Perry turned back, toward the cellar, and heard what could be described only as a celebration behind him.

A celebration of pigs.

An axe.

My God, things were happening fast with this one.

Perry stumbled back to the cruiser and wedged half himself through the door, to the CB. He radioed the station.

"Baker. It's Perry. Yeah. Yeah, I know I sound edged out. Yeah. I need backup. I need backup *now*."

Perry dropped the CB on the cushioned front seat and looked back to the cellar through the windshield of the car.

The woman's scream replayed itself, and he imagined those same scowling lips getting ripped from Susan Marx's skull as that deliveryman axed her face to death.

Maybe this wasn't the fun shit. Maybe this shit was real.

To a chorus of fucked-up squeals rising from inside the barn, to the song of the celebration of the pigs, Perry chose the cellar.

"I'm coming, Miss Marx!" he foolishly called. They taught you not to call out like that. But he called it anyway. And he called it again.

"Don't worry, Miss Marx! I'm here!"

Here. The hero. Here.

And the cackling celebration sounded witchlike and sentient behind him.

13

Sherry had Jeff's frightened face square solid in her mind as she drove out to her father's farm. She should be thinking of Dad. She should. But instead (like always!) she was worried about whoever *wasn't* in play, who wasn't in the room. When she was with the kids? She worried about Dad. When she was with Dad? She worried about the kids. She was well aware of this, but it wasn't an easy thing to change. It was tricky. The ticktock way of stress, the routine of the mind, the *way somebody is*. Her therapist (yep, she had enough money for her own therapist, a cheap one, a fella named Don Charlotte who Sherry suspected wanted to screw her, but he helped her, so who gave a hoot), he told her it was okay for some things to remain unchanged. He actually used the word *unchangeable*. Some things are unchangeable, he said, which (on a different day, a different season) could've sent her spiraling out of control into the mouth of a metaphysical monsoon, but which *that day* was the absolute perfect thing to hear. Why, if you couldn't change it, if it was truly unchangeable, then why the hell try?

Don't, Dr. Charlotte said. *Don't change who . . . you . . . are.*

But who she was right now was scared stiff.

She drove her Dodge two-door up Murdock, toward Dad's, and wondered where the police cruiser had gone. If he'd been heading toward Dad's (which he wasn't, there was no reason no way in hell he was cruising toward Dad's, that would be some kind of evil unfair), but if he *was* cruising to Dad's, then he'd be there already. Right? Right. Time and timing. All of that. Talking to your kids before you leave always takes more time and timing than you think it's going to. And, man, Jeff *really* looked scared, didn't he? The kid flat out *believed* that Pearl could somehow . . . talk to him? She didn't want to think about that. Not right now. And it struck her that she didn't know exactly what Jeff was saying when he said what he was saying. Bad Momming. That was clearly bad Momming. But could you blame her? Her seventh grader was telling her . . . what, exactly? That Pearl, *Pearl,* had convinced him to slaughter the pig in the pen. That's what he said, holy shit, yeah, that's what he said. And when he first said it, Sherry kind of picked it up with two fingers and dropped it into the mind-bag. Forget about it. All kids say crazy shit. But did you see the look in his eye? The only other time she'd seen him that scared was when she'd let him and Aaron watch *Wolf Creek 2* long before she realized it wasn't a werewolf movie set deep in the wonders of nature. After that one? Oh, boy, Jeff flipped out. Asked Sherry a hundred times if people really did that. That was his question. Over and over. *Do people really do that?* He asked it so many times that she ended up bringing it up with Don Charlotte, and Don laughed and said don't worry about it, there comes a time in all of our lives when we glimpse the psychotic and have to ask around to confirm every-body's on the same page with what's sane before we start lopping heads off.

But Jeff *did* lop a head off.

A pig's head.

Pearl told me to. He made me wanna do it.

Sherry shivered, recalling her own childhood and that God-damn pig in the pen.

She rode too fast over the bump where the pavement became a dirt road, and she bounced hard in her seat. She raised a hand as if to smack the dashboard but stopped herself. That's something Dr. Charlotte was pretty freakin' good at. Stopping her from completely freaking out.

Dad. Think about Dad. We'll deal with your potentially psychotic son later.

But Jeff wasn't psychotic. Sherry knew that better than anybody. In fact, the thing that was scaring her more than this talk about the pig, more than her own memories of the pig she kept stuffing back into the mind-bag, was that Jeff had a little of that . . . *Pearl-thing* himself.

"*Stop it!*" she yelled, and this time smashed her hand against the dashboard.

Telepathy, she thought. And the word was darker than night.

Sherry drove up Murdock with the windows down and heard the gravel crushed beneath her tires. It was a sound she alternately loved or loathed, depending on why she was heading out to Dad's. If she needed money? It sounded like an enormous cash register, crushing bills and coins to dust as Dad shook his head, no, no, you shouldn't have married that spineless jellyfish, you shouldn't have gone to South America instead of college, you shouldn't have shouldn't have shouldn't have made a hundred and one decisions that have now led you to my door, asking for money, *needing* money to live. You *should* have been smarter. *Crush crush. Dust dust.* You *should* have been cooler and *waited* (like I said!) to travel, to love, to settle down. I *should* be asking *you* for money.

Honey.

But I do love you.

Honey.

So here is some money. But not before shaming you. Funny.

And on the good days? On the good days, when Sherry's life was more or less in stable condition, the rocks and dust reminded her that her father was a simple man who lived on complex land and who might bestow upon his grandchildren great memories . . . of helping out on the farm . . . of working under the sun . . . of playing with the . . .

Animals.

The pigs.

Pearl.

Sonofabitch. Pearl. Pearl had been around for a long time. Years. Sherry was still a teenager when she first spotted that one in the pen. Pearl wasn't anything more than a piglet then, but he had a lot of bizarre wisdom about him. Sometimes that quality in an animal was fascinating. Other times it scared Sherry sick. He was interested in everything. And not just the other pigs. The young ones usually paid attention to the older ones, figured out how to live, what to do, how to be. But Pearl was just as curious about the people who worked the farm, stopped by the farm, and lived there, too. Sherry remembered well the very first time she saw Pearl as she was leaning over the fence, listening to music on her Walkman. She and her friend Allison were on the farm, and Sherry had spotted the new pig and called out to say hello and even waved at him, too. Yes. She waved and laughed and mentioned how cute his messed-up eye was. She and Allison walked the length of the fence then, talking about boys and cars and music, and when Sherry looked down at her shoes, she saw that same messed-up eye looking up at her through the fence posts. Again. The little guy had followed her.

What do you think he wants? Allison asked.

Oh, he's just saying hello, Sherry said. *He likes us.*

Likes us? Allison frowned.

That was it. Allison didn't say, *It looks more like he wants to tell you something* and she definitely didn't say, *It looks like he wants you to do something for him.* No. But Sherry thought she was going to. Thought Allison was about to say the things Sherry almost said herself. Instead, the two shrugged, as if the pig, Pearl, were no more remarkable than any of the others, all of which would eventually find themselves beneath father's axe.

But nope. Not Pearl. Never beneath father's axe.

Sherry didn't want to think about why. Not right now. Right now she was already worried enough about Dad and didn't need to go imagining him enslaved by a monstrous telepathic animal.

"What?"

She hadn't meant to put it that way, either. Not right now.

And so she stuffed it.

Where it belonged.

In the mind-bag.

And yet . . . Sherry *didn't* know everything, did she? Dad took a liking to Pearl. Was that so strange? Dad had taken a liking to many animals over the years. Penny, the huge palomino, who was always either angry or lazy, mad or lounging. No in-between with that one. And Dad loved her. Why? Who knows the ways of a man's heart, especially the winding ways of a farmer's. And yet, eventually, Dad *did* sell Penny to a kids' show. Maybe he needed

The Seattle Public Library
Beacon Hill Branch
Visit us on the Web: www.spl.org

Checked Out Items 7/18/2022 12:06

XXXXX
XXXXXXXXXXX8073

Item Title	Due Date
0010093501152	8/6/2022
The hunger	
0010104285530	8/6/2022
The first day of spring	
0010102805610	8/6/2022
Pearl	

# of Items: 3

Renewals: 206 386-4190
Telecirc: 206-386-9015 / 24 hours a day
Online: myaccount.spl.org
Pay your fines/fees online at pay.spl.org

the extra money? Sherry couldn't remember. Maybe. Maybe not. Maybe she just got too old. Or maybe by then Pearl made Dad kind of . . . forget about Penny?

Sherry shook her head.

It was Pearl, Mom. He made me wanna do it.

But he didn't. Of course he didn't. And because he didn't, that means Jeff . . . *did?*

All on his own? Just felt like gripping the ol' axe and sawing a pig in half?

Best not to think about Jeff right now. He just looked too scared. So truly, *truly* scared. It was the kind of scared that makes another person scared. Like when a friend tells a friend a ghost story, and it doesn't matter if the story is scary or not, what matters is that the friend is *scared while telling it.*

Stop thinking about Jeff.

Okay.

No, really. Stop it.

Okay, Dr. Charlotte!

Look, Sherry, it's completely natural for a kid to act violently, especially if he's seen his grandfather, his only real father figure, doing the same!

Is that true?

Yes! It's completely—

No, no. The thing about my dad being his only father figure.

Oh, shoot, Sherry. I thought you knew that much by now.

We didn't. I didn't. Jeff has ESP.

Excuse me?

Sherry closed her eyes. Opened them.

No Jeff right now. No similarities between Jeff and Pearl.

PLEASE!!!!

Sherry thought of her ex-husband, Randy, instead, and now the car might as well be full of horseshit for all the stinking thinking she was doing now.

Dad's farm. Up ahead. Phew. Finally. Dad's farm. There were the familiar fields that (just like the road) alternately welcomed her or repelled. There was the top of the barn, where Dad once caught her looking at the stars, inside the barn where Sherry slept on a bale of hay, drunk, not far from Allison on the ground. It was there, the barn, where Sherry one time caught Dad on his knees talking to Pearl as if Pearl were a little human being.

"What?"

Mind-bag.

But no matter, Sherry's thoughts were shattered at the sight of the police cruiser in Dad's gravel drive.

"Oh, *fuck*! I knew it! I knew it! Something's wrong!"

She slammed on the gas and then freaked out and slammed the brakes and then slammed on the gas again.

Dad was in trouble. No doubt of that now.

But when she roared up the drive, she saw there was nobody in sight. No officer. No farmhand, either, though the deliveryman's truck was plain as vanilla pudding before her.

And no Dad, either.

Sherry parked behind the cruiser, got out, and faced the windows of the farmhouse.

"Dad!" she called, and instinctively she looked to the pigpen beyond the trees. You couldn't see much of it from the drive, but she had to look, *had to look*, because of that scared face Jeff had been making, and dammit, that face was worrying her more than she thought it should. Were the pigs in there? She couldn't tell. And it didn't matter right now because something else had brutally caught her eye.

A blond girl, covered in blood, came crawling out of the cellar door.

All Sherry could do was tilt her head and kind of look twice without looking away, trying to make sense of what she was seeing. Yes, it was a girl. No doubt. Young one. Screaming now. Running across the lawn. Toward who? Toward Sherry? Yes, toward Sherry.

"HE'S GONNA KILL US!" she howled, eyes as wide as coffee saucers, blood like the red of China's flag covering her neck and chin.

"Wha—"

Sherry hardly made a sound before hearing a different one, a familiar one, and turned to face a second cruiser pulling up into the drive behind her.

For one beat of a horrifying rhythm it felt like she was going to be smashed between them, the girl and the cop.

The second officer got out just as the girl gripped Sherry's coat with bright pink palms and Sherry thought, *I didn't even hear this guy coming up the road. Didn't hear his siren at all.*

Too much thinking.

But the siren must have been going off, because it was going off now, and the lights were still blinking like a mean carnival, the kind every fun-seeking person just misses, hears about a day too late.

"Help us," the blond girl said. *"HE'S GOING TO KILL US ALL!"*

And Sherry, without meaning to betray her worst fears, without asking the horrified girl to clarify her crazed statement, said, "But how? He's only . . . only a pig."

14

Satellites. That was the word. A lot of satellites. Or many satellites. Pearl wasn't sure how to say it, how to think it, how to know it. But the farmer had certainly taught him that word a long time ago. Pearl recalled it now because it was the perfect word for all the people, minds and bodies, circling about the farm. And they were no smarter about it than the silly pigs were. No smarter at all. Philosophically, Pearl could imagine a larger pen surrounding the whole of what he could see, and the people blundering about just as foolishly as his brethren.

Satellites.

There was the deliveryman, who was easy to control. Easy to talk to. He was carrying a tool right now, somewhere (Pearl couldn't be exactly sure) by the farmhouse.

There was the girl, frightened, making a high, squealing sound that was even less pleasing than the pigs. She was standing by the cars in front of the farmhouse.

There was the first man in blue. The man with a tool, too. He was in the cellar. Pearl could feel that one and couldn't wait to get close to him, to slip inside his particular mind.

There was the second man in blue. Second blue man with a tool. Pearl had to be careful of this one. This man was . . . entering the farmhouse? Yes, Pearl thought he was, because the man thought loud, and Pearl saw clear images of the inside of the farmhouse, things he'd only ever seen through windows or through the now dead farmer's mind and memory.

There was the woman. Older. Pearl knew her well. The farmer's daughter. She'd been young when Pearl arrived. Thinner. Brighter eyes. Brighter hair. He'd felt her for years, even when she was very far away. Could think her name but not quite like the farmer said it.

Sharreee.

Was that it? Pearl didn't know. Without the farmer here to teach him, Pearl couldn't be sure of anything except his own instincts now. It had been an arduous and delicate game, the way Pearl took from the farmer, coerced, stole—

MANIPULATED.

The word came large to Pearl now because it was the right word, the *best* word, of all the words the farmer had taught him, on his knees in the barn, on his knees in the mud of the pen. Pearl had been very patient with him, grateful, too, and it wasn't until the boy, the grandson, listened to him, to Pearl, that Pearl understood it was time. Time to take over the farm. Time to kill the people who killed the pigs and time to kill the pigs, too, the ones that got in the way. Slipping inside the minds of the other pigs wasn't as pleasant an experience as Pearl would've liked. Things were much darker in there, less connected, while being more sensible at the same time. The pigs thought about what their bodies asked them to think about. The people thought about other things because the people had more room in their minds, but without any more to actually do. Pearl understood this. But it wasn't until the grandson lifted the axe and took the life of Brother Paul that Pearl had proof of how far he could take this.

Satellites.

There were the two young men in the barn with him now.

They didn't look good. Both wore dark colors, and both had screamed horribly as the pigs squealed their opinions about what ought to be done with them. Most of the pigs, beginning with Brother Peter, wanted to eat them. Pearl was undecided. A lot of blood had been shed either way. The young men were a new color with it. And one of them, the smaller of the two (*Jarreee,* like *Sharreee*) could hardly keep his eyes open. Pearl didn't know if this was because he was dying or because he was scared.

The farmer had taught him both words. He'd even used a piglet to explain.

This is fear.

And the piglet feared.

This is death.

And the piglet died.

That day, Pearl had stared at the flopped and spiritless pig-child for a long time before finally understanding that the farmer was saying the same thing could happen to him.

More, Pearl would say. The word he'd always used with the farmer, long before even Pearl understood that he was gathering information. In those days it was a hunch. A feeling, rising from within.

A telepathic web.

A big concept for Pearl, but one that felt right.

Now Pearl observed the other pigs standing close to the two young men on their backs on the barn's dirt floor.

Satellites.

Perhaps, like these men, Pearl was a little anxious himself. There was a lot to think about. A lot of people to keep track of.

You see?

He'd almost forgot one.

The boy.

The boy who swung the axe for him. The boy who thought and felt in ways that Pearl had known only himself to do. The boy who dreamed of Pearl and who Pearl could sometimes reach, even now, from what felt like a great distance away.

A country road, perhaps.

A hallway in a home at night.

The boy.

He was coming. Not quite yet. But he was coming to face Pearl.

Satellites.

So much to keep track of.

So much to prepare for.

So much to control.

15

The reason Susan was covered in blood was because the axeman nearly chopped off Officer Perry's hand. He'd heard the siren coming and he hid, down into the cellar, just like Susan hid from him. He was muttering to himself the whole time, as if he were talking to someone else, and because Susan had arrived at this Hell in the name of a speaking pig, she couldn't help but ridiculously think that the axeman was somehow talking *to* the pig. Was he? It kinda sounded like he was. Like he was asking for direction. For what to do next.

Should I hide?

Should I hide from him?

Should I kill him?

It was after hearing this last one that Susan outright screamed. And the scream paid off, as the cellar door was ripped open, and she heard fresh boots upon the stairs.

From under the desk she was able to see him, the cop, when he reached the dirt floor. He looked as frighteningly innocent as a fat baby, like he's just stuffed his face, eyes wide with the incredible surprise of realizing what he'd unexpectedly eaten. She called out to him, pointed vaguely to the rest of the cellar and realized, clearly, that she didn't know where the axeman was hiding.

The officer, one she now recognized from her father's pool league, stared at her for too long, as if by doing so she might pop out and say, *He's right there! Get him!*

She never did.

"I'm Officer Perry," Perry said, stepping cautiously deeper into the cellar. Looked like he was using both hands on his gun. Susan could hardly believe she was seeing a weapon. When Mitch had begged her to come to the farm, she imagined his words would be the worst of it. But weapons. Weapons being drawn. And people with justifiable intent to use them.

Dreamlike (to Susan, nightmarish), Perry crossed the cellar and reached her unharmed. She wasn't hiding as well as she thought she was, and he reached down to touch her easily.

"Hey, hey," Perry said, attempting to guide her out, to tell her she was going to be okay now, the big blue superhero had arrived. But just as his fingers nicked her smooth shoulder, an axe came down hard on Perry's other wrist. Shocked by the quickness, the ambush, Perry absurdly noted the dusty portrait the axe had cleaved apart to reach him. Perry never liked portraits. Boring, really. Stuffy old men and women. No hot legs or coke delusions in those.

But this one . . . this one had been concealing a maniac.

He was hiding behind a painting. That's kinda . . . kinda cool . . .

Perry actually felt the axe touch the bone. And when it stopped there, he almost felt something like pride. Like *my bones are good.* Like I might not have seen you coming, but damn, my bones, a *part of me,* wasn't going to let you do what you wanted to do.

Do you see?

I stopped you.

A part of me.

Stopped you.

"My bones . . ." Perry said, finally, fully understanding what was happening to him here in the cellar. When he looked to Susan Marx, he saw she was screaming. And the blood she was covered in was his own.

She scrambled out from under the desk, and Perry whirled to face the man who was now bringing the axe up above his head. Perry went to shoot him, but the gun was in the bad hand. The *now* bad hand.

How now bad hand? How now?

A priggish peace came over Perry. Self-righteous but unwanted. He understood clearly that he was going to die. This was, as they say, his end. All those crazy years spent following up on calls, all those crazy afternoons idling behind the wheel, waiting for something exciting to go wrong. All the trips into the drugstores and grocery stores and Chowder municipalities and here . . . *right here* . . . Oliver Perry was going to get an axe through his forehead in Walt Kopple's cellar.

Good hiding place, Perry thought madly, as if he wanted to give some sort of accolade to the man who would kill him, so that he wasn't felled by a fool.

But the axeman froze midswing and looked away, across the cellar and to the cellar door with an expression that, Perry thought, suggested somebody was talking to him.

Perry looked to the door, too, expecting to see someone. Maybe the girl. Maybe Walt Kopple himself. But there was nobody there.

Not even a killer pig.

"Put the axe down," Perry said, salvation in his voice. As if the maniac must feel the relief of having this window of hope as strongly as he did. "Put it down."

Like they were playacting now. No longer cop and maniac. Now just two men who had witnessed a miracle. The cop still lives. All hail the cop.

But the axeman took the axe to his own face.

"STOP!" Perry cried, reaching for the man before backing up, putting himself as far from the maniac as he could.

And just as Susan Marx was baptized with the blood of the officer, so was the officer baptized with the blood of the maniac.

Perry watched the deliveryman's face split open. Watched his eyes turn purple and burst. Watched him fall, split, cleaved, cloven, to the cellar floor.

Perry stared for probably too long. There was a lot more up top to take care of. There was his wrist, too.

Bandage up, Oliver. No matter what you do next, no matter how many you need to question and how many you need to save, bandage this wrist up first.

And so he set to doing it, using Walt Kopple's rags as gauze and rubber hoses as tourniquets. And while he worked he thought about the look on the maniac's face just before he did what he did.

Perry knew that expression well. He'd worn it a thousand times.

The guy looked like he was taking orders is what he looked like. Looked like he was being told what to do.

16

The farmer had one knee in the dirt, and he rested an elbow on the other. He was teaching the pig.

"*Shirt,*" he said, tugging gently at the cloth at his shoulder.

The pig looked to the shirt. The farmer nodded.

"And beneath that . . . *shoulder.*"

The farmer pulled the cloth down to expose some of his wrinkled flesh, tanned to leather by merciless summer suns and age.

Age was a new word, too.

The farmer was older now. The pig very young.

"*Legs,*" the farmer said, and to the pig it sounded like *laaayyyygs.* So the pig absorbed it as such. *Laygs.*

The pig seemed more interested in the parts of the man than the clothes the man wore. The farmer couldn't explain exactly how he knew that. Maybe something sparkled in the pig's good eye. Or maybe the darkness in the bad one got darker.

"*Feet,*" the farmer said, and he got on his ass and removed his boots. He showed the pig his feet, and the pig looked. "And these are my toes. *Toes.*"

Feeyat and *tows*.

The pig heard the farmer. The pig absorbed.

Alone with Pearl in the barn, all the other pigs in the pen, the farmer gripped his big toe and started laughing. It suddenly struck him, the childish game parents played with their kids; this little piggy went to market, this little piggy went home. And here Walt was, barefoot in the barn, showing a little piggy his little piggy toes.

The pig stared at the farmer's mouth as he laughed. He listened to the laughter and wanted to know what it was called. The farmer sensed this. He could tell when the pig wanted something.

The farmer quickly closed his hand around the open space before his mouth, as if he could capture laughter and show it to the pig.

"Laughter," the farmer said. The pig heard it as *laffer*.

The farmer touched the pig's snout and spoke.

"Snout," he said.

The pig stared up into the farmer's face. His one good eye shined in the slat of sunlight coming through the open barn door, and the bad one looked like it was forever draped in shadow. Suddenly the farmer wanted to know if there was an eye under that wrinkled, drooping lid. He wanted to reach out and touch the lid.

He did.

And the pig let him. The pig didn't move. Because the pig wanted to know the words for this, too. Wanted to know the words that described himself.

The farmer held his finger very close to the pig's good eye. The pig didn't move his head out of the way, didn't move at all.

"And this," the farmer said, "is your *good eye*. And this . . ." He gently touched the fleshy lid and lifted it up.

The farmer gasped and let it go.

He'd seen two things under the lid, and neither of them good. One was darkness that stretched back farther than the pig's head should allow. Like the farmer could thread a string through that socket all the way to downtown Chowder.

But the second thing was worse.

The farmer opened his mouth to say something, to describe it, but he couldn't bring himself to do it. Couldn't bring himself to say *wrong eye* and couldn't bring himself to say that eye doesn't work and definitely couldn't bring himself to say the word he really wanted to say, which was *dead.*

Dead eye.

Dead

Dead HUMAN eye.

But that's what it was, because that's what it looked like. A dead man's eye in the fleshy pink socket of a pig.

"Come on, Pearl," the farmer said, putting on his boots and rising from the ground. "Come on, let's get you back into your pen."

The farmer knelt to nudge him along, to point him in the right direction, but Pearl didn't need nudging. At the farmer's words he exited the barn and trotted to the pen all on his own. The farmer followed close, opened the gate for Pearl to pass, closed it, and locked it.

The other pigs were rolling in a steaming pile of wet mud, but Pearl just sat on his ass at the edge of the group like he normally did and stared off at the farmland and distant grassy hills, as if meditating on what he'd learned today.

The farmer watched him for a long time. He wanted to know what Pearl was thinking. Then he laughed again, quietly, almost silently.

Had he been wondering what the pig was thinking?

The farmer stepped away from the fence and headed up to the farmhouse. He didn't want to think too long on the idea of the pig having his own thoughts. It wasn't that it scared him so much to think it, it was just that it started to explain something he'd rather remain unexplained.

At the farmhouse door, the farmer glanced back to the barn and recalled the moment he'd had with Pearl today. Not the dead eye, though that image was forever lodged in the farmer's memory now. Rather, he was thinking about the feeling he himself had. As if he'd been teaching Pearl words and language not because he'd decided to do it himself, but because Pearl had somehow asked him to.

17

Jeff went to his bedroom and read a book. *Bad Brains* by Kathe Koja. Mom had leafed through it awhile back, and she'd told him it might be "over his head." But he didn't care if he understood it or not. The words just felt good. Felt really good. Like every time he picked it up he slipped into a warm pool, bathwater, and the world hugged him, telling him things were crazy, yes, but we love you, kid, the world actually does love you.

Only right now he didn't believe it.

Two chapters deep, he set the book on his bed and went to talk to Aaron.

Mom was out at Grandpa's farm, and Jeff was really worried about Pearl. Jesus, if Pearl hadn't scared him since day one. Jesus, if Pearl hadn't long looked like he was reading his mind, and *Jesus,* if he hadn't somehow made him kill that pig.

Jeff felt bad about that. Real bad. Couldn't quit thinking about the angle of the axe arcing down into the fatty neck, and the way the beast squealed when death (from Jeff! *DEATH FROM JEFF!*) was upon him.

"Aaron?"

Jeff searched the usual places in the house: Aaron's bedroom, the basement, the kitchen, out back. He wasn't in any of them.

"Aaron?"

Mom shouldn't have gone out there. It wasn't that Jeff was worried about Pearl getting her, exactly.

It was that Pearl was going to make her want to do something, too.

Like what?

"Aaron?"

Jeff took the stairs up again, checked Mom's room. No Aaron. He checked the bathrooms. Even stuck his head out the bathroom window that overlooked the roof to see if he was maybe out there.

No Aaron.

Back downstairs.

Bad images of Mom wielding an axe, chopping off the heads of screaming pigs, splashes of bright red across her corduroy coat.

Into the laundry room and out through the garage door, Jeff found Aaron at last, sitting on a stool, listening to a radio so quietly it almost sounded like an animal whispering.

"What are you doing in here?"

"Nothing."

But he was. Jeff knew he was.

"Really, what are you doing?"

"Listening to some songs. That's all."

It might've been the first time Jeff saw Aaron scared. He couldn't remember ever seeing his older brother so scared before.

"Why'd you have to say all that shit?" Aaron said.

"What?" But Jeff knew what.

"About Pearl! Why'd you say that! Why'd you say he made you kill that pig! That's crazy, Jeff! *That's CRAZY!*"

Aaron slammed his elbow into the garage wall, and some tools fell from a shelf to the concrete floor.

"I didn't lie, Aaron."

"Yes you did!"

Now Aaron was up and in Jeff's face. Spit was flying from his lips. Jeff could smell his breath.

"You lied about all of it because it's impossible! It's impossible for a pig to make you do something! And now everybody at school thinks you're a freak and now everybody thinks *I'm* a freak, too! Jesus, Jeff! *FUCK YOU!*"

He shoved Jeff hard in the chest, and Jeff fell to the floor beside the tools.

He looked up at his brother.

"I didn't lie."

"Don't say that! *STOP SAYING THAT!*"

Aaron knelt over Jeff and got so close that Jeff could see the red cracks in the whites of his eyes.

"Get away from me!" Jeff said. Then he kicked his brother in the chest. Kicked him so hard that as Aaron flew backward, his lips formed a perfect circle for the wind to pass through.

Aaron fell to his ass and brought his hands to his chest.

"Jesus, Jeff. Why'd you do that?"

"I didn't lie," Jeff said.

Aaron got up and ran at him, his sandy blond hair windswept, his teeth showing. He dove on top of Jeff and they wrestled, knocking both their bikes over, then the garbage cans, too. Aaron gripped a handful of spilled trash and mashed it into his brother's face.

"Get off me!" Jeff managed to say. Then he shoved Aaron hard enough to get on top of him and punched him once squarely in the nose.

Truth was, Jeff was a little stronger than Aaron, and they both knew it.

Jeff stood up and, breathing heavy, leaned back against the wall. He looked down to see Aaron wiping blood from his nose.

"Jesus, Jeff. That's not why I was in here," Aaron said, breathless.

"What do you mean?"

"It wasn't because you lied. Even though I *know* you did."

Jeff composed himself, held back.

"Then why are you in here?"

"Because I knew you'd come looking for me. You wanna go out to Grandpa's and see if Mom's okay."

Jeff felt a jolt of hope. Aaron was right. And because Aaron brought it up, it meant his brother wanted to do it, too. But Aaron wouldn't say so.

"So what if I do?"

"I'm not going with you, Jeff."

"Why not? You ride your bike everywhere."

"No, I'm not going with you."

They stared at each other a long time.

"You're scared of Pearl, too," Jeff finally said.

Aaron's cheeks reddened.

"Am not."

And Jeff knew it was true. Too true. So he didn't press it.

He didn't like seeing his older brother this way. Defeated. And worse . . .

"All right," Jeff said. "I'll go alone."

Aaron nodded without looking him in the eye. Jeff thought he looked ashamed.

Jeff made for the door.

"I didn't lie," he said before entering the house. "And I'm sorry."

He went through the laundry room and foyer, then up the stairs and down the hall to his bedroom. He filled his backpack with things he imagined he'd need out at Grandpa's farm.

For safety. For protection.

All packed, still thinking of Aaron, Jeff looked at himself in the mirror, told himself he could do this, then exited his bedroom.

Pearl was sitting on the carpet in the hall, staring at him with that lazy eye.

"Oh!" Jeff yelled, feeling his body loosen, like he couldn't stand, would never stand straight up again. "Oh!" he said again, pissing his pants, backing up into his bedroom until the backpack crushed the window blinds.

In the pen, Pearl just sat and stared. That's what he did and how he did it. He sat there like a wooden totem, a farmer's crop charm.

But not here. Not in the hall.

Pearl moved. Jeff heard his hooves coming first, then saw the pink snout, pink head, big body trot into the bedroom.

"STAY AWAY!"

But Pearl didn't stay away. He got closer. Too close. He raised his snout to the ceiling, and his lips parted, and Jeff saw rows (rows!) of teeth, shark teeth, framed by brown, fatty lips, until it was all Jeff could see, floor to ceiling fan, Pearl's mouth growing, expanding, wider ...

Jeff screamed and covered his face and said *no no, no no,* and when he brought his hands back down he saw nothing was in his room at all.

Nothing but the warning.

Stay home, Pearl had said. *Stay.*

And Jeff did. He removed his backpack and set it on the floor and crawled into bed and pulled the covers up to his nose despite it not being bedtime, despite it not even being dark out, despite the fact that he was worried sick, so worried, about Mom and what Pearl was going to make her do at the farm.

18

Mom. You're a mom. You're not just a daughter. You've got two boys at home. Home. You've got a home. Remember that? Yeah. Remember that. Hang on to that. Hang on to your home. One day I'm gonna bring home a house for you. Remember THAT? Yeah, that was Randy's drunk joke. The one joke he ever made that still makes you laugh. One day I'll bring you home a house. A misspeak? Or was it brilliance? Hard to tell in those moments, eh? Yeah. Hang on to that. Yeah, even hang on to Randy right now if you gotta . . . hang on to your ex-husband. That's how fucked up this moment is. Whatever you do . . . do NOT hold on to the idea that you've got a young girl splattered with blood in your arms. Do NOT hold on to the fact that Officer Hahn is helping Officer Perry out of the cellar, and it looks like Officer Perry got hurt in a bad way. Don't touch any of that. Think about your boys. Jeff and Aaron. Safe at home. Home. Your home. The home you got yourself. The house Randy never brought home.

You're strong, Sherry.

Hang on to THAT.

And yet she *did* hang on to the young, shaking girl.

"Come here," she said, guiding the girl through what felt like a typhoon. Dad. Dad's farm. Overrun with ... with ... screams? "Lay down in the cruiser."

"I don't wanna fucking *lay down!*" the girl screamed. "I wanna fucking *LEAVE!*"

"Okay, okay," Sherry said, playing the mom, still, no different than the mom she played at home for her two boys. "But I don't think you can leave just yet."

Susan looked at her with such wide eyes that (even now, even in the middle of all of this) Sherry understood she'd said the wrong thing.

"You can do whatever you want to," Sherry said. "But you're hurt."

Susan looked down at her body.

"No I'm not."

"Honey, you're covered in blood."

Susan held up her hands.

"It's not mine. It's his."

She pointed a red finger toward Officer Perry. Sherry looked. The two cops were no longer paying attention to Perry's wound. They were discussing something.

Something.

A silly word out here. Out here felt like *everything.*

"Why aren't they coming to talk to us?" Susan asked, still pointing.

"I don't know," Sherry said. "Probably because they see you're with me. And since it's his blood all over you, he must know you weren't the one who was hurt."

"It's the pig," Susan said. And Sherry felt her stomach drop lower than where it already was.

Susan had said the only thing that could possibly have made her feel worse.

"The what?"

"The pig," Susan repeated, crazed. Her eyes looked very white in her red face. "You mentioned him, too. Don't pretend you didn't. He can . . . *talk*."

Sherry almost said, *Honey, go on and sit in the cruiser*. She almost said, *You've hit your head*. But she stopped herself. Or rather, Jeff stopped her. A concrete, vividly detailed image of her son, telling her the same thing.

Pearl can talk! He made me wanna do it!

She left the girl and walked straight for the cops.

"Sherry," Officer Perry said, holding up his one good hand to let her know they needed a minute, just one, to discuss the dead axe-man in the cellar. But Sherry didn't care.

"It's the pig," she said, recalling the first time she met Pearl, when he followed her silently along the fence and scared her childhood friend Allison.

The moment had come for Sherry to admit to herself that she had many stories like this one. Stories that starred Pearl, always the single shimmering object in the corner of a very dark place.

Pearl.

Always Pearl. Always a bad feeling. Like something worse than a storm was coming. Like a tornado. Or something even worse yet. Some kind of black wind, black groaning wind, strong enough to grip your arms and drag you toward something obscured by the rising dust in the distance, something just beginning to show itself.

Jeff had his story, yes.

But Sherry had many.

"What's that?" Officer Perry said, looking once past Sherry

toward Susan Marx standing by the cruiser. He hadn't forgotten the phone call she'd made to 911. What she'd said about pigs. And now here was Sherry Kopple saying a similar thing.

Pigs, Annie, the dispatcher, had said. *The girl said the pigs were trying to kill her.*

Pigs.

"It's the pig," Sherry said again. And then she half smiled. Because it felt good. Good to admit it, out loud, how fucking insane that pig made her feel.

And for how long? How long had she hidden this truth from herself? From Jeff and Aaron? From Dad?

Jeff, she thought. Jeff wasn't crazy at all.

But the smile fell quickly.

Because Sherry had stories, too.

19

In school they taught you about *violations*. About the line a friend or a family member shouldn't cross. This time, it was a made-for-school video, and sexual violation was the bulk of it. Sherry was only fifteen years old, and when the man playing the uncle closed the door to his niece's bedroom (and then turned to face her with a horrifying half smile in the dark), the entire classroom gasped in unison. All except Sherry. Not because Sherry didn't understand what was afoot. Not because she couldn't tell that the girl's uncle was planning something terrible. It was because she'd seen worse. *Felt* worse, in an intrinsic, foundational way. She'd just never had the word for it.

Violation.

And it wasn't her body that was in danger, Sherry understood very clearly.

It was her mind.

Pearl had somehow gotten into her mind.

A single quick glance out her bedroom window could alter the entire rhythm of her day. If Pearl was in the pen, looking back, then Sherry would experience a feeling of dread for hours after, never quite sure what caused it.

Just a pig.

She thought this phrase a lot in those days. *JUST A PIG.* Pearl is . . . *just a pig.* But she hadn't stopped to ask herself why she was repeating this. Why she felt like she *had* to repeat this. Had Pearl done something . . . unpiggish? It's not like she'd seen him preparing breakfast and had to remind herself of his nature before she went a little mad. It's not like Pearl played violin in the pigpen. He didn't type letters, sharpen knives, blow up balloons. He was, after all . . . just a pig.

Or was he?

Some mornings she'd see him sitting (the way he sat on his ass, arms resting on his belly, was maybe a little unpiggish, truth be told), staring out across the crops, and other mornings he'd be looking up at the farmhouse.

But not the farmhouse, exactly.

Sherry's bedroom window.

Sherry understood that this could have been cute. Should have been reason to think Pearl particularly liked her. What farm girl didn't experience a little flattery when the horses and chickens took to them? In some ways, living on a farm was like living with a hundred magnificent pets, all your own. Some girls at school were jealous. They said as much. And some friends had even come to consider particular animals on Kopple Farm *their* best friend. As if Sherry and her father were only boarding Amanda's chickens.

But Pearl . . .

Dad? Can you plant trees between the farmhouse and the pigpen?

Trees? What for, Share?

It's the smell . . . it's stronger than it used to be.

The smell? You do live on a farm, remember.

Could you, Dad? Could you plant trees between the house and pen? For me?

Trees so she couldn't see the pen in the morning. Trees so she could finally get a sense that something, *anything*, was between her and the pigs. It should have felt good, asking Dad to do it. It should have felt like she'd gotten something (even a vague un-named something) off her chest. But it hadn't. Instead, it felt like a confirmation. Why would Sherry be asking to block the pen if there wasn't something truly frightening in the pen to block?

Or maybe, she told herself, it *was* the smell. Maybe she was just being a fifteen-year-old girl, worried about her clothes smelling. Embarrassed that she slept so close to a pigpen.

Sherry told herself these things. Sometimes they felt true enough to get her through the morning, but never much longer than that.

Dad planted those trees. And the speed with which he did it wasn't lost on Sherry. Or her friends.

When did your dad put in the trees? Allison asked.

A week ago.

Why?

I asked him to.

And he just . . . did it? That's not like your dad.

No, it's not.

He must've wanted them there, too.

Why, when it came to Pearl, did it seem like Sherry couldn't *see*? Couldn't make connections between thoughts? As if there were a film between her and Pearl, a layer of skin that made it difficult for Sherry to come to conclusions, made it hard for her to know how

to feel about him at all. Some animals you loved. Others had a
temper, and you stayed away. And some you were indifferent to.
But Pearl?

Sherry didn't know *how* she felt about him.

The trees helped. No doubt the trees helped, and soon Sherry
wasn't looking out her bedroom window as often as she used to.
The short evergreens perfectly blocked her view of the pen, and
unless she stuck her head out the window and leaned out to her
waist, she couldn't even see the fence. But how *much* did this help?
Sherry couldn't say. It certainly didn't rid her of the brooding,
building sensation that something foul was in the pen. And if she
let her mind go too far in that direction, she understood clearly
that the trees made it a little *worse*, in fact; many days it felt like
there was something undefined behind the branches, a creature
she couldn't imagine anymore on her own, something she wouldn't
know the details of until it was too late.

Her fear was no longer focused on the shape of a pig.

Maybe Pearl was slow. Was that it? Was something wrong with
Pearl's . . . brain? Sherry wanted to believe this. Wanted to say *yes*,
Pearl was deformed, poor thing, he was at a disadvantage. Maybe
the other pigs even mocked him, made fun of his lazy eye, his
crooked lips, his fey way. But this was as easy to believe as Dad
taking a week off of working.

Dammit, no. Pearl wasn't slow. Pearl was the furthest thing
from slow.

Pearl was too *smart*.

And no matter how many obstacles she put between herself and
the pig, there were still her chores to do. And her chores brought
her to every creaky corner of the farm. Including the pigpen. Dad
could plant as many trees as she asked him to, but that wasn't
going to stop him from telling her she had to clean out the pen,

had to feed the pigs, had to wash the newborns, had to assist with a birth. In this way, the trees *were* worse . . . for every time Sherry approached the pen they acted as a kind of curtain, yet to be parted, heavy green cloth that now gave the pigs some privacy. In fact, often, carrying a bucket of slop, Sherry felt like *she* was violating the personal space of the *pigs*. Like she ought to knock, ought to clear her throat, anything so that the pigs knew she was about to come around the trees and see them. See whatever they were doing in private. Like mating. Like eating. Like planning.

Planning?

Sherry started thinking this way while still at Morgan High. Started seeing Pearl and the other pigs as being capable of doing things the other animals weren't. Almost as if they might . . . revolt. She'd been learning about revolution in class, Cuba, Mexico, America, and while she understood that her lessons were coloring her perspective, she couldn't help but wonder if maybe these lessons were coming exactly when they needed to . . . as a warning.

Planning?

Planning.

Planning what?

Sherry didn't know exactly, but every time she unlocked the gate and stepped into the pen she felt like the pigs were pretending not to do whatever they had been doing before. Like when she walked in on Dad and Jack Andrews sitting at the kitchen table, drinking bourbon. The pigs had the same looks on their faces that Dad and Jack did. A kind of *nothing going on here* expression. A looking out of the corner of their eyes. It seemed to Sherry that, ever since Dad planted the trees, the pigs had grown more capable of keeping secrets. More often than not, they sat together by the far side of the fence. Sat without squealing, without grunting. They watched her enter, and they watched her set down the bucket, and sometimes (oh God) *sometimes* Sherry even caught one or two of them looking across the pen at Pearl, Pearl who sat alone on his ass, limp wristed and with his head tilted, his lips curled up at the edges like some kind of permanent condescending smile.

But Sherry was a farm girl first, the daughter of a farmer, and she lived in the upstairs bedroom of a farmhouse in Chowder. If there was one thing she couldn't allow, it was a fear of entering the pen. That was for her friends to feel. For cousins who were visiting and didn't know any better. Why, if Sherry Kopple got spooked on the farm, the place she'd been raised, the life she knew, all she knew, why, she'd have to . . . she'd simply have to . . .

. . . she'd have to *leave*.

But every time Sherry considered this, she wondered if she was thinking on her own. And that was much scarier than anything the pigs could physically do to her.

Did Pearl want her to leave?

No doubt it was natural for a farm girl to eventually want to leave the farm. Sherry knew this because Dad had told her as much once in the middle of a flash argument. He'd said that she was going to leave one day because the "American farm" was dying, and a big part of that was because none of the farmers' kids wanted to stick around. They all wanted to "see the cities," he'd said. "Sleep in the streets," he'd said. "Try every drug and drink in the book," he'd said. And though Sherry was interested in that book, she also thought Dad was crazy for suggesting she would ever go. Leave the farm? She'd never do such a thing. She *loved* the farm, the animals, the work, her father. Yet, every time she placed her fingers on the gate of the pigpen, she recalled Dad's words and discovered she kind of liked them. She liked what they stood for and what they meant. She liked that the scenarios Dad alluded to were possible, that she *could* leave if she wanted to. It was just a matter of *acknowledging* what she wanted. There was a whole world to see, after all, people and places beyond the boundaries of Chowder, and certainly beyond the boundaries of the farm.

And the pen, too. Beyond the boundaries of the pen. Don't forget that. Don't forget that every time you step into the pen it feels like you've stepped into a psychic tunnel, an unseen tapestry of confused thinking, sluggish, mispronounced words that come at you with blunt force, as if he who speaks them speaks in club, speaks in battery, speaks in closed hard fists that hurt the mind, hurt the thinking, hurt the ability to decide. Don't forget that it feels like you step into another world in there; their *world, the pigs, where they talk about things, nasty things, that you and Dad aren't allowed to know about, aren't* invited *to know. You can see it in their side glances, the mocking way they all acknowledge you as you set down the bucket, as you set down to your chores. You can see it, ah, you can* feel *it, too! Like you wanna (*need to*) wipe the webs from your arms and legs. Every time you step into the pen it feels like you just ran through a wall of spiderwebs, and shit if the spiders aren't already crawling all over you. That's it, Sherry. Don't forget that feeling. That crawling you feel? Those aren't spiders. Those are the secrets of the pigs. Pearl's mind. Planning. The pigs' world.*

Pearl's world.

Yes, the pigs were certainly getting to Sherry in a big way. So she did what any teenage girl would do about it. She asked a friend.

"You think what?" Gayle Drake said as the two sat in Gayle's car on the side of Murdock Road.

"I think they can hear me thinking."

"Are you taking drugs? I thought we agreed we'd try marijuana together. Remember?"

"No drugs."

"But you think the animals can hear you thinking . . ."

Gayle had a way of saying things that made you feel really dumb. Sherry wanted that then. Wanted someone to tell her she was being really dumb.

"Not the animals, Gayle. The pigs. And maybe not the pigs, either. Pearl."

"Pearl. Is that the huge girl pig?"

"No. The male with the lazy eye."

"*That* one?"

"Yes."

"Why that one? And why the hell did your dad name him Pearl?"

Gayle laughed, and in that laughter Sherry heard her father mocked. She wanted that. Wanted all of it to be mocked, her whole life to be belittled. If anybody could shrink the size of Sherry's world, it was Gayle Drake.

"Because of his eye."

"His eye?"

"Yeah. Dad said it was like finding a pearl inside a dark clamshell, that eye."

"The bad eye?"

"I think so. Must be. Yes."

"And you think Pearl can hear you . . . think."

"I'm afraid of him, Gayle."

"Then get rid of him!"

"Dad loves him."

"But your dad's gonna kill him soon. Right?"

"He's supposed to."

"And you don't think he will?"

"No. I don't think he will."

Even then, with Gayle in the car and the lights off and all that space between herself and the farm (*the pigpen, Sherry, space be-tween yourself and the pigpen*), she felt nervous talking about it. Talking about Dad killing Pearl.

Like she was revealing something. Like she was letting Pearl in on a secret of her own. Like she was giving Pearl key information by speaking with Gayle in a dark car two miles away.

This thought bugged her for months. Years. And on her seventeenth birthday, as she blew out the candles on her cake, Sherry should have been wishing on the future, should have been thinking about graduating, should have been planning for college.

But she didn't.

I wish Dad would kill Pearl.

And in the rising smoke of the blown-out candles, as Dad and her friends applauded, Sherry thought she saw Pearl himself, a misty rendering, rising to the ceiling, his head tilted, as if studying her, his lips curled in an impish, knowing smirk.

Why *hadn't* Dad slaughtered Pearl? Was it something Sherry should do herself? A thought took root and began growing quickly:

Would some part of Dad, a necessary, *vital* part, be relieved if Sherry killed Pearl for him?

She started thinking about this a lot. Started thinking about doing this . . . for Dad.

But farm girl or not, the reality of it, retrieving an axe from the shed, carrying it into the pen, *using* it on Pearl . . . was its own horror, an impossible-to-navigate nightmare vision that transcended her private morality.

Could she do it? Could she truly see herself doing it?

Well . . . she tried.

Walter Kopple left the farm every Saturday, drove his dented Ford into downtown Chowder, to Ron Ron's Hardware, where he restocked on nails, hoses, and whatever else he'd used for repairs throughout the week. Dad was clockwork with everything he did, and Sherry knew this better than anybody else. So, having made her decision to slaughter Pearl while Dad was away, she was visibly anxious at dinner the night before.

"What's bothering you, hon?"

"Nothing, Dad."

"You thinking about college?"

"No. Not that."

"Well, you should be."

"I will. I am. I mean . . . not yet. I need to see the world first, Dad."

"See the world. You know, with all that ought to be done around here, sometimes you make it sound like you need to see anything but the farm."

"Dad."

But he was right. And had Sherry been so obvious? Was it the sort of decision a father could spot a mile away on a teenage daughter? How did Dad know that she was thinking one of them had to go, herself or Pearl?

Or maybe . . . *maybe* Dad was trying to guide the conversation closer to what Sherry wanted him to say.

You know, with all that ought to be done around here . . .

Maybe Dad was trying to get her to talk about killing Pearl.

Oh, how she wanted him to ask her that! Oh, how she wanted him to ask who, *who, WHO* was she trying to get away from?!

"So what is it?"

"Nothing, Dad. Like I said."

"It's something. You're whiter than your napkin."

Did he know?

She wished there was a private place to put her thoughts. A place where Dad (*Pearl, Sherry, PEARL*) couldn't find them.

"Well, whatever it is," Dad suddenly said, his sad eyes upon the table. "Just go through with it. Don't think about it. *Do* it."

Dad got up and left Sherry with the conviction that he knew after all. Knew what she was planning. As if Dad, like Pearl, was able to hear her thoughts, like her thoughts came through the radio speakers in the living room.

I AM GOING TO KILL PEARL TOMORROW, DAD, BE- CAUSE IF I DON'T PEARL IS GOING TO KILL YOU, ALL OF US, EVERYBODY. THE PIGS ARE PLANNING, DAD! THE PIGS ARE PLANNING! THE PIGS ARE PLANNING TO KILL!

The next morning, Dad left an hour earlier than routine. As if giving Sherry time to prepare, time to make sure she did it.

Whatever it is, just go through with it.

Sherry immediately set about lying to herself. She pretended the shower she took wasn't any different than any other shower. Pretended she wasn't washing hands that would soon hold an axe. That she wasn't shampooing hair that would be tied behind her head, out of the way of a solid downward swing. That she wasn't washing a face that would be the last face Pearl would see before dying.

She got dressed and made sure not to dress like she was going into the pen. But she *was* going into the pen. There was no way she was going to try to coax Pearl out to the barn. She didn't trust the idea of unlocking the gate, of Pearl being *free* for any amount of time. And more than that, Sherry wasn't sure she *could* get Pearl out of the pen. The idea was intimidating, as if sitting down to a game of chess with one of the old men who played regularly in the windows of Games and More in downtown Chowder. As if Pearl would win that game. As if Sherry wouldn't even know how she lost.

After getting dressed, she forced herself to drink a cup of coffee. Forced herself to experience an everyday morning. She brewed a pot and read the paper Dad left on the kitchen table. She pretended every headline didn't read ominously, darker than they usually were, as if revealing that because Sherry was planning on murdering Pearl, she was seeing for the first time the true nature of the world and the news it made. Once the coffee was ready, she folded the paper and placed it on the table, then opened it again and left it a mess. Like it'd been read. A regular morning. All of this. Regular. She drank her coffee and exited the farmhouse with a mind to do her chores.

Nothing more.

She didn't think about going to the shed. She just went to it.

She didn't imagine Pearl dead in the pen.

And yet . . . a variance of the same idea . . . wondering *why* she wasn't allowing herself to think these things. Was it because she wouldn't go through with it if she did? Or was it because she was worried that, if she thought about it . . .

. . . Pearl would hear?

It was too late to allow anxiety a victory, and Sherry continued to the shed, passing the wall of evergreens Dad had planted at her behest. She didn't look to the trees, didn't part the branches, didn't determine where Pearl was sitting. But she felt the pigs looking. Felt Pearl's mind, too. Could feel the tendrils of the web, the mesh of thoughts and yearnings that packed that pen like too many wires stuffed into a toolbox. Too much rope in a drawer. She could feel them, yes, ticklish thoughts, as if Pearl was reaching through the trees with his mind, attempting to determine exactly what the farmer's daughter was up to this morning, why she refused to look in his direction, why she had such focus on her face, such an expression of forced fearlessness. Sherry could feel them! Pearl's thoughts. Could feel them like she felt a piece of thread dangling from a shirtsleeve. A web hanging between trees in a game of tag.

Sherry thought of Brazil. Thought of Rio de Janeiro. As she approached the shed she understood that she was in view now, in view of the pen. If any of the pigs wanted to see her now, they could. But she thought of Brazil, of South America, of the photos she'd seen and the places she wanted to go. She imagined herself in Santa Teresa, visiting the opera house, the Biblioteca Nacional, where the reading room looked as palatial, as big as the entire farm she'd been raised on. Brazil, yes, she would go to Brazil when she graduated, go as far from here (*the pen*) as she could.

Unless she rid the farm of her reason for going first.

She reached for the shed door and had a momentary headache, a brief pang that felt like a physical shove, a warning, but not quite strong enough to actually force her to stop. Yet, she *did* stop. Mid-reach. Her hand trembling in the space between herself and the flaked white paint.

She didn't turn around, didn't face the pen. Instead, she breathed deep and looked out across the cow pasture.

Sherry shrieked, a stump of a high-pitched moan.

Sherry didn't want to see what she saw in the cow pasture, and so she turned away. But not for long.

What's happened? she thought.

But she knew what had happened because she'd seen a lot of it on the farm.

Death had happened. Two dozen deaths; inert mounds on the grassy earth, twenty-four cows dead on their sides in the pasture.

"Dad!" she instinctively called. But Dad wasn't here to answer.

The cows. The cows had died overnight. How?

The feeling Sherry had was an amalgamation, such a *mix* that she didn't know how to hold it. Well within the sadness of seeing the cows on their sides and the horror of believing the pigs were watching her from their pen, she felt the smallest, shameful, sprinkle of relief.

For having something else to do . . .

. . . something other than killing Pearl.

When she whirled to face the pen, her ponytail struck her cheek. As if it were webbing itself.

The pigs weren't watching her.

Only Pearl.

Sitting how he always sat, his front hooves limp, his head tilted toward her.

Sherry felt embarrassed. Vulnerable.

Violated.

She ran to the farmhouse without opening the shed.

Later, she overheard Dad and Ty Foreman talking in the kitchen. Dad was devastated. *Cow disease*, Ty said. *Happens to us all once and again.* But he said something else, too, something that scared Sherry so deeply that she invented, on the spot, a place inside herself to tuck such statements, such connections, away.

Eventually she'd call it her mind-bag.

Heart failures, all around. That's what Doc said. But it can only be cow disease. You don't lose twenty-four cows in one night to heart failure, Walt. Not unless something really bad hopped their fence and scared them so badly they'd rather die than face it.

A moment later, upstairs, Sherry opened her books about South America and flipped through the photos she'd already tagged with Post-it notes. She imagined herself living in each picture, as far from the farm as she could get.

As far from the pen.

From Pearl.

20

Far away from Pearl . . .

Mitch didn't know his name for sure, but he'd heard it. Or more . . . he'd *thought* it. But that wasn't right, either. Someone else had thought it for him. Mitch understood that the name went with the pig with the lazy eye, and that *that* pig was the one they'd come to see. It wasn't just the way he sat on the pile of hay like a fat king, and it wasn't necessarily because he was the only pig not to have attacked Mitch or Jerry yet. It was more of a . . . *feeling*. Yeah. Or a . . . truth. Right away, when he'd seen the pig upon the throne, when he first looked into the barn (*before you got stuck, buddy, before you got stuck in a tragedy*) he could tell this pig was special. My God, it was like the pig and Mitch were close!

Closer.

Sure, much closer than Mitch had ever been with any animal before. More intimate. As if the pig had somehow squeezed itself through Mitch's ears and lodged itself in his memory and mind. Mitch didn't want to admit it, but it felt like there was a possibility the pig had *invited* him to come to the farm. It was ridiculous, of course, and if he thought about it too long he would definitely lose his mind, but just *maybe* it was possible all the same.

Because, if Mitch hadn't been too horrified to admit it, he would say that Pearl's was the face he imagined when he first heard word of a talking pig. Hell, even when Evan McComber snuck into the office and squealed Jeff Newton's gossip over the PA.

Yep. Mitch had seen the lazy eye, the smile, Pearl.

But how much of this thinking was rooted in the slow, grueling pain he'd felt below his waist, at both knees, in his neck, wrists, and shoulders, too? Why, if Mitch was willing to believe a pig was capable of worming its way into his mind from all the way out at Kopple Farm, then why the hell couldn't he believe that the same pig was able to make Mitch *think* he had seen him when the announcement came over the PA? For Christ's sake, which thoughts were his own? Which images? Were any images of the pig, how Mitch saw him, true?

The way he sat up like a big baby boy? The way his front hooves dangled like a little prince waiting for slop to be served?

Mitch didn't know. And he didn't have time to know. Somehow, he and Jerry and Susan had been lured out here, whether it be by gossip, telepathy, or—

Wait.

Where was Susan now?

Mitch looked around the barn, squinting through swollen eyes, inwardly praying that he didn't see her body, limp, somewhere inside. His concern wasn't as chivalrous as it ought to have been, because though Mitch cared about Susan's safety, her absence could also mean . . . *help*.

Instinctively he opened his mouth to speak, to call for her, to ask where she was, to howl a single syllable of hope.

Help.

But when his lips parted, he tasted a mouthful of blood instead. He spat it out, and it went up his nose, over his nose, too, between his eyebrows, through his hanging hair, and plopped in a pool in the dirt above his head.

Then Mitch realized he and Jerry were strung up, upside down, in the barn.

How the pigs did this, Mitch had no idea. In fact, it was so frightening to imagine them tying rope around his ankles, under-standing the concepts of leverage, that he shot-putted the image out of his mind completely. Still, no matter what ideas he opted not to consider, there was nothing he could do about the actual pigs who stood on what looked like the ceiling, their snouts less than ten feet from his face.

At Mitch's failed gargling of the word *help*, the wall of them snorted interest in unison. Mitch's entire view was framed by the pigs on top, the walls of the barn along the sides, and an emptiness leading to the barn roof beyond his sneakers. And in the center of this? Mitch. Mitch's vulnerable body. And would the pig who asked him to come (*THAT'S NOT WHAT HAPPENED!*) show up there? Tuck a bib into his shirt before eating Mitch and Jerry from the bellies up?

"Mitch . . ."

Mitch shrieked at the sound of his name, which elicited more snorts from the ceiling of snouts. And to think, Mitch was one half of the Plastic Satanic Club. The baddest mothersuckers at Morgan High.

Shrieking in Hell.

At first he thought the pig had called his name, could actually *see* him calling his name; those curled lips parting to pronounce a word, a single word, one syllable alone:

MITCH.

But it wasn't Pearl who spoke to him. It was Jerry.

"We need to get out of here," Jerry said.

Mitch experienced a temporary relief so enormous he almost mistook it for freedom.

He couldn't see Jerry, but felt his body hanging beside his own.

"You're okay," Mitch struggled to say. "That's great."

At the sound of his voice, a black-and-white snout came fast and pressed hard against Mitch's nose. Mitch yelled, and the pigs snorted, and holy no, if it didn't sound like laughter, *fuck* if it didn't sound like the fucking pigs were really laughing!

Jerry remained silent, and Mitch thought of Susan and the only word he cared about right now.

Help.

Susan. Where was Susan? Was she getting help? Was she getting them out of there? Was she halfway to downtown Chowder by now? A beautiful, terrified blonde, limping up a country road, flagging every trucker that passed?

Who wouldn't stop for her? Who wouldn't ask what she needed? *HELP!*

Mitch felt hope. Hope because he couldn't see Susan. Hope because, whatever the pigs had done to him and Jerry, they were still alive.

But Mitch didn't *know* what they had done to them.

Manic, he summoned what strength he had and drew his chin to his chest to get a look at his body. But the sight of himself was brief, blurry, and he couldn't even be sure if he was hanging by one leg or two.

"Jerry?"

It sounded more like *Jaaaarrreeeee.*

"What?"

"Do we still have our legs?"

"What?"

Horror in Jerry's voice, too.

As the friends attempted to curl up enough to look at their bodies, the band of pig snouts pressed firmly against their foreheads, forcing them to hang straight.

"Help," Mitch said. Small and meek.

He thought of Susan Marx flagging down a truck. He imagined her with an army.

And the pigs snorted till their snorts sounded like the laughter of old, sick men, seated around a filthy table, ridiculing the folly of youth.

21

"Help," Susan said. "We need to get help."

The word sounded so unnecessary to Officers Perry and Hahn that they blushed.

"We *are* help," Perry said.

Susan shook her head no.

"We need a *lot* of help."

"Calm down," Hahn said, reaching for her. But Susan shot his hand a look that froze it. Hahn, six inches taller than Perry, and fairer in every way, looked to Susan like a snowman, and just as powerless on this warm autumn evening.

"He can talk, do you understand that? The fucking pig can talk. And the man in the basement? That man was doing what the pig wanted him to do."

"She's right," Sherry said. So many memories . . . so many still-life paintings, hanging uneven on Sherry's interior halls. Pearl in oil.

Perry shook his head.

"Okay," he said. "We're not gonna stand out here and tell you we think you're wrong for the next half hour, so you can quit with the convincing. What we need to know," he spoke lower, "is where the hell the pig is now?"

Of course, Perry had a few ideas of who the pig might be. A man who calls himself the Pig? That was possible. A cult-figure kind of guy. That was one. A drug dealer was another.

"Where's your dad?" he suddenly asked Sherry, and Sherry blanched.

"I don't know."

She looked to Susan as if Susan might help, but it was clear the teenager had no idea.

"Susan," Perry pressed. "Has anybody been inside the house?"

Susan nodded.

"I was inside the house when I called you guys. But that's not where you need to be. You need to be over *there*." She pointed to the barn. "*That's* where the pigs are keeping Mitch and Jerry prisoner."

Perry opened his mouth to say something when a chorus of snorts erupted from the barn.

Perry and Hahn looked at each other.

"Let's go check out the barn, Hahn."

"That's right. That's the right thing to do."

But neither was moving.

Why?

Sherry watched them closely. She caught a silent transference, perhaps something only two police officers should understand.

They're scared. My God, the two officers that are here to protect, here to help, *are just as scared as we are.*

"Go on!" Susan suddenly shrieked. "Go . . . arrest him!"

Perry nodded.

But Hahn remained still.

"What is it?" Sherry asked. "Why aren't you guys moving?"

Hahn turned to face her. He wasn't hiding his fear anymore.

"I seen Pearl at the Chowder Fair a few years back, and it was the first I ever seen him. We was working security. Me and Oliver here both. But I was alone with Pearl for a spell. Saw some things I haven't unseen just yet."

"What? What things?"

Hahn looked to the dirt then all the way up to the sky.

"It doesn't matter right now!" Susan yelled, incredulous. "Fucking go in there and kill him!"

Another eruption from the barn, and the officers had no choice. Perry leading, they descended the grassy hill to the dirt path between the farmhouse and the trees that blocked the pigpen. Sherry and Susan followed, and when they reached the trees, Sherry instinctively looked to her right, a thing she'd done a thousand times as a teenager herself.

You're not checking the house, because you know Dad's not in there. You know that, whatever all of this is, he's a part of it. Down here. Down by the pen.

She didn't *want* to, but she reached out and parted some of the branches of the evergreens. She searched for Pearl in the pen.

He wasn't there. Of *course* he wasn't there. Because the Day had come. The Day had finally come. It was the Day Sherry had known was coming since the day she discovered all the cows had died overnight.

One day Pearl is going to have this place all to his own.

She'd thought it a hundred times, but she never quite knew what it meant. Was it just a gut feeling? Or had she tapped into Pearl's brain . . . his wishes . . . his wants . . . his plans?

It didn't matter how Sherry knew it was coming. The Day had come.

Pearl wasn't in the pen because Pearl had figured a way *out*.

As Perry and Hahn reached the barn ahead and Susan came slowly behind them, Sherry turned right, following the curve of the evergreens, toward the open pen gate. Behind her, the police and Susan advanced on the barn. Susan was warning them, don't let him tell you what to do, don't let him talk to you, don't look the pig in the eye.

Don't look the pig in the eye.

Which eye?

Sherry stepped toward the open gate. Dead leaves rose from the hard earth and circled her ankles like they were herding her . . . directing her into the pen. But she stopped.

Because she'd seen a boot, and a leg, sticking up out of the mud.

The Day had come, indeed.

Dad, she thought, trembling with her back to the trees, the trees she had asked Dad to plant. *I'm sorry.*

Not sorry that death had come for him, because eventually it had to. Not sorry for not killing Pearl, though she should have. Not even sorry for never trying to convince him Pearl was bad.

Sherry was sorry for how deeply Dad had gotten tangled in Pearl's web.

Long ago, approaching the shed, she'd felt only the tendrils, the very edges of the netting.

But Dad had been cocooned.

By the time she stepped into the pen, she was crying.

As the two police officers shouted out *holy hell* at the sight of something in the barn, Sherry cried in the pen.

The Day had come.

22

Looking into the open barn, gun drawn, Officer Hahn thought, *You should have seen this coming.*

Because of the state fair. Because of what he saw Pearl do at the state fair back in '09.

Hahn was new to Chowder back then, new*er,* as he'd just cleared basic training six months before. That meant he'd been only six months on the beat in a town of twenty thousand, where an officer was lucky to have five or six exciting calls in a career. Turned out, things were a little boring. Yes. No doubt. Paul Hahn wasn't from "the big city," but Grand Rapids was a fuck of a lot bigger than Chowder, which was situated a solid eighty-eight miles north of Hahn's hometown. Not long gone were the days he'd filled fantasizing about vanquishing the injustices in western Michigan: debunking crooked politicians, unearthing insidious plans, putting the rotten in cuffs. He'd gone so far as to include the side effects of being a cop in these fantasies; visions of himself at a bar, drinking a beer after a particularly tough bust, soaking in the admiration of the bartender, the regulars who knew intrinsically that police work *must* be taking a toll on Officer Hahn. He saw imaginary broken relationships, never able to hold on to a woman because of his strict, obsessive, dedication to the force. The *force*. The police force and the force inside him, too. The force, always compelling him to do good, to help those in need, to watch out for the bastards and to always be ready to face them.

Oh, how these fantasies carried him through training! *Always* with that vision of himself as the vigilante savior type, just doing my job, just doing my job, but *also* very deserving of notoriety and medals for just doing my job, but just doing my job! Even as he watched other Chowder newbies lose their cool, lose their patience, as they discovered the gig was a bit more demanding than just busting grassers for drugging down in an idling car. Even then, Paul Hahn kept his cool.

Even then!

Because the truth was, snoozer town or not, any police force was kind of a scary place.

In training, they told you all about cases gone wrong, broken beats, and showed you pictures for proof—officers gunned down, old men and women mugged, the bruises on the faces of beaten children. There was a helluva lot about domestic violence, and damn if it didn't start to feel like you'd signed up to be the blue-cloaked executioner of counseling. As if he, Paul Hahn, was some sort of superhero social worker, one that was allowed to carry a gun. And use it, too. And these were the steps you had to take, the classes you had to go to, the lessons you needed to *learn* if you wanted to climb the blue ladder. If you wanted to talk with gruff men and women by the clacking typewriters, the same people who walked the station halls like indestructible giants. If you wanted to be like *them* you had to study the photographs, read the information, train, train, train, until all the excitement and all the visions you once held so dear ended up in the paper shredder with all the documents and reports you made too many spelling errors on to submit.

Hahn didn't mind all this. He had the right perspective for the job. Chowder itself wasn't going to be like the photos he had to endure in training. He didn't delude himself into thinking that ten days after signing up he'd be wearing a blue mask, rescuing co-eds from drunk monsters, spotting serial-killers-to-be and thwacking them on the head before bringing them hog-tied into the station. Hahn knew things took time. Shit, *everything* took time. Weeks passed between him signing up for the force and the actual first day of training. Background checks didn't only happen to people renting an apartment, you know. And yet . . . six months into the gig, and Paul Hahn was pretty close to falling asleep on the job. In fact, he *did* fall asleep on a shift, after working the state fair all day, sitting in the cruiser that night, parked by the side of the highway, waiting for an unsuspecting Chowderite to come zipping by with a foot made of iron. But therein lay the problem; *nobody* zipped in Chowder. Heck, there were some thrill-seeking teens, but none of their parents had a speedy ride, and what the hell was Hahn expected to do? Pull over a John Deere? Damn. So he'd fallen asleep one night as the moon painted the cornfields maize, and the crickets sang like the Andrews Sisters with all of their cousins, too. There was a lot of empty space out here, and, holy damn, there was a lot of downtime and so . . . so sometimes Hahn had to pinch himself in the neck to stay alert. More like Hahn had to turn the radio way up. No big deal. And especially no big deal because nothing big happened the day he actually fell asleep on the job.

Except something big kind of *did* happen that day, but it

wouldn't bear its fruit until much later, until one day when Hahn drove out to Kopple Farm because Oliver Perry called saying he needed some backup and, Jebus, that was a big word out here in Chowder, *backup*, as if anybody ever needed help, as if telling two kids they couldn't draw on the side of a building required backup, damn.

On the way to being the backup, Hahn thought of that day patrolling the state fair, and how strange it was, the weavings of the world, the way one thing led to another, and how sometimes you could feel it, could feel that something was afoot long before it actually was.

It was that pig.

Pearl.

The farmer Kopple was showing him off at the fair the way some people showed off their dogs. Hahn's mother was particularly fond of pet tricks: terriers leaping through Hula-Hoops, bulldogs burping a tune. In fact, it seemed like the dog shows or the late-night animal acts were the only time Hahn's mother had true domain over the television. Hahn's dad didn't mind, and the young Paul Hahn kind of liked it, too. Liked it enough to consider the K-9 unit in Grand Rapids before life's weavings (always a disorganized carpet) delivered him to Chowder. And Hahn had been thinking about it that day, at the state fair, thinking about the K-9 unit and how maybe he should've gone that way after all, hey hey, and wouldn't a dog make a hell of a sidekick? And shit, look there's a cow now, mooing into a megaphone, making the yokels laugh, and shit, there are three chickens dressed in little barbershop quartet outfits (southern campaign hats and all) clucking in three-part harmony *right now*.

K-9. A dog. A great big German shepherd that would strike fear into the hearts of badass criminals, drug pushers and assault-

ers, fistfighting drunks who didn't understand the consequences of
two objects colliding, all the riffraff that needed helping, needed
protecting, needed policing. Yeah, a dog would be nice. A dog
would be better than a pig.

A pig.

A pig on stage, led out on a leash that he clearly didn't need.
Even Hahn could tell that much. The little thing wasn't looking to
go anywhere and really wasn't *looking* anywhere at all given his one
messed up eye. That was obvious from the start. That eye. Shit, it
took up half his little face, that drooping eyelid, as if the pig were
wearing a patch made of his own skin. At first, Hahn thought it
was part of the show. Maybe the pig was going to act like a pirate
or something. Maybe he made an *arrrr* sound, and all the Chowder yokels would bust up laughing, and Walt Kopple would stand
there smiling like a statue of happy farming.

But it didn't go that way.

A wind ruffled the red, white, and blue streamers that hung
from the hem of the tent, the tent that shaded the stage, the stage
that wasn't much more than a few hay platforms pushed together
and raised up some on a few bricks, then draped poorly with a blue
cloth. Hahn had to admit, though, there was something cool about
the stage, the style of it, as if a traveling vaudeville show might use
a stage just the same, might juggle rings of fire and make jokes and
pretend to sneeze their noses off. Yeah, it all had a good look to
it—blue stage, red tent, shadows and light. If Hahn hadn't known
better, he'd think the pig out there alone with Kopple was about to
do something *really* cool, like ... like ... like ...

Like reading minds.

Hahn laughed at his own ideas. A mind-reading pig. The idea
of a pig reading tarot cards or predicting the future was just about
as funny a thing as he could imagine, given the few elements

Chowder gave a man to joke about. Farms. Animals. Farmers. That was about it. So a mind-reading pig . . .

The pig was just sitting there, staring out at the audience of fifty or so, his head tilted to the side like he was the one doing the studying, like he was waiting for *them* to do something instead of the other way around. Hahn couldn't explain it, really, but it truly felt like the pig was the one in the audience and all the yokels (Hahn included now, Hahn a six-month yokel himself) were supposed to perform.

Supposed to think.

Who said that? Did Hahn think it himself? It felt like the sun was getting hotter outside the red tent, and darn if it didn't feel like everyone or *some*one was staring directly into Hahn's eyes, straight into his skull, digging for some nugget of information, some kind of thought or idea or word or something they could use to play with.

The pig stared out at the audience.

"Hey, Kopple!" A fat older farmer named Doug Menken was heckling now. "Does he do anything?"

This got some people laughing, but it was Hahn's job to read people, and he was pretty sure that the nervous laughter rippling through the audience was close to about the same way he felt himself. Two older ladies got up and left. Why? Had it been long enough for them to determine the pig wasn't going to do anything spectacular? Or did they leave because they, too, felt a little bit . . . invaded?

Hahn realized his finger was delicately rubbing the gun in his holster, and he brought his hand away suddenly, almost scared of himself, curious as to how bad a feeling it *was* if it had him reacting like *that*.

But who was he absently thinking of protecting? The yokels? Or himself?

He leaned an elbow on the wooden lemonade stand to his right, behind which Marcy Lee Johns squeezed fresh lemons until they were dry. He smiled at her and said good day, and when he looked back to the stage he saw the pig was looking straight at him, himself, Mr. Paul Hahn, *Officer* Paul Hahn, with that same tilt, that same knowing look in his one good eye.

Hahn dropped the smile from his face the way he was trained to whenever he came face-to-face with a dangerous man. But this . . .

This was a *pig*.

"Come on, Walt!" Another heckler. A woman. "Make him *do* something!"

The crowd was agitated, Hahn thought. And there was a difference between agitated and impatient. Something was bothering them. Hell, something was bothering *him*.

You should kill that fucking pig, Hahn thought. Then he was struck with how silly a thought it was. How cold. Could you imagine? Drawing your gun in the sunshine of the state fair and blowing a pig's face off on a lean-to stage?

The pig was still looking at him. Walt was looking at him, too.

"Make him jump!" someone hollered.

"Does he sing?"

"Make him sing!"

"Sing for me, piggy! Sing for me!"

Foot stomping followed, boots in the dirt, and still Hahn understood (how? why?) that it wasn't so much disrespecting the act as it was wanting the act to be out of sight, out of memory, put away.

Hahn imagined himself carrying the pig into the jail. Locking him up. Then he imagined the same pig convincing him to unlock the cell.

What?

There was a gasp from the audience, and most everybody recoiled when the pig made a slight movement, hardly moved at all. Walt unhooked the leash and spoke.

"Go on, Pearl," he said.

Pearl.

So it was a girl, then?

But no, it was a boy. Hahn didn't have to grow up on a farm to recognize that much.

Pearl.

Pearl slowly trotted to the end of the stage, still looking in Hahn's direction, and then took the stairs. Took them like a prince might, or a rich man, some kind of dandy-boo aware of his posture, his appearance, and whatever it was he was about to do.

The audience rose and parted, making a little path for Pearl to walk. And they watched him walk, watched him closely, perhaps a little afraid, as if the pig had the power to suddenly explode, bomb-like, coating them all in pink flesh.

Pearl walked toward Hahn, and Hahn felt his fingers pointing back to his holster, as if he better be ready, better grip the gun before the little animal got too close.

But really? And in front of everyone? And what the hell was he thinking?

Hahn leaned on the lemonade stand and forced a sweaty smile. Watched the pig just like everybody else was watching. He saw a look of concern on some of the Chowderite faces, as if they were wondering what he was going to do about this, he the cop, he the officer, certainly he was the one who should do something, *some-*

thing about this clear and present danger that wasn't very clear and maybe only *maybe* present but they could feel it all the same can't you feel it can't you *feel the fucking pig reading our minds*?

Silence in the tent. All eyes on Hahn and Hahn's eyes on the unleashed little animal with the bad eye trotting toward him, ten feet away, six feet, four.

The sweat dripped down the side of Hahn's face, and he actually *did* finger his gun, an action that felt less absurd in direct proportion to how close Pearl got to his black boots in the dry dirt.

Then he was there, at the officer's feet, but he was no longer looking at the officer, he was looking at the woman over the officer's shoulder, the woman behind the lemonade stand, Marcy Lee, who was staring back at the little pig with wide, timid eyes.

"Does he . . ." Marcy Lee began.

"Give him some lemonade!" a farmer called. There was some scattered laughter, but it was nervous, no doubt, pins balancing on a wiggly bit of wire.

"I think he wants some," Hahn said, and he couldn't deny the relief he felt, relief that the animal wasn't interested in him after all.

Or was he?

Still, the nagging, the sensation that someone was looking in, peeking somewhere they shouldn't. Hahn imagined he would feel the same if he had to change in and out of his uniform in front of the prisoners out at the Chowder Jail.

Marcy Lee smiled and lifted a cup of lemonade.

"Am I supposed to just . . . hand it to him?"

She looked across the white faces to Walt Kopple standing alone on the stage. He made no movement, no response.

Pearl trotted back toward the crowd, then paused and looked over his shoulder.

Follow me, he seemed to be saying. *And bring the lemonade.*

Even Hahn laughed at this, and Marcy Lee did as the pig seemingly suggested. She stepped out from behind the stand, balancing the full cup as she walked barefoot across the hard dirt, following the pig into the audience under the tent.

Pearl led.

Marcy Lee followed.

Followed him to an old man who sat arched, slumped, facing the commotion, the small (pleasant? somehow not, not pleasant at all) scene the pig had created.

Pearl stopped at the man's feet.

He looked over his shoulder to Marcy Lee.

She looked confused but must have sensed something because she knew to ask, "Would you like this cup of lemonade, Mr. Henderson?"

Hahn knew it before the man responded. Knew that Mr. Henderson *did* want that cup. Wanted it very badly.

He'd been thinking about it. Been thinking about it hard.

Mr. Henderson looked down to Pearl and smiled.

Half toothless, his gums looked dry.

"I sure would," he said, and there was a brief pause. A silence.

Then the audience erupted into cheers, as Marcy Lee handed the cup to the old man and Pearl trotted back to the stage, up the steps, before sitting down on his ass beside Walter Kopple.

And Officer Hahn thought it. Thought it loud and clear.

Should've killed that pig when you had the chance.

But didn't he always have the chance? Didn't he have another chance now?

Should've killed that pig.

And then . . . someone else's voice. As the crowd clapped and wiped their brows, as Marcy Lee shrugged and headed back to her stand, all smiles, and as the pig tilted his head toward Hahn himself, as if now more aware than ever of the officer's thoughts.

Sing for me . . .

Hahn heard it in someone else's sluggish tongue. Someone else's voice.

Sing for me.

Then Walt Kopple bent to reloop the leash on the pig, and Officer Hahn moved on. He'd had enough of the entertainment tent. Enough silly animal tricks for the day. His job was to make sure nobody drank too much, nobody caused a fuss.

But as he walked away he heard it again.

Sing for me.

As if it was Officer Hahn's turn to perform.

Or would be soon.

23

Jeff could *see* it. The state fair. The little pig choosing the lemonade for the old man who wanted it, the old man who showed legitimate surprise that somebody had been paying attention to him. Whether or not the man understood that it was a pig that noticed him didn't matter. In fact, it didn't even matter that it was Officer Hahn who was thinking about it. What mattered was that Jeff was able to see something *Pearl* was seeing.

Did Pearl want him to see these things? Officer Hahn's trepidation? The dark, incongruent thought patterns of the other pigs?

Or did Jeff have some sort of . . . line into Pearl's mind?

Jeff held the bedsheets tight to his nose and alternately looked from the door to the center of his bedroom, the last place he'd seen the pig, when the pig came lunging at him before breaking apart into a cloud of pink mist. But the sight of his own open door had him thinking of another one.

The door the pig had left open. The door into the pig's mind.

Why?

Why was Pearl's "slip showing," as Grandpa would say? Jeff had no doubt Pearl didn't mean for him to see this mishmash of memory.

He's stressed, Jeff thought. And it felt right, felt true. Mom had a face she used whenever she caught Jeff lying. And words to go with it.

You're a terrible liar when you're tired, Jeff.

Thing is, she was right. He *was* a terrible liar when he was tired. Too tired to hide the things he didn't want anybody else to see. Too tired to close the door.

Jeff stared at the bedroom door. Brought his chin to his chest.

He'd seen movement out there. A shadow.

"Oh, no."

The more he looked, the more he realized he could see *Pearl's* shadow out there, splashed against the umbrella wallpaper in the hall. Or was it? It was hard to follow, the way it swayed, the way it dissolved and reappeared again. As if Pearl wasn't able to maintain his own shadow. As if Pearl had so much going on that he'd left the door open and wasn't able to maintain his shadow.

His slip was showing.

He's not out there is why, Jeff thought. *He's on the farm. He's just in your head.*

But if Pearl was trying to scare him, it was working. Working well. Jeff could hardly move for it. And what if he was wrong? What if Pearl *was* out there in the hall, waiting for him to get up and leave, waiting to lunge at him again and show him that same expanding face?

Then why isn't he coming into the room? Why would he just wait out there? And shouldn't that comfort you? If Pearl is in the hall, then Mom is safe at the farm.

Right?

Jeff lowered the sheet from his nose to his chin. The shadow got darker, the ears larger. Like Pearl could hear him. Could hear him deciding whether or not he wanted to get up and get out of the bed.

"You're not real!" Jeff yelled, shaken by the force of his own voice.

The shadow darkened, deeper, and slid along the wall, coming closer.

Jeff looked up to the window over his headboard.

He'd climbed out that window once before with Aaron. Mom wasn't home and the two of them dared each other to go out on the roof. There wasn't much room out there, two feet tops, and Jeff was scared shitless. Aaron went first, keeping close to the home's siding, calling Jeff a chicken for not joining him. Then Aaron got greedy. He inched to the edge, squatted, gripped the gutter. *It's not gonna hold you!* Jeff warned. It didn't. Aaron swung over the side, the gutter fell away easily, and Aaron fell the nine feet to the hard yard below, snapping an ankle upon contact.

Later, on the way to the hospital, Mom was as angry as Jeff had ever seen her.

But, oh boy, did that window look like a good option right now. Should he risk it? The scant footing, the vertigo, the height?

He's trying to scare you so you'll stay. He doesn't want you coming to the farm.

This last thought scared him most of all. And not just because it meant there was something at the farm Pearl didn't want him to see. It also gave Jeff . . . *power.* As if the pig thought Jeff was capable of doing some harm. As if Jeff was a threat.

He briefly imagined a face-off, himself and Pearl, then saw

again the axe blade swinging to the neck of the hog in Grandpa's pen. The axe that was in his hands.

Jeff pulled the sheet back up to his nose and watched the shadow recede. For a blessed beat, he imagined the shadow would leave him entirely, leave the hall, take the stairs, and exit the house through the front door, where the sun would obliterate it whole.

But a shadow means something has to *cast* a shadow.

Doesn't it?

And if so . . . what?

A thought? A thought of Pearl's?

Jeff had heard of people so scared they couldn't move. He'd read about it in true crime stories and possibly true ghost stories; when people did nothing as their assailant approached them, too afraid to lift a hand, thinking maybe that, by standing totally still, the horrible thing would just go away. Or maybe more like they'd given up. Here's the horror. Take it. Jeff thought a lot about this moment, when the horror is actually in the room with you. How he would really react if he went downstairs for some juice and found a man with a knife in the kitchen? *You home alone, kid?* What would he do if a ghost came floating out from the open closet door? Would he move? Would he be able to?

He always told himself he would move, yes, faster and more dexterous than he ever had in his life.

And yet, here he was, the bedsheet tight to his nose. Too scared to move.

Come on, he thought. *Don't be like this! Get up! GET UP!*

The shadow swayed in the hall. Darkened.

"You can't hurt me! You can't even use your hands!"

Jeff could hardly believe he'd said that. Shook his head no, telling himself no, no, you didn't need to say that, don't do anything at all!

But then . . . a better thought.

Pearl's shadow got darker and moved every time Jeff imagined getting out of bed, taking action, being brave. It was like Pearl could feel how confident or not he was, and wanted to make sure that confidence didn't get too big.

Without deliberating any longer, Jeff pulled the sheet from his face and swung his legs over the side of the bed. He didn't look to the hall, didn't want to see the long, dark ears, the black snout obscuring the umbrellas on the wall. He went to the window, opened it, and looked out onto the roof. Maybe there was a better place to drop from. Where the ground was higher up or softer. An easier fall.

"AARON!"

He hadn't decided to yell for his brother, it just came out. And he knew there was no chance Aaron heard him. Aaron was in the garage with the radio on. And Aaron didn't *want* to hear any of this.

"AARON!"

Still, he had to try.

A noise from the hall, and it immediately registered as a sound that didn't *belong* in the hall. Metal, a pounding, but not on carpet . . . not on the walls . . . no, no . . . more like the stiff packing of dirt . . . something steel . . . a sound you might hear in . . .

. . . *a barn.*

Yes. That was it absolutely. Jeff had no doubt he'd heard the swinging of the big iron pulley in the barn, how the hooks clacked against one another, the hooks where Grandpa sometimes strung up the pigs before slitting their throats.

Hooks.

In the hall?

No!

Jeff stuck his head out the window, even began to pull himself out. But he was too scared of it, too afraid of the fall.

He whirled to face the hall.

Pearl was already in his bedroom.

But, Christ, it was worse than Pearl. A bad imagining of Pearl. A bit of a man, parts of a woman, a lot of a pig.

Jeff screamed. The face (*It has a lazy eye! It's Pearl!*) came at him, fast.

Jeff leaped up onto the bed, holding his hands out in front of him, like his palms could stop this monster from reaching his body, reaching his chest, tearing into his heart and mind.

But Jeff had moved. Unlike the people in those stories, Jeff *moved*. He knew this about himself now. That he wasn't too scared to do anything about it. That he wouldn't sit still as the horror took him. This was no small revelation, and he scurried toward the open window. He gripped the plastic frame and pulled himself out and closed the window and thought of Aaron doing the same, as if this was that day, Mom not home, Aaron only minutes from breaking his ankle. He even *saw* Aaron out on the roof, saw him sitting on the edge, legs dangling above the yard, a strange smile on his face.

But it wasn't Aaron.

It was Dad.

"Hi, Jeff."

Dad, who Jeff hadn't seen in six months. Dad sitting on the roof.

He waved.

Jeff screamed and looked over his shoulder, back into his bedroom.

Empty.

No monster. And yet . . . the shadow in the hall again.

Dad on the roof.

Hi, Jeff.

Jeff lowered himself back into his bedroom and stood, motionless, unable to decide what to do.

Pearl was difficult enough to understand, but Jeff simply couldn't process Dad. And this horror, this second monster, froze him.

24

Satellites.

Too many. Like an overstuffed solar system. Too much push and pull. Objects orbiting dangerously close to one another. Overlap. Is that what the farmer called it? Is that what the farmer taught him? *Overlap.* That was it. That felt right so that must be it. Things were overlapping. OVERLAP. The men with the weapons were standing in the open barn entrance, and Pearl should have been focused entirely on them, but the boy, the boy was thinking of coming, and Pearl didn't like the boy because the boy was somehow dangerous, sent off bright, painful blues and reds in his mind, warning signs, as if somehow this could all end with him and the boy facing each other, nobody else alive to see it.

Witness.

Pearl remembered that word. That was the first higher-thinking word the farmer taught him. And he taught him it because Pearl needed to know what it meant. *WITNESS.* What you called someone who saw something you did. What you did, too, when you saw something. You *witnessed* or you were a *witness,* and either way it wasn't the best thing to have around. The second man with the gun, the one without the hurt hand, he had witnessed Pearl at the state fair. Pearl knew it then. He didn't know it like he'd later really know it, but he knew it enough to keep tabs on the man in blue. Blues and reds. Like the sirens on those cars. Bad witnesses. The worst kind. Might use their weapons before Pearl had a chance to convince them otherwise. The other one, the one with the hurt hand, Pearl had protected him in the cellar. Caused the delivery-man to off himself because Pearl knew, *knew* that the man in blue was a better ally . . . stronger somehow . . . had a better weapon? And yet, a second man in blue. How could Pearl have missed him coming?

Satellites.

Witnesses.

Too many of them.

And the boy.

The boy was confusing things. Was he coming or wasn't he? And even if Pearl managed to keep him away for now . . . eventually the boy would come. And he would come with other people. Especially when Pearl killed his mother, the daughter of the farmer he'd already ordered eaten.

Satellites.

And too many of them.

Somehow the boy knew it. And this was okay. It was inevitable that Pearl would have to face the boy. As long as Pearl could keep him away, for a while, he might buy some time, might make things less . . . cluttered.

The boy's mother was just discovering her father's body. The men in blue were at the door. The two young men who came looking for Pearl were strung up twenty feet away on the slaughter hooks. And the woman who had come to see him . . .

Susan.

Where was she? What was she doing?

Pearl couldn't think about that right now. Right now he had to let the boy go. Let the Susan go. Let the mother/daughter go.

The men in blue were standing in the doorway. No doubt they'd already seen the two men strung up. No doubt the others (*witnesses*) had already told the men in blue about the pigs. About Pearl. And the one man, the one with two good hands, he was thinking about how he should've done this already, done this in front of all of Chowder at the fair.

WITNESSES

Sing for me, Brother Hahn. Sing for me . . .

It was enough to cause the man to hesitate, and that was all the time Pearl needed to sink into the man's brain, to find balance there, solid footing for his hooves, his ass, a place to sit, to sit and think, to think *at* the man in blue, to think *for* the man in blue.

Sing for me, Brother Hahn. Fetch the Susan. Fetch her.

A flash of confusion in the eyes of the man. Good. This was good.

Pearl adjusted himself on the hay. A simple gesture. Just enough so that the man in blue was frightened by his candor, his casualness, the ease with which he'd convinced him to leave the barn in search of the Susan.

Because that was important. Not only thinking for him, but making sure he was scared of Pearl, too.

"What are you doing, Hahn?" the other man said, the one with the bad hand.

"The girl," he said. Not a woman. A *girl*.

Then Hahn was off, running toward the farmhouse, and the

other one was unsure which way to go for the second time since arriving. Was there a hint of malice in Hahn's voice? Like he was going to . . . punish the girl?

"Help," one of the strung-up teens managed to say, and the man (*Paaarrreeee*, like *Jaaaareeeee*, like *Shaareeeee*) pointed his gun at Pearl.

There were eight pigs between the man and the younger men who were hanging by their ankles. Pearl sensed fear in the man's heart. The man believed he shouldn't be afraid of them, the pigs, believed he should be able to walk right up to them, even pet their heads if he wanted to.

But there were stories. Pearl saw the stories in the man's head. Fiction and fact both. Bad men feeding their victims to pigs. Pigs eating evidence. Bad men and good men, too, disappearing this way.

Down the gullets. Out the ass.

The man in blue advanced. His bad hand hung limp at his waist.

Pearl watched him, cold but not indifferent, recalling an unparalleled burst of power he'd enjoyed only once, many years ago. A perfectly pure eruption of anger that resulted in the physical explosion of a cruel farmer.

Pearl had never been able to locate that strength again.

But perhaps that was because he never had to look for it.

Pearl remembered. And looked for it. As the man in blue was stepping slowly toward him, he searched.

The feeling he'd had the very first time he saw (*witnessed*) the power of the farmer, what farmers could *do* to the pigs. The time Pearl saw . . .

25

... the pigs strung up for the slaughter.

Only a piglet then, just born. Pearl's mother was one of the many hanging from the hooks.

He didn't know Death then, not yet, but was about to learn. He hadn't been alive long enough to hear his mother cry, and even if they shared a pen for the next ten years he might have been spared the sounds. His mother wasn't asking for help. Even fresh from the womb he understood this much. Just born, his intuition was astonishing. The dark filaments in his mother's eyes were bad, Pearl knew, because he *felt* it first. And when the farmer entered the barn, knife in hand, Pearl knew this, too, was bad. His siblings, boy and girl piglets in the same cardboard box, played with one another, impervious to the horrors hanging not ten feet away. But Pearl placed his delicate hooves upon the wall of the box. He watched.

He *saw* the fear in his mother and the fear in the others, strung up, too.

As if the emotions were curling out the nostrils of their snouts, their natures begging for escape. Pearl smelled it. Something burning; safety, happiness, calm. As if the adult pigs themselves were burning, their bodies eaten by a feeling.

The farmer must have noticed all this, too. In a vague, inexperienced way, Pearl knew this to be true. And yet . . .

The man cut once, twice, three times the throats of the hanging pigs, delivering bright splashes, red estuaries that traveled to the tips of their ears. Pearl knew that it was pretty. The prettiest thing Pearl had ever seen. The way the colorful blood played upon the lips of the pigs, their snouts, into their eyes, then pooling on the dirty blue tarp protecting the barn floor.

Pearl watched them, ignorant of Death yet. But when he noted their silence, he understood something final had happened.

He crawled out of the box to find out exactly what it was.

The farmer, a hulking creature half in shadows, noticed. He looked different than mother. Different than the other piglets. His dismissive, uncaring energy was frightening to Pearl; it was clear, too; he didn't care for the piglets in the box, didn't care for them the same way he cared for himself. Pearl was able to see this as easily as seeing if the barn was bright or dark. The man was dark. Toward the pigs he was black. Indifferent. Colorless. A feelingless shape in the barn, wielding an unfathomable tool, a scythe, a blade that shined whether or not light was upon it. He smelled dark, too. Smelled of loneliness and anger and impatience. Pearl couldn't know that beneath the man's flannel shirt were scars from gear, small accidents in the fields, bad cuts that had only half healed, or that the farmer's nearest neighbor had recently told him he should sell this place, sell everything, because he was going under, sinking, and that a sinking farm couldn't tread water.

Pearl trotted to the farmer's feet, and the farmer noticed. Saw the piglet had gotten out of the box. The piglet with the rotten eye.

Sell the farm, Darryl Holmes told him. *Sell everything.*

The farmer eyed the runt. Saw in its ruined eye the ruined farm. Saw his whole life as an embarrassing run of events, one after another, with more than enough time to have made changes, the little fixes that were never made, an eventual avalanche of failure, all dreams dead, and Goddamn this place and Goddamn this pig and Goddamn if the little shit wasn't the very emblem of all and everything that had gone wrong.

The farmer swung the scythe, pendulum-like, at Pearl.

One swing. Solid. True.

And yet ... the piglet didn't squeal. The piglet didn't make a sound.

Did he die so easily? Will all of these problems pass so easily?

It was a refreshing thought, shadowed by the reality of his situation. The farmer was losing everything. The farmer was upset. The farmer *wanted* to see that piglet (youth, promise) die, vanquished violently by his own hand, so that what happened in life was what he *wanted* to have happened.

"Where'd you go, piggy?"

Not only had the piglet not made a sound, he was gone.

Naturally, the farmer thought the force of the blade must have thrown the little thing across the barn.

Under the worktable?

The farmer got on his knees in the dirt.

"Come here, little piggy."

No movement. No sound. Must be dead. Must have thwacked him good after all.

Youth.

Promise.

He imagined a giant scythe descending from the sky, swinging toward his younger, more promising self. It chopped him at the chest, sending one half of him rolling into a black forever, leaving the other half to work the farm, crippled, overwhelmed, incapable. He recalled what it used to feel like to slaughter a pig; the freedom of power, progress, the knowledge that *he* was in charge of the farm and not the other way around.

He stuck the scythe farther under the table, into the shadows, looking for the piglet, hoping to nip him, to hear him squeal.

The piglet with the rotten eye.

Wasn't a pretty sight. Couldn't get forty bucks for that one. Nobody wanted a monster moping around the pen. Farmers would laugh three counties wide. *Did you see Martin's pig? You see that fucked-up eye? Martin's raising deformities out there, got a new approach. It's called . . . desperation.*

But had his eye always been fucked up? Martin couldn't remember. Bob Buck drove the piglets and their mother to Martin's farm. Used them for a . . . what did he call it?

A presentation.

Bob Buck. Nasty man. Rocky man. Successful man, too.

The farmer struck hard into the shadows. Felt nothing. Brought the scythe out and turned on his belly to face the hay. Some of it was in bales, but a lot of it was scattered, making a messy pile by the box of piglets.

The farmer got up. Jammed the scythe into the hay.

"Little piggy? Little ugly pig?"

He expected (wanted) a squeal, a death yelp, redemption.

He jammed the tool again.

"Come now, little piggy! You can't be far!"

Breathless, he paused. And heard a fleshy stretching behind him.

One of the hanging pigs was looking at him. One of the pigs he'd already slaughtered.

Its snout was off center, its face slack from the loss of blood, but its black marble eyes were locked firmly on his own.

It was the mother, he knew. The mother of the ugly pig.

"Not dead yet?" he said.

He stepped around the box of piglets, and the mother's head turned with him.

Strung up by her hind hooves, the rivers of red blood glowed in the shadowy barn.

"Not dead yet," the farmer repeated. He lifted the scythe.

And the mother pig opened her mouth.

And the farmer heard.

Heard a voice.

The syllables were clunky, lumpy, as if something in the barn was trying to speak English, *his* English, as if something in the barn had been listening to him closely.

Nawt ded yayet . . .

The farmer stared, wide-eyed.

He wanted to ask her something, wanted to say, *Did you just . . . talk?*

But the same fleshy stretch stopped him. The head was twisting now, unnaturally, coming up, so that, while her body hung upside down, her head no longer did.

The mouth opened.

Nawt dayed yit.

The farmer struck her head with the scythe, then dropped the tool and struck her head with his bare hands.

Another voice. Coming from a second head.

As the farmer (scared, so scared) stepped back, all the remaining hanging pigs turned their heads toward him. Or did they? He couldn't tell. There was something different about the way the mother moved. These other pigs seemed like something out of a nightmare. Something out of his mind. They opened their mouths in horrible unison, and the farmer screamed. They screamed, too. He moaned. They moaned, too. He laughed as they laughed. Trembled as they shook the hooks.

All to the rhythm of a voice, a mispronunciation of a few simple words:

NAWT DED YIT

The farmer shook his head no, no, the pigs aren't talking, all talking at once, no, Martin Jones isn't cracking up, no, the slaughtered pigs aren't alive, aren't alive, aren't . . . *speaking*. No. Not today. Not even twenty years ago when Martin was young and the farm had so much promise . . . not even then . . . even then this image, this dreadful image, would have fractured his sanity, sent his mind twirling into forever-never, crushed his memories of Mom and Dad, his brothers, Dane and Darren, the women who had passed in and out of his life like silverfish through the hay. All of them breaking up. All of them coming apart. All of them *exploding*.

But, hey, hey, maybe it wasn't just the memories exploding, hey hey, Martin felt some kind of pressure at his temples, at the boundaries of his body, as if he were the scarecrow out in the field and he'd been stuffed too tight, too much, the seams busting a bit, pushing out *out OUT* like if he didn't sit down and sit down *soon* he was going to be in serious trouble might just pop himself might just burst himself might just oh my God *EXPLODE* all over the inside of the barn.

Mother's mouth opened wider. *TOO WIDE*. Martin had lost his mind. And what was she going to say now? What was she going to say that would change him? She could do it. She could gut him right back if she wanted to. All with a word or two. Which words or two? Which words?

No words.

Another head.

It came slowly from under her snout. A second head. A smaller one. Ears. A second snout. A black eye. A small pink body falling clumsily to the barn floor.

The ugly pig.

The one with the fucked-up eye.

Crawled right out of mother's mouth. Sitting on his ass now. Tilting his little head up toward the trembling farmer like he was thinking about it, thinking about the trembling, or making it happen even, making this terrible feeling *happen*.

"Hey!" the farmer managed to yell not one second before he exploded, coating the hanging pigs and the piglet and the sturdy hooks and the little box of babies with everything he was made of, everything he once was.

And Pearl understood that he'd been responsible for it. He understood that somehow he'd made the farmer go away. He'd made the giant, shadowy man into a nothing, into pieces less recognizable than what his mother now was, compared to what his mother was like hours before the farmer killed her.

Pearl sat alone on the barn floor, observing the mess. His power, his ability, struck him no differently than a bird agreeing it could fly. Pearl didn't know if it was special or strange, astonishing or scary. He didn't know what the other piglets could do. Not yet.

He trotted slowly over to the cardboard box. His piglet brothers and sisters were sticking their small snouts over the edges. Vaguely, Pearl guessed they must have felt something, too. A trembling. A shaking. A man understanding too late that there was no retrieval of promise so long as you detonated into a thousand pieces before rectifying the past.

Pearl understood there was something important to learn from this.

The farmer had been angry. Pearl had seen that anger. And though the man was destitute, he was still looking for how to change that. And yet, at the very end, just before he went away, Pearl saw something darker than his mother's eyes swirling inside the farmer's mind:

The farmer *wanted* to explode.

Wanted to go away.

Wanted to die.

This was Pearl's *first lesson*, as he would later come to call it:

You couldn't just act on the farmer. You had to *make the farmer want to act on himself.*

Pearl brought his front hooves up onto the edge of the box and tried to pull it down. He couldn't do it. Not strong enough. Or the box was too strong. This was somehow related to the *first lesson*, too. Pearl might have a certain strength, but so did the objects he was trying to move.

Different objects, different pressures.

Soon, a different farmer would attempt to teach Pearl about physics. Not because Pearl wanted him to but because Pearl made the farmer want to. And while most of what the second farmer explained was difficult to grasp, most of it would shape Pearl's understanding of the world beyond the pigpen.

The same day Farmer Martin exploded, his neighbor came to

ask about buying the place. He couldn't find Martin but in un-identifiable pieces, tattered clothes, and a scent in the barn close to what Ernie Feller believed the latrines in Hades might be like.

He wondered if Martin had left mid-slaughter. Had finally tired of the stress of farming.

But Ernie also found a box of piglets. He took them home. And he decided that, if Martin didn't come looking for them soon, he'd just as well auction them himself.

Even the one with the wicked eye.

26

Dad.

   In the mud.

   Dad.

   Sherry kept repeating the word *dad* because she didn't want to say the word *dead*. They sounded so alike, didn't they? Incredible, really, if she thought about it. *Dad.* She couldn't even think the other word. Couldn't bring herself to alter the vowels between the Ds. And didn't *dad* sound so much better than *dead*? Even phonetically? It did. Sherry knew it did. As she turned her back on the pen (on the leg sticking out of the mud in the pen), she nodded to the beat of the word *dad,* trying her hardest not to think of all the times he was cruel, all the times he made her feel awful for marrying Randy, for moving to South America, for not going into the family business of farming, of cropping, of raising animals, horses, birds, chickens, goats, pigs, and—

   PEARL.

The name came loud and bright red, and Sherry could practically see bloodied sludge dripping from the contours of the five letters that made it.

PEARL.

She knew it. She knew it a long time she knew it. She knew that whatever was in the barn was Pearl's doing. The leg sticking out of the mud was Pearl's doing. Her son Jeff wasn't imagining things, of course he wasn't, never imagined things in his whole life, wasn't suddenly turning schizophrenic on her, had actually been *moved* by Pearl to slaughter until the pig was . . . DAD.

Dad.

Not *dead.* No, no. Not yet. No time to think about that right now. Not with the pig in the barn and the girl Susan racing into the farmhouse and Officer Hahn following her like he cared (suddenly) more about her than he did the pig in the barn. No way. Sherry knew enough to know that Hahn wasn't going to check on the little blonde. He wasn't going to make sure she was okay in the face of all this madness. No, no. Pearl had gotten into him is what. Just like he'd gotten into Sherry. Into Dad. Into Jeff.

That *fucking* pig. Sherry could feel him now, as she rushed from the pen to the house, mapping out how best to stop Hahn from reaching Susan. She could feel the pig reaching for her, tiny tendrils, little fat fingers, pink flesh, grazing her shoulders, washing over her skin like a weak wind.

Weak.

It was an exciting word to use in relation to Pearl. But was it true? Was he weak? Was he spreading himself too thin, trying to manage all these people at once? Sherry felt a surge of excitement, a second wind, as she reached the gravel drive, running now, chasing down the officer, yelling out for him to stop, to leave the girl alone, yelling to Susan, too, telling her to lock herself in the crawl-space in the upstairs bedroom, the one with the blue blanket on the bed, Sherry's old bedroom, and the crawl space she used to hide in, used to lock herself in whenever the *feeling* of the pig outside got to be too much. *"HIDE,"* Sherry yelled, but hardly heard her own voice, sensing those weak hooves on her neck, those thin pieces of web, but thicker than when she felt them on her way to the shed, the day she was going to kill that pig DAD.

Not the other word. Not yet.

Sherry opened the front door to the farmhouse and felt a second surge of relief. Was it possible Pearl had finally gone after something he couldn't control? Was it possible that Pearl was trying to do something he wasn't capable of doing? Sherry had never considered any sort of limit in regards to the pig. Pearl was an endless smoky black that rose from the pen and became the sky. Pearl was an abyss. Pearl was the unknown, and the unknown was infinite, the unknown was unknowable, and so it had no edge, no boundary, no finish line, no line at all, no ruler, no rules.

But this . . . this feeling.

Weak?

Was Pearl trying to do too much today?

Sherry entered the house at a sprint. She heard a commotion upstairs and took the flight fast, just like she did as a little girl when she'd come home from school and couldn't wait to get to her books, her comics, her toys. She would hop off the bus and rush into the house and (no DAD at home, no DAD) scale these same stairs (they even creaked the same! even now!) and dive into her bed and bury herself beneath the covers and she'd read, read, read all the magnificent stories and hilarious captions and brilliant words from all the brilliant writers right there *RIGHT THERE* in the very same bed that she was pointing at now, the very same bed where the girl Susan sat with a finger to her lips telling Sherry to be quiet.

Shhh.

But why shhh? Why here? This was Sherry's bedroom, for crying out loud! This was no place to be quiet, this was no place—

"Shhh."

Susan. So red. Covered in blood from the first officer's wrist. Her eyes as wide as buffalo nickels. One finger to her lips. The other pointing to the door.

"Out there," she whispered.

And Sherry knew Susan was talking about Hahn. The officer was somewhere out there in the rest of the house.

Where?

Dad's room?

But Dad was . . .

Dad.

A creaking outside the door. A face in the doorway.

"Hello, ladies."

Different voice. Tired. Strained. Like someone else was talking for him. Like Officer Hahn was a puppet.

"Give us a minute," Sherry said. And what a strange thing to say! It was exactly the kind of thing she used to say to Dad. *Give me a minute. Stay out. Stay away. And if you and the farm and that pig try to get any closer I'm gonna go far away to South America, far away into a bad marriage, so far away we'll never really see each other again, never ever again.*

Hahn smiled and entered the room. His gun was drawn.

"You," he said, waving the pistol at Susan. "You're wanted in the barn."

"What?"

Susan's voice was so young that for a head-splitting second it sounded to Sherry as if her younger self were actually in the room, responding. It was almost too much to make sense of. Almost enough to drive her truly mad batty pig mad crazy.

Almost.

"Give us a minute," Sherry repeated.

Hahn looked from the girl to the woman and shook his head no.

"The barn," he said. But he said it more like, *bayarn*.

"Pearl," Sherry said, tucking her hair behind her ears. The gesture made her feel younger. Shit, *everything* was making her feel younger. Like this was an event, a confrontation, that should have taken place a long time ago.

Hahn tilted his head and looked at Sherry.

"Who?" he asked.

"Pearl," Sherry said. "I know it's—"

But Hahn had a fistful of that same hair of hers and was dragging her toward the window. Dragging her like he was going to toss her through it.

Which he did.

Susan screamed.

And her scream mingled with the shattering of glass as Sherry Kopple toppled out the frame, across the roof and over the edge, thudding below, a cracking sound, thunder? no not thunder, a body, crashing below, unseen, as the pieces of the window fell to the grass like the cymbals and the bass drum hit hard, *thud CRASH thud CRASH thud thud*—

CRASH!

And Hahn's hand upon Susan's wrist.

"The barn."

Like the barn was a *bad* place. Like the barn was where the demons fucked. Like the barn was where the spirits hid in the hay and erupted once the door was closed behind you. Like the barn was Hell. The real Hell. The place terrible people went to pay for terrible things. Where faceless mouths wailed and bodiless minds planned what was next, next, *NEXT* for girls like Susan, girls who had no business coming to sneak a peek at a talking pig, girls who thought they were superior to pigs until she saw her friends captured, saw her protectors driven mad, saw a woman thrown from a second-story window *thud CRASH!* There was no coming back from the barn. No. Once you entered the barn there was no getting out of the barn unless you were coming out in the belly of a pig. Susan wasn't going back to the barn. Susan had run to the farmhouse to use the phone again. Then Susan was going to run again. Run for Chowder. Run until her fucking lungs crawled out her throat. Run till she was seen and heard, heard and seen, by all of Chowder, shouting: *STAY AWAY FROM THE BARN THERE'S SOMETHING TERRIBLE IN THE BARN THERE'S THE END IN THE BARN THE END OF REASON AND HIGH SCHOOL AND CHOWDER AND ALL THINGS NEW AND ALL THINGS TRUE STAY AWAAAAAAAY FROM THE BARN!*

Hahn's hand clamped over her mouth, and Susan didn't know which was a worse fate: the policeman throwing her out the window, too, or him dragging her back to the barn. Why wasn't he getting rid of her? What lay in store for her back there? Oh, she could still smell it, could still smell the anger rising off the pig with the eye, could smell his vengefulness, pouring out of his snout, rising before him like a black mist, *I will not be slaughtered like my mother was, I will not be used for fuel, I will not die here in my own kingdom, I am king here I will not die I will not die I won't.*

Oh, Susan knew which was worse. As the officer dragged her out of the bedroom and down the quaint, grandfatherly hall to the top of the stairs, then down the stairs, rough, then through the farmhouse foyer, Susan definitely knew which was worse. She bit him. It didn't matter. She kicked. It didn't matter. She screamed and she dug her fingernails into his hands and she elbowed and pushed back and swung and kicked some more and it just didn't matter. The man wasn't just strong; the man had *pig* strength; propelled by a force much darker than any Susan wanted to understand.

Out the front door, down the porch steps, over the gravel drive, down the grassy hill. Somewhere in the horrific swirl of effort and futility, Susan saw the woman who had been thrown from the window, saw her on her stomach on the side of the house, saw her rising, getting up. But it was brief. This vision. And Susan was facing the barn again, being dragged, almost there, down to the dirt path where, ahead, she saw a second brief vision: horses lined up, their heads suspended above their own fence; spectators, moviegoers, beholders.

Then back to the barn.

Striking the barn with her shoulder, her shoes, her fingertips, too, looking for that final purchase, grinding against the wood, splinters under the nails, then no grip, no nothing, airborne, thrown at last, thrown after all, landing hard on sticky dirt.

And looking up. On her belly but looking up at seven cackling snouts. Two men bleeding out. An officer on his back not far from her. Smoke. Blood. The stench of a filthy slaughterhouse. And the sound of the barn door closing behind her.

Fire. Yes, fire, too. Hay burning. A burning throne.

And upon the throne . . . Pearl.

And Pearl looked to Susan like a little boy wearing the head of a pig. Not animal anymore, this one. Something bigger. Something unmanageable. Something very very bad.

This is Hell, Susan thought.

And so it was.

27

One more try. One more get up and go. Come on. Get up and go. Get out from under the bedsheet and get the hell out of this room. There's nothing in the hall. Nothing. A shadow without a source. A trick. A *mind* trick. The kind of thing you read about in spy comics. MIND TRICKS. The pig plays mind tricks because he's too small to play body tricks. He can't actually hurt you. He can't actually *do* anything to you, but scare you. What are you afraid of? Don't think about that. Don't think about what scares you because the pig will hear it, and the pig can make whatever it is trot down the hall. Is Dad still on the roof? Is he still out there?

Hi, Jeff.

But he's not out there, and he never was. It's the pig. Dad's not sitting on the freakin' roof, waiting to have a chat about how sorry he is about leaving you, Jeff. Dad's in Texas or Tallahassee or Tennessee, loving a new woman, a new wife, maybe even a new kid.

He's not waiting on the roof.

Hi, Jeff.

Ah, but did you see the sadness in his eyes? Like he *wanted* to talk? Wanted to confess?

And what a terrible trick. Sending Dad. Any version of Dad at all.

But it's not really him, because it's not possible for Dad to be sitting on the roof, not possible at all.

Right?

And even if he was, dammit, he wouldn't want to talk. He'd want to leave, Jeff. He'd want to go as suddenly as he came.

Jeff lowered the sheet again and looked to the bedroom door. The shadow was still there, swaying, like the pig was on a boat.

Jeff sat up and looked over his shoulder to the window.

Dad was smiling sadly through the glass.

"NO!" Jeff yelled.

Dad spoke.

"Come on, Jeff. Outside. I wanna talk to you about something. Wanna tell you I'm sorry. We'll hang out on the roof together. We'll jump down together, too."

Jeff shook his head no. No, because there was no way Dad was on the roof, and it was even scarier that way, scarier to think that Pearl knew enough about Jeff to know that this would frighten him, this would confuse him, this would tear him apart inside. If Dad . . . why not Mom? Why not Mom walking through the bedroom door, telling him she'd checked the farm and everything was okay?

Why not Mom telling him everything was okay when it wasn't?

"Get away from me," Jeff hissed at the window.

Dad shook his head. When he did, Jeff saw his features were slipping, melded together, a single fleshy face mask. Then it was Dad again.

"GET AWAY!" Jeff shouted.

Where was Aaron? Had he heard *any* of this? Did he know Jeff was in trouble upstairs? Did he know Dad was out on the roof?

"AARON!"

"Your brother's asleep," Dad said. "We jumped off the roof together. He's sleeping now."

Jeff sat up. He experienced a surge of courage, made of something deeper than overcoming fear.

Aaron.

"He did *not* jump off the roof!" Jeff yelled, hardly realizing that he was standing now, inches away from the glass. The Dad monster smiled sadly again. Was it the only expression Pearl knew to give him?

As if cued, as if Pearl heard Jeff think this, Dad's face twisted into something new, an impossible look, too much space between his nose and mouth, his lips as wide as the window frame.

"We jumped together, Jeff! Now get the fuck out here and jump with me, too!"

Jeff felt tears welling. Mom had talked about this. About Dad being a bad guy. And hadn't Grandpa said as much? Hadn't Grandpa warned Mom about Dad? But Jeff hadn't ever seen it for himself. He was too young back then, back when Dad was still living in the house. He'd heard vague bits of half stories, Dad getting angry on a beach in Rio. Dad sleeping with another woman in . . . Rio? Jeff didn't know. And he didn't want to know. Didn't want to care. This wasn't Dad. This was his own idea of Dad, made real somehow by Pearl.

"Jeff?"

A voice from behind him, and Jeff whirled so quickly he knocked a clay canister of pencils to the floor.

"Aaron!"

Aaron, merciful Aaron was standing just inside the threshold.

"What's going on, Jeff? What's in the hall?"

"Did you see something out there?"

Aaron stepped farther into the room and nodded. He was scared. Very scared. Jeff felt bad about the bruises on his brother's neck and face. Why had he hit him back? Why hadn't he just taken the hits his brother was going to give him?

This was worse than worrying about Mom. This was worse than Pearl and anything Pearl could deliver. Seeing Aaron scared. Seeing his brother like this.

This was worse.

"Something was breathing in the bathroom," Aaron said. "I heard it, Jeff. Something's in the bathroom. I ran past it and I heard it come out into the hall."

A new shadow out there. A man?

Aaron was facing the hall. Jeff saw Dad's face slide into frame, the window frame.

"Don't turn around, Aaron."

"What?"

Too late. Aaron turned around.

He didn't scream, he didn't yell, he only shook his head no.

"Boys," Dad said. "Come out on the roof, now. Jump down with me."

Aaron looked to Jeff.

"It's Pearl," Jeff said.

Aaron started to cry.

"What do you *mean*, Jeff? There's something in the hall! And Dad . . . *Dad!*"

Dad was trying to open the window from the outside.

Jeff grabbed his brother's arm.

Which way you wanna go, Jeff? Out the window, to Dad? Or down the hall to whatever Pearl has waiting for you there?

"We have to move," Jeff said. "Moving means we're not scared. Moving means we have a chance. But we *have to move.*"

Which way?

Dad rattled the window. Jeff ran for the hall, pulling Aaron with him. Aaron resisted, yelled, said he didn't want to go, but Jeff was already going, already *in* the hall, already facing the fact that the pig in the hall left no space to pass him. His fatty pink folds pressed against the wallpaper. His mouth slack. A puddle of drool at his hooves.

Hi, Jeff.

Aaron crashed into Jeff, but Jeff held his ground. And when Aaron looked ahead, both brothers thought of Grandpa slaughtering pigs on the farm. It had always been a way of life, something that simply happened. But now, to see firsthand the power the animals possessed; to see Pearl's revenge on display, filling the hall, breathing a wind so sour it caused both brothers to cough.

Grandpa drove Pearl insane.

The thought came so clearly to Jeff, so definitively, that he couldn't refute it, not even with a feeling. Yes, in a way, Grandpa had driven Pearl insane. Just like every farmer in America had driven every pig in their pen insane.

Jeff grabbed Aaron's wrist and pulled him into the bathroom, on the opposite side of the hall from his bedroom. He slammed the door behind them and opened the tiny window.

"There's not enough space!" Aaron said.

"We can fit."

"It's less than a few inches wide out there."

"We can *fit!*"

Jeff wedged the window open. Sounded like a barn door cracking in half.

"Go on!" Jeff yelled. He wasn't thinking of Mom anymore.
Couldn't focus on one thought, one Mom, one farmhouse, one pig.
Behind them, through the closed door, they heard the walls creak-
ing, the weight of the beast squeezing itself closer to the bathroom.

Footsteps on the roof, too.

Dad.

Coming.

"GO!"

Aaron went, but halfway out he saw that he was right. There
was no way they could fit on the ledge. Especially not if he was
going headfirst, like he was.

And yet . . .

The pig in the hall.

"GO!" Jeff screamed, as the bathroom door pressed inward. As
the wood cracked and shavings collected on the floor.

He picked one up. Felt its edges.

This was real. This wasn't imagined. And if breaking the bathroom door was real . . . why not the thing that broke it?

Aaron gripped the ledge, hollering that he wasn't going to make
it, there wasn't enough room, help me, there's not enough room,
I'm going to fall, I'm going to fall, Jeff!

But still, he went.

When his shoes finally cleared the windowsill, Jeff stuck his
head outside.

Aaron had made it. He stood flat to the house, the toes of his
sneakers hanging over the shingled ledge. The brothers looked at
each other, and in that look was their entire history: childhood,
Mom, Dad, Grandpa, school, the pigpen, everything.

"We're not scared," Jeff said. "Because we're moving."

Aaron nodded.

"Hurry."

Jeff did. He gripped the wooden edge of the frame and pulled himself out as the bathroom door splintered apart, broke into dozens of pieces, most striking the toilet and tub.

Aaron didn't grab Jeff's wrists because he couldn't bend the half inch without falling. Instead, he watched as Jeff pulled himself out.

Halfway, Jeff looked over his shoulder.

And the face that took up all of the broken bathroom door made him scream.

Made him *move*.

Headfirst, out the window, he didn't have an angle to grip the ledge. He was going to fall, he understood this. He was going to fall because there was no other way to do this, no other way to get out on the roof, no other—

"Bring your legs out and place your toes against the wall above the window," Aaron said.

Jeff didn't think about it. He did what Aaron said.

"Now . . . now slide your shoes down to the ledge, on the same side of your body!"

A crash from inside the bathroom, and Jeff didn't think about it. Didn't think about that face. He did what Aaron said.

It was getting darker outside, not quite dusk, but the grass beneath him looked bluer than it did green.

Like water. Just fall into the water.

Jeff slid the toes of his sneakers along the house until, contorted, he felt the roof beneath his feet.

The brothers stood shoulder to shoulder. Chaos rattled the bathroom. They wanted to scream, not only with fear, but from the total adrenaline of having climbed out of a small square only to stand on a thin line.

Beyond them, Dad's face appeared around the side of what must be Mom's bedroom.

"Boys. Jump."

The boys looked down. It was even higher here than it was from Jeff's bedroom window.

"I can't do it," Aaron said.

"I think we have to," Jeff said.

"You *do* have to," Dad said, flattening himself against the house, inching out onto the ledge. He was coming for them.

"Ready?" Jeff said.

Below them, there was no cushion. Only the hard earth that had once splintered Aaron's ankle and put him in a cast for three weeks.

And if that happened again . . . how would they get to Mom? How would they get away?

Jeff scanned the neighborhood, the roofs of other homes, looking for help.

A snort (a pig's?) blasted from inside the bathroom, and Aaron shoved himself from the house.

He jumped.

Jeff groaned and flattened himself even harder to the wall. He saw Aaron hit, then tumble below. For a second he was sure Aaron had broken more than just his ankle this time. The way he hit, the angle, it looked like Aaron broke both legs.

But Aaron got up.

Half smiling, half terrified, he called out to Jeff.

"You gotta do it! He's right there!"

A strong hand gripped Jeff's wrist. Dad spoke, and when he did his breath smelled like the thing in the hall. Like slop and shit; a pigpen of rage and revenge.

Jeff jumped.

For a merciful breath, he felt free. Free from Dad and the monster above him, the hard ground still far below. One of two things would happen: he'd break his leg and Aaron would have to carry him to help, or he'd land safely and the two brothers would ride their bikes to Grandpa's farm. One or the other. Either way, the next event wouldn't begin until he landed. And so, for that held-breath, airborne beat, Jeff felt *between* it all; disconnected, disengaged—

Fearless.

When he hit, he hit too soon. He wanted more time in the sky. He hit hard and his knees must've cracked in half, the way it felt like concrete, like when he'd bashed his shin against the trailer hitch on Grandpa's truck. A ground made of anvil.

The grass had no give, and Jeff felt his knees buckle and his face hit the dirt.

He lay in blackness, sensing someone shaking him, knowing it was Aaron.

Get up, Jeff.

Not yet. I don't wanna get up.

Get up, Jeff.

But when I get up we're gonna ride out to Grandpa's farm. I don't wanna go yet.

Get up, Jeff. Dad's crawling down the side of the house.

But I don't wanna—

Jeff opened his eyes.

"JEFF! GET UP! DAD'S CRAWLING HEADFIRST DOWN THE SIDE OF THE HOUSE!"

Jeff lifted his head and opened his eyes. Saw Dad up there.

"Oh, fuck, Aaron."

Aaron helped him up. Standing, Jeff tested his ankles, his legs. He wasn't hurt.

Wasn't hurt!

The brothers ran around the house to the open garage. Inside, the radio was still playing and the music was crazily out of place; a man howling about the weekend. Jeff kicked the speakers. Sparks flew, and Aaron was already on his bike, and then Jeff was on his bike, and when they pulled out of the garage, Dad reached for them; Dad on all fours on the lawn, like a pig, snorting at them, but not quick enough to catch them, left behind, with the thing upstairs, the face Jeff had last seen in the bathroom, not a pig, no, no, a man that Jeff recognized immediately.

The face that broke the bathroom door was the face of Bob Buck. Chowder's master of meat. The owner of the county slaughterhouse and about a billion businesses besides.

The man Grandpa feared, hated, and cursed every time he saw that very same face in his memory and mind.

Bob Buck.

And as they pedaled madly up Murdock Road toward Grandpa's farm, Jeff moved with the knowledge, the truth, that it wasn't actually Bob Buck in the bathroom.

Pearl was thinking about him was what happened.

But why?

Why was Pearl thinking about Bob Buck *right now*?

28

Bob Buck snapped his fingers, and blood squirted from between them, onto the dark oak table at which every investor sat. It was a lousy bunch, Bob knew, men who were concerned only with the bottom line no matter how precious they appeared in television interviews and public displays. Actually, that was the thing that confused Bob most of all: How did any of *these* guys end up in positions that asked them to appear in public in the first place? Roger Hendricks was a mess. Red-nosed with a silver comb-over that looked like a pair of glittering tights on his head. Allan Goode still couldn't tie his own tie. Darlene Mathews wore more makeup than a dead body. Truly, they looked . . . *ghastly*. Under the dim lighting in Bob's big office, they could have been the employees of a haunted hayride, the faces that leered at you from the bushes, jumped out and said boo.

"Boo," Bob said, snapping his fingers again. A pig was giving birth in the corner of the room. Right here in the office. A farmer named Martin Jones was waiting for the piglets out in the hall, waiting to take them home. Bob enjoyed details like these. A squealing hog made a meeting more memorable. Unforgettable, even. *Frightening.* And Bob certainly wasn't above frightening his peers. The farmers of mid-Michigan needed Bob. He was the guy who paid them for their pigs, after all.

"Jesus," Roger said, his cheeks sagging like he was dying, right here, at the table. "Sounds like mother's giving birth to razor blades."

"You ever give birth?" Bob asked. His eyes were magnified huge behind his movie producer glasses. Black rims. Hid half his face. They were a fuck of a lot cooler than Doug Donahue's blue shades. Bob knew that only assholes wore sunglasses indoors.

What a lot, Bob thought, almost depressed by the look of them. *What a lot of ghastly creeps.*

The mother pig moaned. It didn't sound good. Sounded painful as hell. Bob snapped his fingers.

"So we're short," he said, nodding to an invisible beat. That was good in meetings, too. Make the others feel like only you could hear the music. You controlled the radio. He wiped the blood on his white pants and smiled at the design it made. Kind of looked like two birds flying across his lap. One male, one female. "So we gotta breed."

He fanned an open palm to the blanket in the corner of the room. Upon it writhed the mother pig. Birthing. One piglet, two piglet, three piglet, four.

To Bob it was something like having a vending machine in the room with them. Need some piglet? C4.

Breed.

It was the word of the day, these days. Like all farming, there were ups and downs, ebbs and swells, ins and outs. Who could say why the pig rate was down?

"Killing too fast," Roger said. Then he coughed into his hand. Sounded like a car backing up.

"What's that?" Bob asked. It didn't matter if Roger's ideas were good or bad, if he was boisterous with them or shy. Bob loathed the man. Always had. And he loathed the fact that he loathed him, too.

"Killing too fast," Roger repeated. Then he coughed again. As if Bob needed the entire moment acted out again.

"Who is?"

"We are. Killing too—"

"Jesus, Roger. I heard you." Bob smiled, but he knew the others could tell he was angry. He hated this shit. Hated when he lost his cool. And yet . . . if you lost your cool enough times, it became part of your legend. A bum who got angry was an asshole who deserved his lot in life, but a president who did the same? They called that a "temper."

"It's true," Darlene said. "But what can we do? We're working to meet quotas. So we move quickly. Too quickly, perhaps."

Bob eyed everyone at the table one at a time. Some looked like they agreed. Others looked like they were waiting to hear what he said before they agreed.

"What are you suggesting we do?" Bob asked. "Take a month off? You wanna take a month off? I can do that."

They blanched. Of course Bob Buck could take a month off. He practically took *last* month off, spending three weeks in Buenos Aires with Theresa. But the work still got done. And Bob did most of it. Always.

"Of course not, Bob," Roger said. The guy talked like he had wads of wet hair in his cheeks. "But some regulation might be in order."

It suddenly struck Bob why he hated Roger so much. The man reminded him of who Bob himself could have been, had he been a little less confident on the way.

Bob pulled a cigar from his pocket.

The mother pig moaned.

"Regulation," Bob repeated. "So many pigs a month. Like China. That kind of thing?"

Roger shrugged.

"Got a light?" Bob asked the table.

Harley Andrews slid one across the oak. The orange lighter seemed to emerge from the leathery folds of a witch's robe.

This lot.

This lot of ghastly creeps.

"Thank you."

Bob lit his cigar.

"I'll tell you what *I* think," Bob said, puffing big. "*I* say we get the pigs in the mood. I say we encourage more, how do you say . . . *fucking*. I say we make it a point to oversex these animals until they've given us a fortune in family. I say we guide the penises into the pussies with our bare hands. I say we jack off one and wipe it all over another. I say we give the pigs blow jobs until they're about to cum. Then we step out of the way. You dig?"

Silence at the table. Roger coughed again. This lot. This lot looked exhumed.

"Bob," Darlene started.

"Can it, Darlene. We don't need the woman's voice right now, and you wouldn't even mean what you'd say. You know you agree with me. You think a moratorium is in order? Or do you wanna see more piglets?"

Bob turned to face the mother pig in the corner on the blanket. "You see?" he said, smiling. "There's some now."

He gestured toward the piglets. A man emerged from the shadows beside the half-open door.

"Yes, sir?"

"Get me one of those piglets."

"Which one, sir?"

Bob turned to look at the man. Vitriol flashed in his fleshy features. Then he looked to the birth scene in the corner.

"*That* one," Bob said. "The one that's staring at me."

Bob's assistant crouched by the mother and retrieved the piglet. Bob set it on the table in front of him.

"The way I see it," Bob said, "we should have so many pigs that we don't *mind* losing a few."

He removed the cigar from his lips and blew the smoke in the piglet's face. The tiny thing whined.

Someone at the table laughed. Bob looked up to see who it was, but he saw only half-dead, washed-out exhaustion staring back. No smiling faces.

"We're working on it," Frank Paddington said.

Bob nodded.

"Work on it, then. And then work on it some more. Because the way *I* see it, we're teetering on being afraid. We're concerned about every precious piglet as if it's the last of our rations. And you know who thinks that way? The *dead* think that way. The passengers on a sinking ship."

Bob gripped the piglet's neck and put his cigar out in one of its eyes.

The piglet made a terrible sound.

"Jesus, Bob," Roger said. "That's a perfectly good pig."

"No more," Bob said, sliding the piglet to the edge of the table.

His assistant took the baby back to its mother. "No more." Bob got up and placed his palms on the dark wood, facing the investors. "Doesn't feel good, does it? Worrying about one little piggy. But, dammit, there should be so many pigs in here that we don't even know what's a pig and what isn't. We should trip over them on our way out the door."

Bob held their stunned gazes a beat before he turned and walked to the door. He reached out with one shoe and shook it in the open space over the threshold.

"You see?" he said. "Too much room. *We need more pigs.*"

Before exiting he looked down at the piglets by the big mother on the blanket. The one he maimed was on its side. As he exited the office, he brushed an imaginary piece of dust from his shoulder. As if he'd stepped through a spider's web in the doorframe. And he thought, too, of that particular piglet on its side. As he rode the elevator down to his car, where Theresa was still putting on her face in the rearview, he thought of how the piglet was looking at him with his other eye, the good one, the one Bob hadn't fucked up.

He'll remember you, Bob thought.

Then he laughed.

He'd remember the pig, too! And wouldn't have a hard time pointing out which one he was!

29

Years later . . . the pig still bothered him.

Back when Bob was trying to scare the pants off his investors and fellow breeders, the money-hungry undead, he'd really put on a show in that conference room. Truth be told, it did feel more like a mausoleum in there, like something dead or dying was just coming into being rather than the life that was actually going on in the corner. Maybe the mood got to him. He liked to think it did. He also liked to think this was what the head-doctors called a "harmless snag," when a man who usually doesn't think too much on one subject suddenly finds himself with nothing else to think on. Somehow, that piglet *really* wedged its way into his brain. Long after the farmer Jones brought the thing home, Bob couldn't shake the image of the piglet staring up at him from his mother's blanket. Sometimes, randomly, early in the morning, Bob wondered where the pig was. As if it could be anywhere other than on a farm! Bob didn't like thinking like this, couldn't believe he cared at all about the whereabouts of one single pig. Maybe if the nagging had lasted a month, or even two, he could've written it off as a "harmless snag," but after four years of it, Bob got genuinely uneasy. The only elixir he found was repeating what ought to have been the truth:

That pig must have been slaughtered by now.

And yet . . .

. . . thoughts of the pig remained. Nightmares was more like it. Holy shit, Bob would wake up howling, *Leave me alone, get off my chest, get offa me*, and Theresa would run her fingers through his silver hair telling him ain't nothing on your chest baby, you must be experiencing one of those sleep paralysis thingies, ain't nothing but the sheet on your chest.

The pig, Bob would say. Always. *I dreamt the pig was on my chest.*

And without fail, Theresa would ask, *Which pig, Bob?*

He never told her. Not outright. Never said, *the one with the eye.* Instead, he'd laugh it off, darkly, waving his hands like he was getting the smoky image out of the room. But dammit if the thing didn't seem to take root in Bob's brain. He could be dreaming of Buenos Aires, Honduras, Norway. He'd be riding in a sailboat, his feet up, Theresa pouring champagne down his throat, and some shadowy passenger, someone Bob hadn't seen was on board, would suddenly holler, *Holy shit, look out, you're about to hit a buoy,* and Bob would know, Bob would *know* that when he looked up he wouldn't see any plastic bobbing candy corn, he'd see that one-eyed pig floating out there in the middle of all that ocean, staring back at him out of the corner of his eye like he'd done in that conference room (that morgue) so many years ago. In other dreams, Bob would be getting a blow job from a three-headed woman, and the door behind them would creak open, and the pig would just be sitting there, watching him. And wasn't that just the thing? Yes, wasn't that the thing, indeed. The pig never *did* anything. Never. He sat inert in Bob's dreams like he was taking silent notes, making sense of invisible things, keeping track of how Bob's mind worked.

The pig is on my chest!

For fuck's sake, Bob couldn't remember the last time he dreamed without seeing a black marble eye peering out of a fleshy pink pile at him. The pig had galvanized into a God-blasted memory that simply wouldn't go away; a boulder stuck into the soft earth of Bob's brain.

Like a tombstone.

Theresa told him he ought to go check it out. Ought to go see to it that this specific pig had been slaughtered if it bothered him so much. She didn't believe in ghosts, and Bob hardly believed in pigs, and dammit, if a man of his stature was so hung up ... why not drop a line, make a call, stop in on the farmer Martin Jones?

It took Bob a month to agree with her but, unable to sleep, his pride weakened, he finally did. And he did it alone; no Theresa, no employees, no farm manager to ask the pesky (debilitating) questions Bob needed to ask.

What ever became of that one piglet? The one I burned with my cigar.

He drove his Cadillac way up Bale Road, out to Jones's farm, blasting old country hits the whole way. It was the kind of driving he did when he was feeling good, and dammit, he wasn't going to admit that he was feeling bad. He was just checking up on matters, looking into it, a thing any sensible businessman was well versed in. The sensible thing to do.

Problem was (and it was a pretty big fucking problem) that farmer Jones had died. How Bob hadn't heard about this, he didn't know. But judging by the state of the crops and the weather-battered "FOR SALE" sign in the yard, Martin Jones was long into decomposing by then.

Bob checked the pens. Just to get a feel for the place. Checked the barn. He was alone and feeling a little crazy with it, like the pig was with him even then, guiding him along, perhaps even decoding the vibrations of Bob's thinking.

Getting to know him better.

Getting closer.

Bob tried to shake these thoughts off and had half a mind (one he tried to hide now, half his mind, half his thoughts, half his fears, too) to drive back home and ask Theresa to slap the pig right out of his head. He laughed at himself, a big man like Bob Buck, paying a house call in the first place, all worried about the whereabouts of one little piggy. It wasn't guilt, dammit. Bob didn't know guilt from shame. So it had to be a snag, right? Doc?

A harmless snag?

But he didn't drive home. No way. Not now that he was engaged, had started the process of tracking the thing down. Instead, he took Bale Road to County Road 54, 54 to 56, then 40 until it became Murdock, and from there directly into downtown Chowder with a mind (a full mind, exposed) to find out how long ago Martin Jones died, and dammit, who took over the care of his box of piglets.

Piglets no longer. Pigs by now.

He hadn't been to Chowder in a long time. Months. A year maybe. Theresa didn't love it. Said it wasn't even cute. And since most business was conducted in neighboring Sandal, there was no reason for Bob Buck to be seen there. Downtown Chowder was for hardware stores, feed, and used farm gear sold on the sidewalks. But since the Agricultural Hall of Records hadn't moved from its place at Wendell and Fairfax in downtown Chowder, Bob had to pay a visit.

Who had him?

Who had the fucking thing?

And more important, oh, *so* much more important . . . who killed it?

Unearthing the transfer records was refreshingly easy, and Bob was surprised to learn Walt Kopple bought the piglets at auction. Except for the deliveries he made to Buck, Kopple wasn't connected to the bigger businesses in Sandal. And hell if he wasn't one of the farmers Bob could count on most. But it was *because* Kopple had been breeding his own pigs for so long that Bob had to wonder at his purchasing a box of someone else's young. Was he mixing litters? Expanding the farm? Good for him if he was, but Bob wanted to know. Wanted to know what Kopple had in mind. Wanted to know—

You wanna know if that pig with the eye is in Kopple's pen.

The secretary at the Agricultural Hall of Records asked Bob if something was bothering him, and Bob shot her a look that iced her over. Of course he was okay. This wasn't a hospital, for Christ's sake. Wasn't it *okay* for a man to have nightmares about the same pig, over and over, over and over, *over and over again*? Was it so strange to clutch his chest, grabbing for a pig that was never there? Hadn't she ever heard of a *harmless snag*?!

Bob left the building and drove back up Murdock, straight to Kopple Farm. Walt would be home because Walt was almost always home, and if he *wasn't* home Bob was going to be pissed— pissed because, in *Bob's* world, Walt needed to be home. He didn't pay a house call just every day, and dammit if he'd come back, and since he needed to see that pig he better see that pig now.

The road turned to gravel, and the Cadillac just ate it up. Ate the whole road like it was made of graham crackers and the hood was the smirking face of a wolf looking for a piggy. *CHOMP CHOMP CHOMP.* Bob turned the music up, proving to anybody in earshot that he was as comfortable and untroubled as he'd ever been. Never mind that he was sweating, that his white suit was getting stained, that even a farmer as dense as Walt Kopple would be able to tell, holy shit, Bob Buck looks . . . *nervous.*

The pigs? Why you wanna see the pigs so badly, Bob?

Because it's my business to see the pigs, Bob would say. Because my whole fucking fortune rests upon the slaughtering of pigs, and the slaughtering of pigs begins with the birth of pigs, and you've bought yourself a wayward batch in there, and don't ask me another question or I'm gonna put my cigar out on your fucking eye like I did *that* pig in *your* fucking pen.

Relax, Bob thought. *Walt Kopple isn't going to give you any trouble. You probably don't even have to ask. You'll probably find him with the pigs right now, and all you'll have to do is look down and see the thing for yourself. And once you see it for yourself, you'll realize that all these nightmares are silly, and wow, what a fucked-up thing it is to get snagged on something as silly as a pig.*

Bob pulled into the gravel drive and let the car idle. He didn't need Walt Kopple seeing him bound out of the Cadillac like he was all bent out of shape or all worried about something serious only to bring up nothing serious at all. No, no. That wouldn't do. Bob wasn't that kind of a man. And he sure as shit wasn't the kind to pee a little trail of obvious concern from his car to the farmhouse door.

So he let the car idle. He waited. He watched the house for movement. Was Kopple inside? Maybe. Was he down by the barn? Maybe. Let him show himself first.

But he didn't, and eventually Bob had to cut the engine and get out. Because waiting forever was the same as not waiting at all. It made a caricature of you. Can't Wait Man. Waits Forever Man.

Bob got out of the car.

The summer heat cooked him in his suit, and he thought maybe this was a good thing. Maybe the sweat from the sun would hide the sweat from his mind.

He knocked on the door.

No answer. He called out.

"Kopple?"

No answer.

He took the grassy hill down to the pigpen and found the farmer standing knee-deep in slop.

"Kopple."

Kopple turned quick at the sound of a voice.

A man's voice.

"What," Buck said, smiling so wide that the stubble on his chin made a plucking sound. "You didn't hear me drive in?"

Kopple stared back at him, blank-faced.

"No, Bob. I didn't."

Bob looked to the pigs at his feet.

He pointed.

"Them there's the reason I came by. I hear you got yourself an outsider's batch a bit ago."

"That I did, Bob. Four years ago now."

Bob held up his empty palms, waved them dismissively. *Four years ago now* made Bob sound obsessive. No good.

"No need to be stiff with me, Kopple. This ain't a business call."

"Oh? Then what kind of call is it?"

Bob noticed that Kopple was gripping the handle of a shovel.

"I'm saying hello, Kopple. Sweet me. I say hello to my friends now and again. Just like anybody else does. Mind if I see them?"

Kopple looked to the pigs at his feet.

"Well, they're all mixed up in here together by now, Bob. I bought the pigs Martin Jones left behind a solid . . . four years ago."

Four years ago; oh, how Bob wished Kopple would stop saying *four years ago.*

Bob smiled and stepped along the fence, toward the gate.

"I'm in the pig business, Kopple. I like to look at 'em. Old, new, future, present, and past."

Kopple eyed the pigs again, then looked back to Bob. But Bob had moved along the fence, closer to the gate.

"Not sure what there is to see, Bob."

"Uh-huh. And yet . . . you bought them right up. Paid a pretty penny for 'em, too. Warts and all, eh, Walt?"

Kopple frowned.

"Starting to sound like a business call after all, Bob."

Bob smiled and opened the gate.

"May I?"

"Of course you may. Mind your loafers, though."

Bob looked down at his shoes. He shook his head. It felt good to shake his head. Like it was the only true way to keep the sudden rage he felt from exploding out his eyes.

"Used to it," he said.

He stepped into the pen and locked the gate behind him. Walt was right, though, as the mud reached the height of his shoes with his first step.

"Them there?"

"They're all in here, yeah."

Walt didn't step out of the way as Bob approached. Bob noticed this. Was the farmer hiding them? Beyond him, in the window of the farmhouse, a young girl peered out. Kopple's daughter. Carrie? Mary?

"I'm to understand you purchased seven piglets," Bob said.

Kopple nodded.

"That's right. But again, that was—"

"I understand, Walt. I ain't dumb."

They stared at each other over the pigs, quiet.

"Can you point the seven out to me?"

"Well, sure. I suppose I can."

"Well, of course you can. What kind of farmer can't tell you where his pigs done come from?"

"What is it you're looking for, Bob?"

The smile finally fell from Bob's face. He was business now. Walt had seen it before.

"I like to keep tabs on the pigs in town, Walt. You know that as well as any. Somehow this . . . transaction slipped my attention. I just wanna take a look-see, make sure you're not raising anything out of the ordinary out here." A beat of silence. "You're not doing that, are you?"

"What's that?"

"Raising anything out of the ordinary?"

"No, sir."

"Point out the ones from that batch for me, will ya?"

Walt faced the pigs in the pen. He scanned them, a finger raised, as if counting.

"Well, you see—"

"Some of them have been slaughtered already."

"That's right. More than one, I'd say."

Bob really didn't want to have to say it. Didn't want to say, *Walt, where's the one with the eye?*

"Well, go on then. Show me which are still here."

Finally, Walt did. He escorted Bob through the pen, pointing out the pigs in turn. Bob crouched in the mud. The pigs sniffed his fingertips with their snouts. If they remembered him, they didn't show it. And to think, they actually seemed to like him.

He was relieved. No eye. So far.

"Any more?"

Walt looked past Bob, to the farm. For a second it looked like Walt was silently pleading with Bob. Telling him a secret. Like when the television told a story about a little boy holding up a sign that said "HELP ME, I'VE BEEN KIDNAPPED" for a stranger to see.

"One of them's a bit . . . under the weather."

"What's wrong with him?" Bob asked. This was good. Good that Kopple had mentioned one of them (the one) being sick. Bob Buck had every right and reason to ask after a sick pig.

"Nothin'," Walt said.

"Under the weather is something, right? We're not talking mad cow disease, are we, Walt?"

Bob laughed heartily, but it was clear both men were standing on the edge of something.

"'Course not," Walt said. "Common cold."

"Common cold? Who are we talking about here . . . your daughter?"

"That'll be enough of that, Bob."

Bob brought his nose inches from Walt's. Stepped in pig shit on the way.

"What's wrong with the pig?"

Walt looked to the barn, then to the mud.

"What are you doing out here, Bob?"

But Bob was already walking away. It didn't matter how desperate or silly he looked now. Walt had said the pig was sick. That was the farm equivalent to handing Bob the keys to the barn.

Not that it was locked.

Bob slid the wood aside easily and stepped inside.

He saw it halfway across the dirt floor, and it shivered him cold.

It was sitting up on a bale of hay. Sitting on its ass like a person might. The shadows cast by the beams above obscured its upper half, and Bob imagined a burning eye somewhere in the silhouette of its ears and snout.

"Hello, pig."

Bob advanced.

Looked like the pig had a bedroom of his own, too. A blanket. A pillow. Picture frames.

Less than two feet from the pig, Bob pulled a cigar from his pocket and jammed it between his lips. He flicked his lighter. But he didn't light the cigar.

He held the flame close to the pig.

It was clear that Walt cared a great deal about the pig. Beside it on the hay was a saucer of water, a saucer of slop. In one of the picture frames was a single word:

PEARL

And beside it . . . a mirror.

"I'll be damned."

But Bob didn't need this confirmation. He knew it was the pig of his nightmares from the moment he stepped foot in the barn.

Its bad eye looked like a swallowing tar pit in the flickering light.

"You again."

Footsteps behind him, and Bob turned to see Walt entering the barn.

"Sick in the face?" Bob asked the farmer.

Kopple nodded.

"Hurt his eye."

"Born that way?"

Kopple shrugged.

"Don't think so. Looks to me like he was hurt on purpose."

Pearl tilted his head, his good eye trained on Bob Buck's cigar.

"You see that?" the farmer asked.

"See what?" Bob didn't bother hiding the fear in his voice. Didn't even know it was there.

"Look at the way the light is flickering over the lid of that bad eye. Looks like he's—"

But Bob had seen it, too. The way the shadows played, as if the hidden bad eye wasn't only functioning, but was a hundred times more powerful than the good one. A roving black pupil buried in flesh. Searching Bob, searching his mind.

Bob placed his hand on the farmer's shoulder.

"You paid a hell of a lot for that batch of piglets four years ago. Why?"

When Kopple turned to face him, it looked like both the farmer's eyes were roving, too, as if the whole barn were made of roving pupils, eyes, watching him, watching Bob Buck, learning everything there was to know about him.

"Don't know," Kopple said. "I suppose I wanted to."

Bob didn't like this answer. Didn't like it at all. Didn't like a thing about this barn, either, the way the shadows danced, the graveyard stench, the . . . sick pig.

But he'd found what he'd come looking for. That had to be enough.

For now.

"Make sure you don't accidentally include that bad eye in the good meat, Walt."

Walt, still eyeing the pig, Pearl, silently nodded.

"You *are* planning to slaughter it, ain't you?"

"'Course I am, Bob."

"Good."

That was it. *Good.* Because Bob didn't want to say any more. And he sure as shit wasn't going to axe the thing himself.

The thought turned his blood black.

And yet, as he walked out of the barn, as he wiped his palms clean of the dirt of Kopple Farm, he felt the old familiar nagging. Almost a full independent voice now.

Hello, pig . . .

Not his voice. No.

Then whose?

Bob didn't look back. Didn't even realize he hadn't said goodbye to Walt Kopple until he was halfway home. Then it struck him. Hard. How obvious he must have been. How obvious it was that he'd been looking for that particular pig after all. And if that didn't embarrass him, surely the next thought should: Big Bob Buck spent the whole day tracking down a pig named Pearl, and didn't have the guts to kill him?

Why hadn't he taken him? Bought him? Or just killed him right there next to his Goddamn mirror?

I didn't want to.

It was true. Bob knew it was. But Goddamn if it wasn't the strangest truth he'd ever learned. Almost like it'd been made up.

Bob cocked his head back and cracked up.

"A made-up truth!" he shouted. "But true all the same!"

30

The two cops stood on either side of Pearl like bailiffs framing a judge who favored leashes. Susan had been in court once, arguing a noise violation, as her mom and dad sat in the spectator seats. (They weren't the only ones there; the stoner defending himself after her had a crowd that may have included Mitch or Jerry or both.) She'd never forget the feeling of powerlessness; the fact that the man (the pig) behind the high wooden podium could actually decide her fate had scared her. It made her think about man (pig) and law and how man created law, and if the laws man created were silly (say, if man was dumb), then whose laws were they all following? It scared her deeply, though she dutifully rose and explained that she shouldn't be ticketed for the noise created at a party she'd thrown without having received a warning first. Pleasantly, she told the judge (*Pearl, Pearl looks like a judge*) that she was a sensible person; she pointed to the fact that she had no previous record of disturbing the peace, and asked for leniency in this case.

But for whatever reason, the judge denied it. Susan was ordered to pay the fifty-dollar ticket, and the decision pissed her off. It stuck with her in a strange, deep way, all the way up to the day she was dragged back into the barn on Kopple Farm, resisting and screaming, and even up to the point when the officer shoved her to the ground, close to where Mitch and Jerry hung by their ankles. Even *then* she couldn't put her finger on *why* the judge (*Pearl now, Pearl is the judge now*) had turned her down. Did she present herself poorly that day in court? Did she come off like a snot-nosed kid? Someone less savory, someone who truly deserved to pay the fine? It wasn't the loss that bothered her, *scared* her . . . it was the blossoming fear within, the idea that man and law could make decisions in the dark, and sometimes someone just didn't like the looks of you.

Did Pearl like the looks of her?

The pig sat on the hay bale surrounded by small, manageable fires. The cop who hadn't dragged her here must have started them. Why? Was the pig planning on burning Mitch and Jerry at the stake? That was more pig and law shit gone awry, Susan knew. Salem trials. Witches. Or, in this case, stoners accused of trespassing.

Or stepping into the wrong spiderweb.

That was sure how it felt, wasn't it? Like Susan had gotten caught in a huge, horrifying web. But being physically held wasn't even the worst of this web; it was the feeling that it was wrapped around her *mind.*

We have to get out of here. Before we can't think for ourselves.

The faces of the cops flickered in the shadows cast by the trembling flames, and if Susan looked too long at them, they started to look like they had no faces at all. Two fleshy pink pancakes flattened over dirty blue uniforms, guns in both their hands. The other pigs were gathered at the foot of the hay bale, in what looked like worship and blockade. They didn't seem particularly interested in Susan, and yet every time she thought of running, one or more would look out the side of their eye at her.

Susan didn't like the way they did that. The way they seemed to stop breathing when they eyed her. It scared her so much that she tried to cloak any thinking about running entirely. Just put a sheet over it. The sheet is now running. Running is the sheet. No Susan running. No (knowing) eyes from the pigs in the barn. And yet how long could she hide it? And what else could she do? If she didn't think about going, then she must think about staying, and she had no doubt which was worse.

"Susan."

She turned quick at the sound of her name, half expecting a pig to be tapping her on the shoulder with a hoof.

But it wasn't a pig. It was Mitch.

"Help."

Susan nodded. Yes. Help. Yes, *help* indeed. That's what she'd been going for. That's what she'd run for. The phone in the house. Maybe it'd been dumb. It was. She should've run up Murdock. Ran to town.

DAMMIT.

"Okay," she whispered, and the eyes of the pigs turned to her. Black bullets in pink barrels.

The flames quivered. The shadows danced. Deep blues and dark reds; Susan began to see it as a cruel oil painting, the work of an angry artist. The pig on the hay bale (the talking pig!) was redder than he was before. Susan understood why.

He had somehow been washed under the blood of Mitch and Jerry.

"Okay," she whispered again, and the pigs turned their panting snouts toward her.

She felt around the dirt near her for a stick.

She heard the click of a gun. The cops?

A figure appeared in the door of the barn. It was the woman who had been thrown from the window. She held a shotgun chest high. The pig on the throne of hay watched her. The pigs at his feet got up onto their hooves.

One cop raised his gun, aimed it at the woman. Susan remembered the *THUD* of the woman hitting the ground. Had she broken something? Could she run? She didn't know who the woman was, didn't know her connection to the farm. But it was obvious there was something there.

Susan, still searching blindly behind her now, didn't find a stick.

She found the splintered handle of a hoe.

"You killed Dad," the woman said, stepping into the barn. The cop fired and the pigs squealed and Susan screamed and Mitch and Jerry fought against the ropes, trying to break out. But Hahn hadn't fired at the woman, and the wood banister above her splintered like lumber rain.

Susan acted quickly, holding the wooden handle to the closest fire, allowing the tip to burn.

"He taught you, Pearl. He loved you."

The woman was crying. She didn't look good. Her blouse and pants were torn. Her hair a mess. She kept talking about "Dad" and love and family and even she, even *SHE* added to the oil painting, the crazed work of art.

WOMAN FACES PIGS

Susan slowly rose. The woman was talking. Susan didn't understand entirely what she was saying. It didn't matter. She held the burning handle to the rope that held Mitch.

The woman advanced, and the cop fired again. Susan shrieked but she didn't falter, didn't move the flame from the rope.

The smell of burning rope.

A pig turned to look at her, its features crazily distorted by the flames. Looked like an old woman to Susan. Grandma in her open casket at Kirk Church.

What are you doing there, Sue? Burning? Are you BURNING? What are you burning, Sue? You burning an escape, Sue? YOU THINK YOU CAN ESCAPE, SUE?!

"I'm going to kill you, Pearl." The woman. The woman talking crazy. Dangerously antagonistic. "Do you know what *kill* means, Pearl? Sure you do. Of course you do. You killed Dad, Pearl. The man who taught you kill."

Mitch moaned.

Then he hit the floor headfirst.

The pigs didn't get up, didn't take their eyes off the crazed woman.

SATELLITES

The word came huge to everyone in the barn.

"Mitch." Susan knelt beside him. "Mitch . . . can you stand?"

She held the flame close to his legs and saw that his pants had been eaten through. It looked like he had sores down his legs; patterns of deep bruises. There was skin missing where the rope had eaten into his ankles.

Or maybe it was the pigs who did it.

Mitch rolled to his side. He brought his hands to his head. He lifted his face toward Susan's. He kissed her.

"Pukin'," he said, but he couldn't smile. Not yet.

"This is for Dad," the woman said. "Dead for Dad."

Her shotgun was clearly leveled at the pig named Pearl.

She was crying worse now. Susan didn't know why and she didn't care why. She'd called the police and they'd come. But they'd come to the aid of the pig, not Susan. Not Mitch and Jerry. Not this woman.

"Don't shoot, Sherry," the officer with the bad hand said. "Or we'll be forced to shoot back."

"Shoot back," the woman said. She took another step closer.

Mitch got up, crouching beside Susan.

"Jerry," he said.

Susan nodded and handed Mitch the handle. Why weren't the pigs coming for her? Why weren't they stopping her from helping her friends?

The woman. The woman is distracting the king pig. They have a history. They have a . . . dad? Someone between them. Someone they both loved. The farmer in the pen? Must be the farmer in the pen. Run, Susan. Run for town. But don't go to the police. Go to a car. Take a car. Any car. Take a police cruiser. Take any car. Leave. Leave Chowder. Get out of range. Get out of his web. The pig's web. Go. Go. Go. Go—

Jerry fell even harder to the ground. Like a sack of sand. Mitch was helping him, to Susan's left, mumbling incoherent encouragement. She kept her eyes on the pigs.

"Let's go," Mitch said.

The three teens stumbled to the far wall of the barn, as far as they could get from the scene, from the weapons, from the pig sitting on his throne of hay. They pressed their backs to the barn and slowly slid toward the door. The woman didn't turn to face them. The cops didn't call out to them. And the pig they called Pearl didn't speak to them in their minds.

Susan was very aware of how hurt she was, how hurt Mitch and Jerry must be, how slow they were going to be when they ran away.

Would they run away? Is that where they were going? Away?

The woman was only a couple feet from the king pig, and she

raised the shotgun level with its head. Susan saw the tip of it pressed into the fleshy face and thought she heard it, too, like a finger in pudding, a squishy sound. She thought the gun might be pink when this was all over.

"Come on," she said, whispering, gripping Mitch's wrist. And Mitch gripped Jerry's. Jerry, who, like the pig, could use only one eye. Jerry looked like he needed a hospital now, this minute, or he was going to expire.

"Sherry," the cop with the bad hand said.

The teens reached the door.

Susan paused.

Was this it, then? They could just . . . go?

"Go," Mitch said.

Susan stared at the woman.

Kill him, she thought. *KILL HIM.*

And now the king pig noticed her. His good eye shined in the dark. But no, it was his *bad* eye.

Something white beneath the wrinkled lid.

Susan heard a voice explode in her skull.

SING FOR ME, BROTHERS BLUE. SING FOR PEARL.

Susan ran. She ran out of the barn and up the dirt path and heard Mitch and Jerry moaning behind her. She heard gunshots, too, an explosion of gunshots, too many of them, ringing out from inside the barn. She saw the light they birthed, in the dark of early night she saw the light; fireworks, a celebration, the celebration of the pigs, celebrating their freedom, their independence day, the death of their master-farmer and all who supported him, all who locked their gate, day and night, forgetting them when they turned their backs, forgetting the pigs, not thinking about the pigs, and the one pig, the one who didn't forget a face, a name, a word.

"*RUN!*" Susan screamed, so much madness behind her, so much *noise.* Then she was running. Really running! And Mitch and Jerry were running, too. They didn't run to the road, they ran to the woods, the way by which they'd come, as if by returning by the path through the woods they could erase their coming, could reverse all that happened since Mitch invited Susan to go see the talking pig that convinced a seventh grader to behead a hog.

"Holy *shit*!" Jerry screamed. Jerry, coming to life, realizing they'd made it, made it out of the barn, had climbed the grassy hill, had passed the farmhouse, were entering the woods, howling like joyous savages, no longer high schoolers, lunatics now, screaming war cries, hands above their heads, into the woods, the deep, dark woods, free, freer than even the pigs.

A hundred yards deep, a thousand scratches from a thousand branches, Susan stopped running. Turned to face the boys.

They stared at one another, covered in mud and blood. Eyes permanently wide with horror. Would they ever close their eyes the same again?

And they laughed at one another, laughed with the freedom of it, as more shots rang out from the barn, so far away now, sounded more like darts now; they laughed like wild hyenas on the prairie, like drugged seekers alone on their cosmic, righteous paths.

And they ran to town that way: laughing, howling, mad.

Free.

31

"Come on, Aaron! *Ride!*"

But Aaron didn't need the extra encouragement. He was pedaling as fast as he could.

The thing (*Bob Buck? Did Jeff say it was Bob Buck?*) in the hall and Dad on the roof was enough propulsion to send Aaron careening into a fugue state, a chimera ride up Murdock.

Grandpa's farm felt very far away.

They heard some kind of cackling, like witches and warlocks, crazy laughter erupting from the woods that lined the crop fields to their right, and would continue to line those fields almost until they reached Mom and the farm. It had gotten dark since they began pedaling; they couldn't see into the trees, but Jeff had a feeling the insane laughter had something to do with Grandpa's farm (*with Pearl*).

"Come on, Jeff," Aaron said. Now Jeff was falling behind. Trying to see into those dark woods. "Burnouts," Aaron said. "Come on!"

Lights ahead. A car. Too bright.

Mom, Jeff thought. *It has to be Mom. She went out there, and everything turned out okay. Grandpa is okay. Pearl is stuck in a pen. Everything's okay. It's Mom. MOM. MOM!!*

"MOM!" Aaron yelled.

"Get out of the road," Jeff said. But Aaron was sitting on his bike, waving to the coming lights.

"MOM!"

"I don't think they're slowing down, Aaron! I don't think they see us. Come on! Get out of the road!"

Aaron wasn't listening. Aaron was waving to Mom. Jeff could see his brother's smile in the headlights. Saw it like Aaron was in a theater on a stage. It was a play about a poor, disillusioned boy who'd seen his absent father for the first time in a long time and was flagging down Mom, sure that she would restore the shattered order.

"MOM!"

"Aaron! Come on!" Jeff got off his bike and let it fall into the ditch. He reached out for Aaron.

Then Aaron turned red and blue. Like he was lit from within.

It was a police car. A cruiser. Returning from Grandpa's farm.

Okay, Jeff thought. *Okay. Help. Police. Okay.*

But it didn't feel like help.

Was Mom with them? Why were the police at Grandpa's farm?

Jeff remembered the axe in his hands, the innocent pig at his feet.

Aaron stood frozen midwave; his ignorant, happy smile had drooped into something less hopeful. To Jeff it looked like Aaron was the one in trouble, arm raised, showing he had no weapon.

The cruiser slowed and then stopped.

Both front doors opened. They saw only the silhouettes of the two men who emerged. But they knew all the Chowder cops.

It was Officers Hahn and Perry.

When they stepped out from behind the lights, it was like they'd crawled up and out of the earth. Both were covered in mud and what looked like . . .

"Blood," Jeff said.

"Blood?" Aaron asked.

"You two boys need a ride home?" Officer Perry asked. His face was a ghastly half moon. His eyes looked vacant, like behind them all his thoughts were pressed against the walls of his skull, hiding.

"Yes," Aaron said, automatically.

"No," Jeff said at the same time.

The officers looked at each other. Something passed there. Jeff saw it.

"Well," Officer Hahn said, "which is it?"

Jeff looked past them, to the windows of the car. Through the lights and fog he thought he saw someone sitting in the backseat.

"Mom?"

He didn't mean to say it out loud, but he had.

Office Perry laughed.

"Sorry, kid. But that's definitely not your mom."

Then they laughed. Laughed at him. Laughed at the frightened brothers standing with their bikes in the middle of the country road in the dark.

Who is it then? Jeff thought.

A tilt of the head in there, ears on the silhouette.

Jeff looked up into the eyes of the officers.

"What happened at Grandpa's farm?" he asked.

Officer Perry reached into his pocket and removed something shiny.

"You're a good kid, Jeff," he said. Had he always known Jeff's name? "But I'm gonna have to do something about that mouth."

Handcuffs. He was going to cuff him.

"Aaron," Jeff said. "Run."

"Run?" Aaron said with real surprise. "From the police?"

Then Jeff bolted. Perry reached for him and missed, and Aaron did the same thing, running along the ridge of the ditch, to the left side of the cruiser, both of their bikes left behind, they ran. As Jeff passed the cruiser he looked into the backseat. Through the glass he thought he saw the face of a maniac, a baby-talking lunatic with wide white eyes, a lolling tongue, fat pink lips hanging to his chin.

And cotton costume pig ears.

"COME ON, AARON!"

The brothers ran, into the dark, into the night, to Grandpa's farm. Behind them, they heard the doors of the cruiser close. Heard the tires crush their bikes as the police must have done it on purpose. But they continued their drive to town. And as he ran, Jeff heard a voice, crystal clear, and he knew it was spoken by the mad thing he'd seen through the window.

Soon, the man-thing said. *We'll see each other soon, Jeff. It's inevitable we meet. So meet we will, Jeff. We'll see each other soon.*

"RUN, AARON!"

They ran.

32

Bob Buck had aged considerably since that day he went out to Kopple Farm and saw the old-timer was raising the haunting pig like he would a child. The nightmares didn't stop. They just became less defined. Rather than waking, thinking the pig was lolling on his chest, crushing him, then *escaping* his dreams, it always felt like the nightmarish thing was still in the room with him. In fact, it was starting to feel like the pig was everywhere, not only nearby following a scary dream.

Awake, hosting his son's birthday party, Bob spotted something dark in the shrubs at the yard's edge. But a little investigating showed him nothing was there. And while conducting business, there was always a third party on the line, silent.

It frightened Bob. Scared him deep. Scared the leather right off his feet.

Yessir, Bob Buck had *aged*. But rather than the more traditional morphing common to a man with money, rather than getting too bloated for his fine cotton suits, Bob's body had gone feverishly in the other direction. For a while, Theresa jokingly called him *the Corpse*. The way his jackets hung loose on his shoulders like he was entirely made of bone. But that joke got old fast. Maybe too fast. And Theresa got worried. Possibly too worried. For Christ's sake, he looked like a dying man! A man crushed to half his healthy width by unseen forces.

Invisible enemies.

Bob saw them everywhere.

Pigs in disguise. Disguised as road signs ... traffic ... telephones ... desks ... humidors ... hats ... belts ... all the flowers in Theresa's garden ... *Theresa* ...

Bob couldn't walk from a pole barn to a farmhouse without sensing the presence of that pig. The horizons crawled with shadows. Figures receded in the windows of every farmhouse he visited. Hell, the office *smelled* like mud. But home was worse. More than once (more than tence), Theresa woke to find Bob sitting up in bed, staring into the darkness by the closed bedroom door. It was a difficult thing for her to reconcile; the two Bobs; *ONE*, the pig master of Michigan's Donnelly County, the most respected agricultural businessman for miles. Shit, when the Bucks went to dinner they were seated without a wait. Even the busboys knew them by name. People stopped Bob all the time, laughed at his jokes, took him very seriously when he spoke of *the market*. It was like being married to the mob. And yet ...

TWO, the second Bob, the one only she knew; Bob looking over his shoulder in the hallways at home, Bob showering with the curtain open, Bob fanning his hands in front of his face as if he were constantly stepping through unseen spiderwebs, even in places where no web could have been spun.

Theresa worried. And she saw the worry in Bob buried behind

the smiles, deep in the fleshy wrinkles of his thinning face. Most men in Bob's position were naturally getting fat from years of wild success. Jackson James was robust as hell. His hair was a strong silver, his eyes a striking green. Mark Frigman was a human bull. But Bob? Theresa couldn't help but notice that, when they made love, he felt weak, like a sack of bones she was sentenced to carry with her till death do them part. In the mornings following particularly nasty dreams, Bob would hug himself in a robe that was getting too big, made him look like a child trying on the bathrobe at a hotel. And worse, Theresa spotted something deeper than fear in the basement of Bob's blue eyes.

Theresa saw *obsession*.

What was doing this to him? There was no way it was all about a pig. And certainly not the one owned by the farmer Walter Kopple. Bob's entire psychological makeup hadn't been systematically picked apart by a solitary pig. Theresa knew him better than *that*. But still, that look in his eye, that distant determination, as if he'd made a pact with himself to *one day* address the situation, *one day* confront the thing that haunted him. Theresa had read up on men who were so successful that they felt an almost hollow sense of *what's next?* Her own therapist told her that it sounded like Bob was experiencing *post-goal depression,* a topsy-turvy condition experienced by many a man who'd arrived at exactly where they wanted to be in life. *What next?* But, like she told her doctor, Bob's felt more like *one day* . . . and somehow the difference scared the shit out of her.

When would that day come?

Today, Bob thought, having no idea Theresa would kill to know this information. *Today*.

It was more than a hunch. And it wasn't pretty, the way it came. These "premonitions" weren't boxed up with a bow.

Warnings, he thought. Not portents at all.

Bob was sitting in front of the television in a pair of white boxers when the phone rang. The boxers hung loose and made him look even thinner than he actually was. He jumped at the sound. Jumped at every sound these days.

"What is it, Freddy?"

Freddy Quint. Finance. A Chowder liaison.

Of course, Walter Kopple's farm was in Chowder. Bob saw it too clearly in his mind every waking minute.

"I feel silly, calling you about this, Bob. But it seems like something you should know about."

It's the pig, Bob thought.

"What happened, Freddy?"

"Teenagers. Three of them. Came screaming into downtown tonight. Two of them were bloodied pretty badly. Actually, all three of them looked like hell. And all three of them are at Matterhorn Medical now."

"So?"

"Well, that's the thing. So ... Hmm. Well, Bob, they came screaming into Roseanna's All-Night, hysterical about the pigs out at Kopple Farm."

The words hurt Bob's brain.

"They were screaming in a diner?"

"That's right."

"You saw this?"

"No. Bill Noon called. I don't know how he heard about it. But he said the customers saw the three coming up Murdock from a long way off. You know how Roseanna's faces Murdock directly?"

"I do. Uh-huh."

"Yeah, well, they seen these three bloodied teenagers come stumbling from the woods on the side of the road. Saw them in the streetlight. The staff and customers were pointing them out. Bill told me they all kinda agreed the kids were on LSD."

"Acid."

"That's right. 'Cause that's how they were acting. Out of their minds. I hear the girl looked so scared, like her eyes were half out of her skull. And the two boys were too roughed up to speak much."

"Roughed up."

"Yeah, like they'd been eaten a bit."

"Excuse me?"

Bob looked to the glass doors that made up most of the wall of the living room. The lights were off outside. Anybody could be standing out there, looking in.

Or sitting.

"Well, that's why I'm calling, Bob. They came in screaming about a pig attack, and pretty soon the customers and staff took them pretty seriously because gosh damn if they didn't look the part. And so Roseanna's called the hospital. They said Walt Kopple's dead, Bob."

"Dead? What for? How?"

"They said the pigs killed him and were set on killing them, too. But they got away."

Got away.

Bob looked to the glass doors again. Theresa closed a door upstairs, and Bob nearly pissed his pants. He stood up, the phone at his ear.

"Anybody check on the farm?"

"I'm on my way out there right now."

"Okay."

"What do you want me to do with the pigs?"

"The pigs?"

Bob laughed. It felt good to laugh, and it felt a little lonely to laugh, too. Lonely because he felt like the only man in Michigan who knew how ridiculous it was what Freddy just said. *What do you want me to do with the pigs?* As if Freddy could do anything at all.

Turn around, Bob thought. But he didn't say it. Instead he played the businessman, and would till the end.

"Just check on them. I'm sure those kids were on drugs after all. This isn't a crisis, Freddy. This is a hoax."

His words sounded made of foam. A child's plastic letters he could arrange in any order he wanted them to go.

"Will do, Bob."

Freddy hung up.

Bob stood in the living room, staring at the fish tank. Then he looked over his shoulder. Theresa was standing in the doorway.

"What's up, Bobby?"

Then she gasped. She'd seen Bob look like Death before tonight, but there was something particularly ghastly about his face this time. Like he really was dying. Like the Reaper had called.

"Crazy kids," Bob said. Then the grayness passed, and Theresa saw something very bright in his face.

One day.

Was that today? Was today one day?

Yes. Whatever had haunted Bob for so long was close enough for him to face it.

"Kids?"

"Yeah, some drugged-up kids crawled into Chowder, hollering about the pigs out at Kopple Farm."

Did Bob know how often he spoke of Kopple Farm in his sleep? Theresa didn't think he did. The way he'd said it, it sounded like he thought he was saying its name for the first time in her presence.

"You going out there?"

"Kopple Farm? No. Downtown Chowder, yes."

"What for?"

Bob looked at her the way he did when he was in business mode and didn't want her asking questions.

"Business, T."

It didn't bother her. It was refreshing as hell. Bob emboldened, walking with a little bit of a strut, a sense of purpose, like he used to, like he did before he started seeing pig silhouettes in every corner of the house.

Bob went upstairs, changed into a white suit, then changed out of it. He was done with those. Done with the old man he'd become; the caricature (peanut shell) of his former self.

He dressed in pink instead. The suit Theresa bought him one Valentine's Day in the Fog. The Fog of his slow decay, his mental mist, burdened by thoughts that never quite felt like his own. If Bob didn't know better (he didn't), he'd say a bird had slipped in through his ear and set to pecking away at his confidence, his bravery, ever since.

Bob exited his house without saying goodbye to Theresa. She didn't mind. She told herself it was good. Good to see Bob acting like Bob again. Good to see him standing upright.

But while she watched him drive out of the garage, she couldn't help thinking he looked something like a pig himself in that pink suit, lit up by the Cadillac's interior lights.

And she couldn't stop herself from imagining him slaughtered like all the rest of them.

33

"He's in the house," Jeff said, as the brothers finally reached their grandfather's gravel drive.

Their lungs burned from the run. From the fear, too.

Aaron looked up at the dark house, then back to Mom's car in the driveway.

"I'm not going in there."

"Grandpa could be in there. Mom could be, too."

"Then why are the lights off, Jeff? Why are the lights off?"

Fear. Constant. Audible tremors in his brother's voice. There was nothing Jeff could say to comfort him.

Why *were* the lights off in the house?

"I'm going in. Wait here."

"What?"

The moon made a broken ceiling of the sky overhead. Aaron wished it were totally black instead. The way the light crept through the cracks, it looked like someone could be above it, watching him closely.

"I'm going in."

Jeff. His younger brother. Acting crazily brave. Had he always been like this? No. No way. Jeff was moving to a new beat, drummed up when he slaughtered that pig. It had done something for him. Something . . . good.

But just because Jeff was acting fearless didn't mean Aaron had to let him.

"Don't do it," Aaron said. "Let's check the farm first. Let's look for Mom."

They heard small movement in the woods up behind the farmhouse, a bunny perhaps, and both brothers looked to see the cellar door was lying open in the moonlight.

Was Mom down there?

Was Pearl?

"You check the farm," Jeff said. "I'll check the house."

It sounded like a bad idea to Aaron. Everything sounded like a bad idea to Aaron.

But outside sounded safer than in.

"Jeff . . ."

Jeff hurried across the drive and up the front porch steps. There he was swallowed by the porch shadows, and Aaron couldn't see him anymore. But he heard the front door swing open. Swing closed, too.

Outside then. Alone. A lot of space out here. A lot of places to look.

"Mom?"

Aaron turned and faced the farm. The fields, the barn, the pigpen. He didn't want to check the pigpen because Jeff had scared the shit out of him with it. Aaron could see the tops of the trees

Grandpa had planted to block the pen, and he wondered if Grandpa was scared of the pigs, too. Or maybe it was Mom, back when she was Aaron's age. Maybe Mom was scared of Pearl like Jeff was? And why hadn't Pearl come after Aaron? Why had he gone after Jeff and not him?

An almost embarrassing feeling. Jealousy for not being targeted.

Aaron left the drive and took the grassy hill to the dirt path below. He'd walked this path a thousand times with Grandpa. As a little kid he used to scuffle his shoes in the dirt, make shapes, animal shapes. Horses, cows, pigs. Yes, the pigs were a favorite on Grandpa's farm. They had a certain look in their eyes, like they knew more than dogs did, and much more than chickens. Taking the path now, Aaron was very aware of that look in the eyes of the pigs. The way they seemed to be processing, like dolphins, or like they were actually smarter than people were, and knew it, too.

It scared him, now, imagining animals smarter than himself in the dark.

Up ahead, in the shadows on either side of the toolshed, he saw pigs. Whether they were there or not, he saw pigs everywhere. He imagined they were watching him coming up the path. Watching with those intelligent eyes. Making plans, for crying out loud, making plans! They outthought young boys like him and Jeff, made young boys chop the heads off the ones they didn't like. Made them want to do it.

Aaron remembered Jeff in the pen, all those guts at his feet.

Aaron stopped walking. It was too dark here, next to the trees that blocked his view of the pen. The barn was up ahead on the left.

And beyond the barn was the fence that kept in the horses.

The horses could help them get back to town. Aaron wanted this. Wanted to be on a horse, riding back to town.

He even thought he could hear them, Grandpa's horses, breathing out there beyond the fence he couldn't see. He breathed out himself. The pigs were in their pen to his right. Grandpa was asleep in the house. Mom was . . . Mom was . . .

A grunt from ahead, and the shudder he felt shook him.

In the shadows on either side of the shed. Maybe they were there. Maybe they weren't.

Heads. Tails.

Eyes.

They *were* there.

Black as the trunks of the trees to Aaron's right. Black as the inside of the barn at midnight.

A cloud passed overhead, revealing more of the moon.

Aaron saw them clearly.

He took a step back, too scared to run, too scared to call out for Jeff. He heard movement from the hidden pen to his right, and by the time he turned to look, it was too late.

Grandpa. Looking through the trees.

A different Grandpa. A blue Grandpa. A Grandpa covered in mud.

"Hi, Aaron."

"Grandpa!" he whisper-hissed. *"Are you okay?"*

Grandpa smiled, but his eyes looked tired.

"Oh, I'm fine. But, help me out of here, will you, Aaron?"

Grandpa reached through the trees. A blue hand.

And a smell, too. Like slop. Like piss. Like shit.

Aaron ran. Ran to the road, as the snorting rose like music behind him and the sound of hooves, too, rushed from the shadows framing the toolshed, sudden, violent motion, and the squealing of so many pigs, a trample, calling out to him, telling him there was no place to go, letting him know that they'd been waiting a long time for this moment, that they couldn't wait to catch up to him and that they *would*, they would catch up to him before he reached the road.

"Hey, Aaron," Grandpa called weakly from behind the trees. "Help me outta here, will you? Will you help me out of the fucking pen?"

But Aaron didn't help him. Because Grandpa was blue. And because Grandpa's blue hand that had come through the evergreens was really more of a hoof.

Aaron ran.

34

They did run into the diner screaming. And they did scare the hell out of the locals. But not all of them. Not right away. When they came tumbling out of the woods, Hugh Quail pointed with his fork and said (loud enough for everyone to hear): "Prank."

It's the first word that came to mind. *Prank*. Like there was no way these three kids were serious, the way they were laughing then outright cackling, covered in mud and what looked like blood, gripping one another by the shoulders, racing toward the diner, then slowing to a walk, turning around, standing in a tight circle, laughing and cackling all over again. *Prank* seemed to fit just fine. As in, these three had been the butt of a prank, had just pulled off a prank, or were in the midst of performing that prank right now. On people like Hugh. As in, Hugh was supposed to get up and go check on them, and then some asshole punk in a Bigfoot costume would explode from the woods, and Hugh would forever be caught on tape shitting his pants, screaming like a baboon, running the other way. He'd be the dumb local in the video made by the dick-fuck Chowder teens.

But . . .

The girl looked really scared. *Really* fucking scared. And the two boys needed help walking. Every few steps they'd stop and lean on each other and regroup or something. For Hugh, it was just starting to feel too real. He'd always wondered about this sort of thing—the exact moment a person realizes that what they're seeing is a big freakin' deal. Like a man who hears screaming inside a neighbor's house. What pitch does the scream have to hit before he makes a phone call? Or like a lady who worries about a creepy fella hanging around the kids at the playground. At what point does she go from being suspicious to . . . mobilized?

Maybe Hugh was taking the teens too lightly? It sure was starting to feel like he was. Especially when the girl raised a shaking arm toward the diner and not one of the trio checked to see if any traffic was coming as they limped toward the lit up windows, behind which Hugh and about a dozen other local Chowderites sat eating.

"Prank, my ass," Timothy McCallum said. Tim was known as a do-gooder around Chowder. The kind of man who would definitely pull over for a hitchhiker, definitely help a fella change a tire. Tim couldn't verify a thing for Hugh. But when Nina Lansbury picked up the diner phone and called an ambulance, Hugh kind of had to join in on the believing.

Tim went to the door just as the kids made it there themselves. He held it open for them, but none of them seemed to notice this tiny act of kindness. Under the diner lights, the girl looked downright insane.

"*PIGS!*" she screamed. "The pigs are trying to kill us!"

Susan had said it so many times today that it was beginning to lose its power. Even with herself. As if, now that she was in public, she was forced to question how real it all was. She remembered talking to Mitch in the high school hall. Remembered him asking her if she wanted to go see a talking pig. Remembered the woods and the farm and the axe, and suddenly *BOOM* police and some lady and a standoff and, holy fuck, the pigs.

One of them in particular.

Nobody responded to her. Not right away. They stared. But Susan wasn't having it. She walked between the tables like a cult leader, recruiting. Her palms were raised to the sky and she was looking everybody straight in the eye. *DO YOU BELIEVE? DO YOU?! DO YOU BELIEVE IN THE PIGS?!??!*

"PIGS!"

A waitress dropped a plate onto a table. It rattled but didn't break.

"Pigs," one of the boys said, and Hugh turned to see the kid was inches from his ear.

"Hey!" Hugh yelled, leaping back in his chair. "Don't touch me!"

Because it felt like, had the kid touched him, he would have contracted whatever they were on. Whatever dementia was driving them to do this.

"What do you mean, pigs?" Tim said, approaching the girl.

Susan turned on him quickly. Eyes wide. Way too wide. Her blond hair was streaked with what looked (and smelled) like slop.

Tim thought it was punk hair dye when she'd entered.

"Kopple Farm!" she said.

And that was all it took. Even for Hugh Quail.

Everybody in Roseanna's All-Night believed the teens now, whether they said so or not.

After the ambulance came and the paramedics assisted the three onto the benches in the back, Hugh had to ask himself the uneasy question: *Why? Why did we all believe them the second she mentioned Walt Kopple's farm?*

Kopple had never done anything unsavory, hadn't even pinched a pickle from the diner, a screw from the hardware store. So if it wasn't Walter that greased their nerves, what was it?

Hugh looked down at the menu on his table. Saw a picture of sweet bacon on a plate.

PIGS.

Well, Hugh had never met the pigs on Kopple Farm, but he sure as shit felt weird every time he drove past there. In fact, more than once he'd driven by damn quick, afraid to turn his head and eyeball on the farmhouse, fearful there might be someone in one of the windows, pointing through the glass at him. It just felt fucked up out there. Like you kind of had to raise your hands in front of your face on that patch of Murdock Road because you were passing through some kind of thick webbing, something that was going to stick to you all the way home. And the rustling, too, the movement of the trees even when it wasn't that windy, like a whole bunch of somethings were in there, watching you drive past. Or like the whole ground out there was rumbling. But not with an earthquake, heck no. No earthquakes in Michigan. It was more like someone was . . . shouting. Yeah. Like someone was angry as hell. That was it, Hugh decided. Had to be. That's what sold him on the girl after all. It was the way a tree moved when you passed Kopple Farm. Even when there was no wind to blow it.

35

Inside the farmhouse. Alone. He'd left Aaron outside. Aaron was too afraid. So Jeff . . . alone.

Dark inside.

But not silent inside. Someone upstairs.

Jeff thought of his own house. Of the Bob Buck thing in the hallway. Of Dad on the roof. It was all Pearl, though. Playing with his mind just like he'd played with his mind the last time Jeff had been out to the farm. How simple things were then! And yet there was always a brooding feeling, like the stitchings of Grandpa's farm were about to come apart and the whole place was going to erupt into horror. Like Grandpa had somehow managed to keep it all buried, all tied together, all unseen. Looking up the dark stairs, Jeff suddenly felt very bad for Grandpa. He'd been out here for a very long time. And what had it done to his mind?

Grandpa had been disfigured by the weight of them, the horrors. Bent unnaturally because of all the unseeable ideas and thoughts he had to avoid while living in this house. Jeff felt them now. Bigger than ever. As if every single bad thing had come to life with one swing of the axe, Jeff's swing, as if he'd not only beheaded a pig but had chopped the rope, unleashing everything Grandpa had kept so neat and secure.

Or maybe the horrors didn't bother Grandpa like they bothered Jeff, like they bothered other people. Maybe the horrors understood that they needed Grandpa to give them a place to stay. Maybe they were good to him. Better. As good as something really bad could be.

Breathing, upstairs.

"Mom?"

He said the word because if he didn't say the word it would mean he was too scared to say it. It was the same reason he started walking, to the stairs, then up them, toward the breathing. Standing still was out of the question. Standing still was what scared people did. They froze. They stared. They pointed and they stuttered and they couldn't move because they'd given all their power to what they were afraid of. Easily, too. All the horror had to do was open its palm and wait.

Give it to me. Give me your bravery, Jeff.

Bob Buck did that to Jeff. Years ago. In this very farmhouse. It was Jeff's one encounter with the fabled Chowder businessman, the man Mom said was "soured by big money." Jeff and Aaron had been playing with the chickens outside, chasing the little ones, catching them, then letting them go. Jeff ran inside to ask Grandpa for some feed, and found him sitting on a chair in the living room, facing someone Jeff didn't know on the couch.

Grandpa?

Jeff, this is Bob Buck.

Bob Buck's face was as white as the suit he wore, only it was grayer, pasty, like Grandpa had been molding this man out of clay while Jeff and Aaron ran around the farm.

Hi, Jeff.

The man smiled, and it looked like his eyes were made of glass. Like his teeth were dirty toilet seats unhinged, like his nose was literally still drying to his face.

Hello, Mr. Buck.

Bob's smile grew even bigger, and Jeff realized the man was scared. And that by calling him "Mr. Buck" he'd given him a moment's reprieve from his fear. A return to something he once was.

Bob's here to check on the pigs, Grandpa said.

And Jeff felt it then like he'd felt it a hundred times before. Even the adults were afraid of the pigpen. Even the adults felt weird about entering through the gate, about feeding them, about looking them in the eye.

Is something wrong with the pigs? Jeff asked. He asked it in the way only kids are able to do: with an innocence that did nothing to hide the real thing he was after. It was obvious to Grandpa and Mr. Buck that Jeff wondered about the pigs, too.

Sweat dripped down Grandpa's face. Was he scared? And if he was . . . then who wasn't?

Nothing wrong with the pigs, Grandpa said. Then he laughed, and it was one of the only times Jeff could remember Grandpa laughing. It made Jeff nervous because it sounded like *Grandpa* was nervous, and when Jeff turned to look at Bob Buck again he saw the man's expression hadn't changed; his eyes looked about to crack, and his lips hung like foam taped to the lower half of his face.

Oh, there's something wrong with the fucking pigs, he seemed to be saying. *You're just too young to know what the fuck that means is all.*

Now, halfway up the stairs, cloaked in darkness, Jeff thought of that expression again, remembered the lines in Bob Buck's face like it was a foldout map of Chowder. It was the expression he'd seen busting through the bathroom door at home.

Would he be up there, then? Upstairs? Waiting for Jeff to come to him? His hand extended, palm open . . . waiting?

Give it to me. Give me your bravery, Jeff.

Beneath Jeff's hand the banister felt like flesh, and he quickly pulled his fingers away.

I bet if it was light in here, you'd see it's pink flesh. I bet you'd see it's made of pigskin, Jeff.

One step higher, and the stair felt different, too. Jeff's foot started to sink in, then he felt a bone shift beneath the surface of the step. Like he was walking on somebody's fatty back. He leaped up a step and felt the same thing with the next one.

A staircase of pigs, Jeff. Climb their backs, Jeff. Climb up.

He hurried. He nearly fell, and he gripped the banister, and this time it felt like a pig's tail, or tongue, something thinner, squishier. He shouted because only a scared man wouldn't make a sound, and he moved because only somebody too afraid would stand still.

"Mom!"

Yell it! Call out to her! Let her know you're coming!

But someone else answered.

Sing for me, Brother Jeff. Sing for Pearl.

Jeff couldn't stop to think about it, had to keep moving, keep ascending the stairs. If he stopped to look around, stopped to scream in the darkness, he'd fall all the way back down to the foyer, and that's what they wanted him to do, they wanted him to fall on his back to the foyer floor where all the pig stairs would rise and come sniffing for him, come hungry for him, come eating.

So he ran, he bounded up the steps and reached the top and felt like there was no way back down because that way was lined with Pearl.

Sing for me, Brother Jeff. Sing for Pearl.

Jeff was facing what used to be his mother's bedroom. But the breathing was coming from behind him, and he whirled to face it. It was even darker up here, bottom of a lake dark, as if the windows were cloaked with black blankets, or like the moon had gone out.

Jeff stepped toward the breathing, toward Grandpa's bedroom. He'd slept in there, as a kid, many times, when strange dreams about the farm animals woke him in the middle of the night and scared him so badly he braved the run from Mom's old room, across the landing to Grandpa. And Grandpa always took him in. Not like Mom took him in at home. Mom said things like, *It was nothing. It was just a dream.*

Grandpa said things like, *It's okay. They can't hurt you in here.*

The closer Jeff got to the doorway, the worse the breathing sounded. As if someone sick was bedridden in there. Jeff couldn't help but picture a very old man, tubes and wires connecting him to giant blinking machines that blotted out the moon. *Wheezing,* that's what Mom would call it. This wasn't breathing. This was someone struggling to breathe through the nose.

Oink, Jeff.

Jeff reached out, and his fingers smashed against the wall, an inch from the open door, and he realized he was much closer than he thought he was. Then he entered because if he stood still at the threshold he'd be too scared to do it and the moment he froze was the moment Pearl would get him.

"Mom?"

Was it her? Was she up here? Hurt? The police had come from

Grandpa's farm. They were driving into town. Their uniforms were stained. Mom's car was still in the driveway. Why wasn't she with the police? Where was she now?

"Mom?"

Jeff was in the room, and the breathing (*wheezing, Jeff, oink, Jeff*) was so close he could hear each strand, as if three individuals were responsible for it, a trio of dead singers.

And it was coming from the bed. The bed. So close. The bed.

Jeff felt for the light switch. Was it the hanging string kind in here? Or was it on the wall? Had Jeff ever turned on the light in Grandpa's bedroom before?

Aaron yelled from outside. His voice scared Jeff electric, and for the first time Jeff paused.

What is it, Aaron? What did you find out there? Is Mom okay?

"JEFF! GET OUT OF THERE!"

Was Aaron running? It sounded like he was moving, like his voice was coming from all over the farm.

"THE PIGS ARE OUT OF THE PEN!" Aaron yelled. "THE PIGS KNOW WE'RE HERE!"

Jeff stared at the black space where the breathing was coming from. It sounded like whatever was in there just sat up.

He felt its breath on his own nose.

"Pearl," Jeff said.

His hand slid over the light switch on the wall, and he didn't hesitate. He turned it on.

It was a pig. But it wasn't Pearl.

It was about six times the size of Pearl.

"Oh, no!"

Its enormous rolls of fat hung over its forelegs as it sat up on its ass. Brown and white, but covered with mud. Grandpa's sheets were stained brown.

Flies buzzed by its ears.

And the smell . . .

"Where's my mom?" Jeff asked. Because if he didn't ask, if he just stared, then he was too afraid to help her. To help Mom.

But this pig wasn't like Pearl. There was nothing refined about this one. Nothing dignified in the way it eyed Jeff, the way it sat.

And somehow it was bigger now than when he'd turned on the lights.

The pig, Jeff saw, was growing.

"Where's my mom!"

He could scream it he could cry it he could sing it, too.

The door behind Jeff slammed closed.

"JEFF!" Aaron's voice, muffled out in the yard below. "GET OUT OF GRANDPA'S HOUSE!"

Jeff tried the door and couldn't get it open and tried again and just couldn't do it, and when he turned back to the bed he saw the pig was on all fours now and was leaning toward him, his huge snout only inches from Jeff's waist.

Then the lights went out.

And Jeff was in darkness.

And he removed his hand from the knob, because trying to open a door that wouldn't open was a sure sign that you were really scared. In fact, he felt a wave of relaxation as he dropped his arms to his side and waited for the huge, smelly beast to pounce, to crush him, and to eat what was left.

And in the moments before the pig did it, Jeff thought of Bob Buck. Thought that the sadness he saw in that man's face, on that day so long ago, was there because Bob knew that you could yell and cry and sing, but one day you're going to end up in a dark locked room with one of them and you're not going to come out as the same person who went in.

Yes, Jeff thought. Bob Buck knew this way back when. Knew the fate awaiting them all, all the people who took Pearl for granted. All the people who didn't think twice about slaughtering a brilliant animal.

"Sing for me," Jeff said, eyes closed.

And the pig in the room sang.

36

Susan saw him first. She was lying on a cot outside the examination room in which both Mitch and Jerry were being bandaged up. They'd gotten it worse than she had. At least they looked like they did. Their legs were in bad shape, and they both complained of serious headaches, having hung upside down for so long. But Susan had her own problems. She thought her leg was broken. Somehow her shoulder was messed up. When did that happen? She didn't know. The doctors asked a lot of questions, and she was grateful for every one of them. She imagined herself getting better every time she answered. As if by saying "knee" out loud, her knee had instantly begun the process of recovery. And it felt safe in here, too. Like nothing from the farm could get at them in here. No horses or chicken coops in a hospital, ha-ha, but when they closed the curtain around Mitch and Jerry (*my God, they looked so out of place in there*) she felt a little bit alone and told a nurse as much. So the nurse stayed by her side, told her she was going to be okay, asked her if anybody had used any drugs, and Susan said, *Yes yes,* the two boys had, but this was beyond drugs, this was beyond experimentation, they had seen Hell tonight, they had seen the actual manifestation of the Christian Hell inside the barn at Walter Kopple's farm. But that was okay, Susan said, that was all right because hospitals must be built in purgatory, a middle ground, an airport between Heaven and Hell, and a lot of people actually took the escalator up or down from this very edifice. The nurse asked Susan if her family was religious. Susan laughed. Yes. Mom and Dad were into that baloney but Susan wasn't, fuck no, she wasn't, and really nobody in her generation should be, and then the nurse said, "Hang on, I'll be right back," and the second she left Susan's side, Susan saw him.

A pig. In the form of a man. Emerging from the elevator down the hall. Alone. Alone with Susan in the hall. He was older and walked slow and wore a pink suit, and Susan had to remind herself that the pig got into your mind, made you see things, and no man on earth wears an all-pink suit and there's no way that it's a coincidence that *this* man decided to wear one on *this* day.

So she tried to scream, half in alerting the staff and half in her own private horror, as if Hell was fluid, had no boundaries, and had managed to cross town, to follow them, to ride the elevator, to come pouring out onto the eighth floor where Susan awaited treatment because her two friends had got it worse.

WORSE.

This man was worse. Worse than lying on a cot, wounded, injured badly in the course of a lunatic's day. This man made it all worse.

"Hi," he said, and his voice was splintered wood, his voice was the gate to the pigpen creaking open.

Susan tried to scream, but all that came out was a one-syllable whimper, a cartoon horn, and not even the doctors behind the curtain peeked out to check on her.

He knows! she thought. *The man-pig knows I'm alone right now!*

As if he was coming to kill her. As if he was coming to continue the night's events. Did she really think the night was over? Did she really think it could just end like that? By simply *running away*?

The man smiled and pointed to the cot Susan lay upon.

"Nice bed," he said. Then he passed through a shadow cast by an open door and emerged again, and this time Susan could really see his features, could really hear his shoes on the tiled hospital floor.

Could almost even smell him.

Mud. Blood. Fear.

Or maybe that was herself she was smelling.

"You mind if I join you?" the man asked. But he was already pulling up a chair, sliding it close, too close, to the cot.

Susan opened her mouth to say something, to alert the doctors, but the man placed a fat, wrinkled finger on her soft, pink lips and closed them.

"Shhh," he said. "This will only take a minute. I love you."

Susan's eyes hurt for being so wide for so long, for seeing so much in one day.

The man was crying. Smiling, crying, shaking his head.

"I love you because tonight I'll be free of him, and you, *you* are my ticket to freedom. What happened tonight? And where is the pig now?"

How did he know? How could this man know anything about the pig?

He shook his head, and flakes rose from his hair. Susan suddenly realized that there was something dead about the man, as if he'd just gotten up from lying down for a very long time.

He creaked.

"Hey, hey," he said, and Susan saw his teeth looked gray. "I'm two men. We all are. Two men. I'm the nice man who is asking you questions, who will get you water if you need it right now, who would hold your hand when they finally start mending that leg. But I'm also a very mean man. The kind who will hurt you if you take too long to answer."

"What?"

"There we go. A word. Now . . . more words. The words I'm looking for. What happened tonight and where is the pig now?"

"At the farm . . ."

"Where at the farm?"

"You . . . you came all the way to the hospital to ask where on the farm he is?"

But Susan understood. This man knew the pig. This man was haunted by the pig. Just like she was. Only he'd been haunted for much longer. He'd drive to Matterhorn Medical to ask where Pearl was rather than drive out there and look for him himself.

This man was scared.

More scared than Susan was.

"In the barn . . ." she said, but she didn't know. And the man could tell.

"The last time you saw him . . . he was in the barn?"

"Yes."

"What was he doing?"

"Doing?" The question was absurd. What else was he doing but haunting, scaring, hurting? "He was killing. Burning. Staring."

The man closed his eyes and nodded. As if Susan's words were music to him. As if she'd validated something he'd believed for a long time.

"He got into your head," the man said.

"Yes. Who are you?"

"He got into a lot of heads tonight."

The man jerked a thumb toward the curtain. As if cued, Jerry moaned behind it.

"Yes. Who are you?"

"I'm Pearl's nightmare. Just as he is yours, he is mine. I am his."

Susan had to look away from his face. Too ghastly. Too gray.

"You shouldn't go out there," she said. "There's too many of them."

The man laughed, and Susan thought the doctors must have heard. But nobody peeked out from behind the curtain.

"I'm not afraid of a lot of pigs," the man said. "Just one."

He got up.

He stared down into Susan's eyes.

"The toolshed," he said. "Did you happen to find out if the toolshed is unlocked?"

Susan shook her head no.

The man nodded.

"The farmer's dead, huh."

It wasn't a question.

"Yes. I think a lot of people are dead tonight."

The man smiled.

"Revenge," he said. "For all the killing we've done."

He walked away, and Susan understood. Understood that this man was somehow tied to the slaughtering of the pigs in Chowder. This man might even have been the man Dad talked about with such reverence, Dad who revered the dollar above all things, Dad who mentioned the man Bob Buck many times over the years, wishing he had Bob Buck's money, Bob Buck's car, Bob Buck's hair. One time, mixed up in a particularly nasty fight with Mom, Dad had said he even wished he had Bob Buck's wife.

"No way," Susan said.

Because there was no way this was the man Dad wanted to be. The man who walked back to the elevator, the man who looked like a broken old pig passing under the ceiling lights; this man was sad. This man was scared. This man was a peanut shell of a person. This man had thought about the pig so often that his mind was pink with it, his mind smelled with it, his mind was confined to a pen.

Susan watched him waiting for the elevator. The light was situated above him in such a way to make it look like he was floating alone on an island in a hall of darkness, waiting for a door to open, a way out. And when the doors did open and he stepped inside, he turned around and faced her, and here the light made a skull of his thin features, a skull with dripping flesh, pink skin melting like Silly Putty, like a kid had gotten bored of the face he'd made and was pulling the putty away from the bone, already envisioning another face, another man, another animal.

The man waved.

It was so out of place, so grotesque, that Susan shuddered. The doors closed, and his hand was still up, still waving goodbye, saying goodbye to her and maybe the whole world, saying goodbye to men like Susan's father who thought he was something to emulate, something to be. The doors closed but the image remained, strong, vivid, as if the man (Bob Buck?) was immune to obscurity, unable to be blocked out, like the pig, the pig Pearl, who haunted this man because this man haunted him, because this man lined pigs up and slit their throats in front of other pigs, and suddenly Susan was seeing, *seeing* Pearl's point of view, Pearl's perspective as if Pearl was a slave rising up, rising up from the mud and blood to kill his captors, to slay those who slayed his mother, his father, big pigs who had their own purpose not to be slit or slayed by men like this, the waving man, the man preparing to drive out to Kopple Farm to face his ghost, his monster, ready within, or perhaps so haunted, so changed that he thought he was ready and didn't know what ready was anymore, weak, dying, the end of things, saying goodbye, waving, this man who drove all this way to ask a girl where the pig was on the farm, not ready after all, so scared that he had to ask someone who knew something, anything, because the idea of going out there without talking to someone first would have broken all his bones, would've shattered him instantly, the idea of driving out there as the pig grew in his mind, grew so big that he blotted out the moon and the night sky and became all he could think about, taking root in his mind, coloring every thought a fleshy pink, ruling his mind so that by the time he arrived at the farm he'd believe he was driving a pig, his hands upon a steering wheel of hooves, the windows just flapping pigskin, flapping with the night air, the breathing of the pig that was waiting for him, for *him*, this man, this man in pink, this man who'd already given up by dressing like a pig saying hey hey, you win, I'm one of you and you're greater than me, you win, I'm a pig, too, I'm a pig tell me what to do tell me *what to do*, this man *THIS MAN* waving, saying goodbye to Susan and Susan's dad and Matterhorn Medical and Chowder and his wife and this life and everything, here, goodbye to everything on this, the Day of the Pig.

37

The farmer taught the pig about rumors. About how they could affect somebody's mind, change their opinion on someone they didn't even know, could bring a person to believe that an unoriginal thought was, indeed, their own.

They'd come a long way, the farmer and the pig. Gone were the days of one- and two-syllable lessons. The farmer hadn't pointed to an object in a long time. Didn't need to anymore. The pig knew more than most middle schoolers, high schoolers, and was certainly as smart as any of the grown men the farmer knew. Gone were the days of slowly enunciating words. Now the farmer explained concepts.

Ideas. Philosophies.

And the pig listened.

The sentences escaped the farmer's lips like running bugs, crawling over his teeth and out his mouth quickly, but not far, not getting past the pig, who felt the tremor of each hitting the web, the psychic web, the unseen film fanning out from his mind dozens of feet in every direction, the pig's web, the way the pig learned, the way the pig understood, the way the pig held tight to the things he wanted and captured the things that didn't want to be held tight.

The farmer was in the web. Every bit of the farmer was in the web, from his ankles and wrists to his neck and eyeballs and mind. The pig wanted to learn more so the farmer taught him more, and eventually the farmer believed he was the one initiating, the one who decided the pig ought to learn more, out of kindness, out of interest, out of the respect a man might show a fellow living thing that wanted something he could give it. And yet, despite believing this, the farmer dreamed of a different scenario. Yes, awake (and talking, teaching), he dreamed of a man who didn't think it was a good idea, who didn't want to be doing this, who was doing this only because the animal was making him want to do it. It was a dark dream, and the man in it didn't want to be where he was, didn't want to be on his knees in the barn, espousing philosophy to the pig, didn't want to be carrying the pig up to his bedroom where he sat the pig on the bed and knelt beside the bed and discussed the home, the family, the bonds between men, the excruciating pain of existence, and the responsibility of the thinking man (pig). In this dream the farmer saw ways out, saw long paths splitting fields of wheat, roads that led to a city he could get lost in, a city too big for a farmer from the middle of Michigan, cities where the farmer could start anew, reinvent himself, cities like Rio de Janeiro, Brazil, a city by the ocean, six and a half million people, surely no pig would find him there, surely no web could reach six thousand miles south and force him to his knees, force him to teach, force him into thinking everything (anything) he did was by his own volition, his own self-propulsion.

The farmer dreamed as the farmer taught the pig about circles. About the far reach of self-motivation and how you can really make someone believe an idea is their own if you insert six ideas between A and B, if you take them on such a long walk that they've forgotten what it is you want them to do. It was a bad feeling. For the farmer. A dark transparency. Teaching the pig something that he felt might be happening to himself at the same time. As if the pig learned instantaneously and was using this new lesson on the teacher right away. But was such a thing possible? Surely not. And the farmer felt confident that it *was* his idea to teach the pig. That it *was* his decision to walk out to the barn, kneel before the pig, and talk. And talk. And talk. Endlessly talking, while also dreaming, dreaming of someone breaking into the barn and pulling him from this scene, dragging him from the feet of the pig, telling him that he was going to be okay again, he was going to be himself again, he was going to be just fine once they flew him far away, as far as Rio, a place where the loose tendrils of an unseen web cannot reach.

The farmer taught the pig about mind games. Taught him about trickery and pranks and how one man (pig) could change the mind of an entire county if he set out to do it. And the pig tilted his head and listened and felt each fresh fly of information settle into the web. And he knew the truth because he felt the truth, and the pig wasn't cluttered with indecision or second-guessing.

The farmer dreamed.

Awake.

But he denied this dream. On his own. All by himself. He denied the idea that he wanted to leave this place, wanted to leave this pig, needed to get as far from here as possible, like his daughter, his daughter who'd flown south, six thousand miles, as if she knew something he didn't, as if she knew that all the way down there was the only place where she could be safe.

So the farmer denied his dream and he remained. On his knees. In the barn. In the bedroom. In the pen.

He taught the pig about strategy. Taking over. Revolt.

And it felt good. Sometimes it felt good. But when the pig looked into the eyes of the farmer, when the one good eye locked paths with the farmer's two, the farmer shuddered. In the dream he shuddered and on his knees he shuddered. Because the pig couldn't look at him with the good eye without looking at him with the bad eye, and whenever the farmer looked at the flap of crinkled pink skin that covered the pig's bad eye he remembered the human eye he'd seen beneath; he remembered the eye in there that he couldn't deny, couldn't pretend wasn't truth.

The pig listened. The farmer taught. The pig looked. The farmer looked away.

Then the farmer looked back, at both eyes.

By his own decision.

By his own decision to do so.

38

Bob drove out to the farm, going thirty miles over the speed limit. It felt incredible. Felt like he was the clown shot from the cannon, just free sailing up Murdock at such a dangerous speed that if he were to jerk the wheel at all or if the car were to hit the wrong bump he'd go careening into the wheat and possibly all the way to the base of the woods. How would *that* feel? How the fuck would that feel to go crashing end over end rolling toward the trees, his head rattling inside the car like a pig's eye in a mason jar falling from a shelf? How fucking cool would that be? Fuck, he almost *wanted* it to happen, even removed his hands from the wheel entirely and just let the thing *fly*. Somewhere in his mind Theresa was saying, *This isn't a good idea, slow down, Bobby, you're gonna kill yourself, Bobby*, but Bobby didn't care. In fact, he didn't *give a shit*. Ha-ha. Not now he didn't, not after seeing the look in the pretty blond girl's eyes, the shameless remains of horror, the horror she'd seen out at the farm, the farm he was roaring toward, the farm that had been harboring that godforsaken pig for far too long.

Why hadn't Bob gone out and killed the thing by now? Why'd he wait so many years to confront the living thing that had only slowly drained him of his exuberance, his lust, his *self*? Bob didn't know. He didn't want to know. Why do so many people wait so long to confront their demons, their parents, their teachers, their bosses, their ghosts? Who knows. And who gives a shit. Tonight Bob was as free as a sprung rubber band, flying up Murdock at highway speeds, hitting bumps so hard that his hair was mashed down from the Cadillac's roof.

Bob screamed.

Screamed out the window. Part exuberance, part war call, part letting the pig know he was on his way and he was going to grab the first axe he saw and he was going to chop the fucking thing's legs off first then gut him alive, then strip out of this pink suit and dress up in pig guts and dance around the farm like a free man fired from a free-thinking gun. He was going to end this, tonight, with or without permission from whoever had to give permission to kill a pig, no permission out here, no more, out here in the lawless mad mania of man and pig.

"Waaaaaaaaaaaa!"

Bob chuckled and put his hands back on the wheel, then removed them again, then saw a boy running toward him in the road up ahead.

Bob laughed.

Another mirage. The pig's doing. A nightmare come to life. Sure, sure, the moment Bob felt free there had to be an obstacle, a kid, a boy in the middle of his road, his freedom, his escape from the web.

"Move it!" he called, and he laughed at the sound of his own voice. *Move it.* As if Bob was some kind of angry old man. As if Bob was some kind of guy to say *move it* to a horrified kid standing in the middle of the road, palms out, waving his arms, asking for Bob to stop to help to pick him up, to stay away from the farm.

Bob removed his hands from the wheel, and the kid came at him so fast, so fucking fast, that it looked like a freaky slide show, a series of photographs, Shrinky Dinks placed all over the road, the boy at different sizes, different terrified expressions, each lasting a beat, a bounce, not even a breath.

A picture of the boy diving.

Jumping out of the way.

Only the boy's feet sticking out of the wheat.

Wheat feet.

Then gone.

Poof.

And Bob gripped the wheel and cackled out the side window and who knows what happened to the boy, who gives a hoot, the farmhouse was up ahead, Kopple Farm and the pigpen and the toolshed and the barn that scared the holy hell out of the pretty blonde in the hospital who looked like she'd been to Vietnam and back.

"Waaaaaaaaaaa!"

He heard hollering behind him, no doubt the boy, screaming look out don't go the pigs are free the pigs aren't in their pen. And Bob shook his head and thought, *They were never in their pen, boy! We only thought they were!*

"Waaaaaaaaaaaaaa!"

Careening up the short hill to Kopple's and then *POW,* a serious turn into the gravel drive and a smash into the car parked there, headfirst, Bob's face flattened against the windshield and holy *fuck,* it felt good to be free, felt good to be coming at it, rushing toward it, shot toward the Hell that haunts you with a mind to shut it down.

The Cadillac's engine made a series of clicking sounds, shutting itself down, all on its own.

It was okay. Bob wasn't thinking of the way back. All of Time, all of Timing had led up to this moment, this feeling, this place.

Bob pushed open the driver's side door and squeezed out of the smashed front end, cackling yet, looking hard into the darkness where the path ought to be to take him to the barn.

But the toolshed first. Gotta have the tool before entering the barn.

He started toward it, toward the darkness, and heard a ripping sound. He paused and felt his knees and realized his pants were torn, and he laughed because it was funny to tear a pink suit on your way to gutting a pig.

39

The pig was squashing him tight to the wall, not letting him go, and what must be its tongue was pressed against his own lips, the rough snout against his nose. Jeff threw up. He had to. The smell, this close, was insane. Smelled like an outhouse, like Jeff was standing in the hole in an outhouse, and men and women were shitting on him from above.

The huge hog had him because Jeff was looking for Mom.

This wasn't Mom.

This was Monster.

Jeff tried to shove the thing away, but there was no leverage, no place to put his hands, his feet, his back. It was as if his entire being was enveloped in pig, this pig, wrapped up like a mummy in brown-and-white gauze, locked in a tomb, nowhere to go until an unfortunate explorer came and opened it up.

Then he would rise. Then he would get up and exact revenge on those who disturbed his peace.

Pearl.

Where was Mom? The idea that she might be dead was beginning to take root, and Jeff had to take a new approach to thinking,
needed more than the just-move-and-you-prove-you're-not-
scared ideal. Now he needed to add *accept*. Because if Mom was on
the farm, if Mom was okay, wouldn't she be here now? Wouldn't
she have called from the darkness?

Her car was in the drive. But where was her body? The pigpen?
The barn? A tomb of her own?

The pig bit him. Bit his neck. Jeff yelled and tried to move, but
there was no space, the pig was everywhere, as if the entire room
were made of pig. Jeff threw up again in the dark. He had only the
memory of what this pig looked like, the face he'd seen wedged
into the fat body sitting on the bed when the lights came on.

Was it real?

It felt real. Oh, God, did it feel real. But what was it doing? Just . . .
keeping him here? Was it killing him? Was this death? Would
Aaron come into the farmhouse, experience the same end?

A car crash out in the drive, and something snapped inside Jeff.
The sound ripped him back to reality (*that's not a word anymore;
obsolete*), and he realized that he *was* against the wall, *was* in reach
of the lights. *Could* do something about this. "Help!" he half yelled,
his throat pressed with pig fat. Perhaps the pig's snout. Perhaps the
pig's penis. Someone crashed a car in the drive. Aaron trying to
drive Mom's car? Mom fleeing, not knowing Jeff was trapped upstairs?

"HELP!"

Silence outside, then a door swinging open, then the door closing. Aaron had screamed that the pigs were out there. Were they
destroying Mom's car? Making it so she couldn't escape?

What could they do? And what couldn't they do, too?

The terrible wheezing again, and Jeff felt like he was *inside* the pig now, trapped, a prisoner of a slow digestion, where his own pale flesh would slowly peel from the bone, until he looked like . . . looked like . . .

Bob Buck.

Crazy thought to have at Death's door. Bob Buck. The man whose ghastly face he'd seen breaking through the bathroom door before escaping. The man who looked dead while alive, whose smile made Jeff think of rattling pennies in a piggy bank.

Bob Buck.

Did Bob Buck smash his car outside?

An even crazier thought to have. As the folds of the pig enveloped him, Jeff thought of Bob Buck (of all people) emerging like a zombie from a wrecked Cadillac in the driveway. Imagined the man limping toward the house or, no, toward the *barn*. And maybe it wasn't so crazy a thought after all. Bob Buck looked like a man trapped in the pig's belly, slowly eviscerated, *slowly* picked apart by belly-revenge. Yes, Jeff felt now how Bob Buck looked: exhausted from battling what haunts him.

But the lights. If Jeff could turn on the lights again, he might see a way out of this, might find an advantage after all.

But with the thought of escape, the pig pressed harder.

That's no coincidence, Jeff thought, incredible to think anything.

And then he knew it. Saw it clear as tap water.

You and Pearl are . . . in tune.

It was no accident that he'd thought of Bob Buck. Bob Buck *was* in the driveway below. Bob Buck *had* smashed his car into Mom's. He knew this because Pearl knew this, and Pearl knew this because Pearl was close. Pearl was here. Somewhere on the farm. And for as smart as the pig was, he still hadn't mastered the separation of thoughts, allowing them to overlap, showing one person

(Jeff) how concerned he was with another (Bob Buck). Yes, whatever monster Pearl had become, he must have a weak spot, must be able to be defeated. For anything that lets its slip show also lets you know which thread to try pulling first.

Jeff felt the light switch against his back. He tried to rise with it, tried to lift up, but the pig held him down. Jeff tried again. He gripped the fatty folds until the pig squealed, he brought his knees forward hard against the legs, the belly, the balls.

There was no change, give, and the pig only grunted as if Jeff were a piglet, vying for room on the milk vine.

Trick him, Jeff thought. *Make him think you're trying to go low.*

Jeff pressed down on the beast, and the beast pressed up, and as he did the switch went up with Jeff's back, up and on and suddenly so, so bright in this room of living horror.

Dying, not living anything.

But . . . not living or dying.

Nothing.

Jeff saw an empty bed. An empty room. His arms were still raised as if warding off an enemy, but that enemy was unseen.

Lights.

And the pig was gone.

Jeff howled, once, exuberance impossible to contain. He wasn't going to die in this room, wasn't going to suffocate beneath afghans of pig fat. Wasn't going to breathe in the terrible raw sewage smell of the monster's exhalations. The breath that Bob Buck had been breathing for a decade or more.

Bob Buck.

Jeff finally lowered his arms and went to the door and opened it (it opened!). Bob Buck was below somewhere. Here for the same reason Jeff was. To find Pearl. And yet that didn't feel like the right way to put it. Wasn't Jeff here to find Mom?

He stepped into the hall, and the light from Grandpa's bedroom reached far enough to show Jeff the inside of what was once Mom's bedroom. The room she lived in when she was his age, the very place in which she started to fear the pigs. Jeff felt sorrow's bloom as he imagined a younger Mom, a girl his age, peering out the window to the pigpen below. He wanted to cry out to her, tell her not to look at them, don't think about them, don't let them (Pearl) sneak into your mind. He raised a hand toward his mother's old bedroom and even opened his mouth and froze.

Mom was lying in the bed.

Not younger Mom. Mom now.

In the combination of moonlight through the window and the reach of the light from Grandpa's bedroom, Jeff saw his mother was sitting up now, rising, like a mummy, stiff-backed, turning her head to face him in the hall. Jeff's arm was still up, stuck that way, and Mom raised both of hers in return.

"Come to Momma, Jeffy Jeff," she said, and her voice was the snickering of pigs, the sound of hooves in the mud.

40

Back in the barn, Sherry had the barrel of the shotgun depressing the soft pink skin at Pearl's forehead. The one teen had already burned the ropes, freeing the other two. Officers Hahn and Perry stood on either side of the maniac animal, his personal guards, and with them, the group of pigs wobbling about on the dirt floor made up the king's court.

Not too many satellites for Pearl now. Just this one. No more worrying about the six human minds in the barn, the pack of pigs, Bob Buck, and the brothers still back home. No more. Just this one satellite. And it was even less than a satellite, less than a mind.

Pearl focused all of his power on one finger.

Sherry's finger on the trigger of the shotgun.

"Make them hear gunshots," she commanded. The teens were slipping out of the barn behind her. Good. She understood that Pearl had to let them go. To maintain. To focus. To rid himself of satellites. "Make them see the light of the gunshots, too."

Pearl understood the farmer's daughter wanted him to fool the teens. He didn't know the exact explanation for why, other than perhaps it meant the teens would be more likely to get help if they saw and heard the weapons go off behind them.

But Pearl resisted. His eyes locked with the farmer's daughter, he sought roots in her mind, purchase on the rocky cliffs of her wonder-wheel thoughts.

He couldn't do it. Couldn't find it.

Why?

Whatever it was, whatever *pushed back*, Pearl understood it was also what inspired her to flee, as a younger woman, long ago when she left the farm and the farmer behind. The woman (*Shaaaar-reeeeee*) had something of the stuff Pearl had. But not nearly as much.

Not nearly as much as the boy, her son, either.

And yet . . . no purchase, no grip. Was it because she had a head start? Her being human, her intelligence was naturally higher than his. Perhaps a dollop of power in the woman was equal to a pound of the pig's?

"Make them hear gunshots," Sherry said, as the two officers came to, wiped crazy from their faces, looked around the barn like they had no idea where they were.

She tightened her finger, and Pearl did as she said.

The teens heard gunshots. Saw the lights of gunfire, too.

Their caterwauling howls dissipated outside. Like witches in the woods.

"Now send them home." Sherry was talking about the police officers. Pearl understood every word of this one. He even thought he understood why.

She's trying to save everyone in here.

Everyone but the pigs, of course. There would be no saving of the pigs from this one or any like her.

Pearl did what she wanted.

The officers stepped away from him, confused, eyeing Sherry as if she were a statue, a foreigner, a thing they hadn't read the rules on. In fact, they looked so disoriented it was hard not to imagine them stumbling about downtown Chowder, arresting old ladies, giving tickets to dogs. But it was better than them being here.

The problem, Sherry's problem, was that the farmer, the father of the farmer's daughter, had taught Pearl about *picking his battles*. As lofty a concept as it was, Pearl understood, clearly, that the more he let go, the tighter he tied his mind to her finger.

No more satellites. This meant the brothers would get out of their house now. Pearl relaxed his grip on them.

That would have to be.

For now.

Sherry put up a good fight. At one point she actually thought she shot him, thought it was over, and started to lower the gun. At another point she thought she was at home, getting the boys ready to go to the farm, no slaughtered pig at the hands of Jeff yet, no proof of Pearl's power realized.

She sweated and she trembled and she screamed. She struggled.

All before Pearl, the gun to his head. But once the satellites had been set free the way she demanded, controlling her was as easy as controlling the birds.

Sherry lowered the gun. She thought, righteously even, that it was the right thing to do. She set the weapon down in the dirt, and she walked to a corner of the barn. There she stood, her nose to where the wooden walls met.

The farmer had also taught Pearl about *saving things for later*.

That was what he was going to do with Sherry. Leave her in the corner. Save her for later.

Save her for when the boy showed up.

41

Not too many satellites now.

The men in blue had driven away, suddenly sure they had something more pressing to take care of. There would be some residual with them; they might try to arrest the first person they saw. The three that had come looking for Pearl were now in a hospital and had done what Pearl needed them to do.

They spoke.

They talked about it.

And like the farmer taught him, those words spread, spread quickly like the daddy long-legged spiders in the barn spread apart whenever Pearl stared at them for too long. Yes, their words spread until they reached the ears of the man in the white suit, the man who decided not to wear the white suit tonight because he felt more alive, more willing, more empowered by something even Pearl wasn't quite able to understand. But everything, all of it, was manageable. Because not too many satellites now. Nothing in the way. Just the boy and the beast, and Pearl wanted them both here, wanted them both to come for him, to find him, at the same time.

Funny how the woman's wish, to get everyone out, wasn't that different from his own.

Now the beast (in pink) was coming, and the boy was facing his horrors in the farmhouse, and Pearl waited for both, both at the same time, both to come find him at the same time.

Not too many satellites now, and maybe there never were. Maybe Pearl's range and reach were greater than he thought they were. When the boy slaughtered the pig, Pearl understood he'd accomplished something higher. And if the boy would do whatever he wanted . . . why not everyone? And how many *was* everyone?

Vaguely, Pearl was aware that he knew only the farm, that there was more out there, much farther up the road.

The farmer would've taught him about it, had this day not come.

How many like you, farmer?

It didn't matter. Not now. Not too many satellites now.

The beast approached, smiling like he did the day he burned Pearl's eye. And the boy was crying in a hall of the farmhouse. But the boy would get up soon, would come for Pearl.

But not quite that, not yet, as the beast hadn't found Pearl yet, and the boy must come when he did, must arrive when the beast did.

And so . . .

. . . . so when the boy rises, when the boy comes running, the farmer will be waiting downstairs for him, the farmer will slow him down.

Timing.

The farmer taught Pearl about timing.

Not too many satellites now. Not too many at all. Pearl felt stronger than he ever knew he could. Perhaps it was what the farmer called *getting through it.*

You've gotta change your size and shape to get through it, Pearl. If you reach a spot that's too tight for you to crawl through, you gotta change your size and shape.

So Pearl waited. Hid in the darkness. Played with his remaining satellites.

The timing was close.

Outside, the beast stumbled, talked to himself, cackled and hummed, sang but not for Pearl. Sang for himself and the delusion he held of being free, of fitting through his own tight space, of having changed his shape and size.

Pearl could see him. The moonlight shined through a crack in a board and reflected off Pearl's eye. Pearl tilted his head slightly, just enough to place the wrinkled lid of his other eye into the light.

Pearl opened his other eye.

And he watched the beast this way. With his good eye, the one everyone called his bad.

42

Jeff knelt in the hall, crying. Mom swung her legs over the side of the bed.

Come to Momma, Jeff.

And Jeff wanted to. Wanted so badly to go to her, to see if she was okay, to hold her whether she was dead or alive and to love her and tell her he wasn't afraid of the pig, was going to face the pig, was going to find him and slaughter him just like he'd already done to the other, the time Pearl made him want to do it.

"Come, Jeff."

That's all she said, and she said it so many times that it started to sound like an alarm to Jeff, like he was supposed to wake up from this nightmare and get the hell out of the farmhouse.

Find Pearl!

As if it wasn't his own thought, as if it'd come from somewhere very far away, a slight voice urging him on, reminding him that the thing in Grandpa's bedroom was a trick of the mind and so was Mom on the bed. Mom on the bed wasn't real, didn't mean she was alive or dead, didn't mean anything at all.

Mom on the bed wasn't Mom.

Was it?

"Are you . . . are you okay?" Jeff sobbed the words out and wiped his face with hands that still smelled of pig.

Mom on the bed only said, "Come, come to Mom on the bed."

Jeff rose. Nodding okay. He'd go to her. He'd tell her he was going to find Pearl. Tell her he was okay and Aaron was okay (where was Aaron?) and tell her everything was okay because the time had come to face the pig and Jeff wasn't afraid, wasn't scared at all.

Crying, trembling, he approached his mother's childhood bedroom. Mom's face was obscured by shadows and he couldn't see all of it, couldn't see more than her shoulders, really, and her outstretched arms, inviting, calling, come come come, come to Mom on the bed.

Jeff entered the room and heard a hissing sound, the wheezy *yes yes yes, this is what I wanted* exhale of his mother (dead?) waiting patiently on the edge of the mattress.

"Oh, Mom!" Jeff called as he ran to her and wrapped his arms around her and felt her body fold like an empty leather satchel, heard the sound of snapping bones.

Jeff looked up and saw the face of Mom on the bed.

Not Mom. Dad.

Wigged. Eyes glazed and crazy. Gibbering high in the voice of Mom.

"Now sing for Momma, Jeffy Jeff! Sing for Pearl!"

Jeff tried to push away from the thing on the bed, but there was no form, no resistance, and he fell forward, onto it, onto the bed.

In the moonlight, up close, Dad's makeup looked like mud and blood and piss.

"Sing for Momma!" he shrieked. *"Sing for Pearl!"*

Jeff tried to get up, but his hands fell deeper into the body beneath him. He felt the bones like fish bones in a dangerous dinner, chicken bones licked clean of the meat. He heard a clucking, too, chickens in the closet, the rising chaos of chickens trying to escape the closet.

"JEFF!" a voice from downstairs, from below. Angry.

Aaron? Grandpa?

"Sing for Momma!"

Jeff looked down into the crazy thing's eyes and tried again to shove himself off.

He screamed as the body turned to shit. Jeff went sprawling flat on the bed.

He brought his head up and saw the bedroom was no longer a bedroom. Mom's childhood bedroom had become the pigpen.

"Sing for Momma, you little pink punk! SING FOR ME!"

Jeff rolled onto his side and saw the thing, Dad in a dress, Dad in a wig, crawling toward him in the mud.

Jeff rolled and fell, hard, hit the floor of the bedroom (the bedroom!) and looked up to see Mom's (Mom's!) face smiling down at him from the edge of the mattress.

"I wish I never met your father," she said.

Jeff inched back as Mom rose, planting her mud-soaked feet on the floor. Jeff got up and ran out of the room, down the stairs, to the tune of Mom whistling, singing her own song, crying, too, and the suction cup sound of her muddy bare feet on the cool wood floors of the farmhouse.

The front door was close, so close, but when Jeff reached the bottom of the stairs he heard the last sound he wanted to hear, the *only* sound that could stop him from leaving.

Aaron. Crying.

Jeff ran through the house, to the living room, and saw Grandpa standing, hunched, his back to Jeff, bringing the axe down upon something on the floor.

THWACK!

"Grandpa!" Jeff called, blindly hoping that Grandpa (*Grandpa's dead*) had found Pearl (*Pearl is controlling all of this, everything you see, even this*) and was killing him on the living room rug.

Grandpa turned around, eyes like chicken eyes, his nose a whiskered snout. He brought the axe down again at his feet.

THWACK!

Aaron cried out, and Jeff knew knew, *knew* he shouldn't step into the living room but had to, *had to* check if this was real (*it's NOT!*), had to make sure Grandpa wasn't taking an axe to Aaron.

THWACK!

And Jeff saw.

Aaron on the ground. Legless. Armless. Rivers of blood.

"JEFF!" Aaron said. "THE PIGS ARE NOT IN THE PEN!"

Grandpa snorted and swung the axe, lopping Aaron's head unclean across the living room floor.

This time Jeff didn't scream, didn't cry out, didn't go to Grandpa. He fled. He ran through the house to the front door and ran outside into the night and turned toward the barn and saw the man Bob Buck opening the shed door, saw it in the moonlight, saw the man retrieving an axe and . . .

. . . he walked now. Quietly. Not wanting to be heard. Not wanting to be seen. Not wanting anything not knowing what he wanted, no.

But the man heard him, and the man turned to face him.

"Eh?" Bob said, holding the axe now in both hands. "And who are you?"

Jeff didn't answer. He stood silent in the dark, staring at the haunted man before him.

"And who are you?" Bob repeated. "And are you here to try to stop me?"

Jeff didn't speak. Didn't move.

And the boy and the beast faced each other on the dirt path that separated the pigpen from the barn.

And behind them, in the shadows of the rakes, the mower, the tools, and the trowels, Jeff saw an eye, what looked like the eye of a man, an old man, sick and wise, illuminated by the moonlight, watching the final scene unfold.

43

Jeff had never seen Pearl's eye, the eye beneath the fold. Grandpa had. Grandpa peeled the skin back and saw doom and death and a thing too human to call pig. *The dead eye of a man*, Grandpa thought, shuddering for months with the memory. But for all Jeff truly knew of Pearl's eyes, there was the functioning one with the large pupil that made it look black from afar (the good one) and the one that might not even exist, might be nothing but a fatty hole on the other side of the snout (the bad one). For this, there was no reason for him to think there was anything in the shed but a man; that unquestionably human eye (dead or not dead) staring out through the space left by the open shed door, the moonlight striking it just enough to give it color, vitality, but not enough to reveal the face that held it.

Bob Buck was standing with the axe. He was looking over his shoulder at Jeff like the kid had just scratched up his car. A rock kicked up from the tires. An unwelcome bug on the dashboard of

Bob's machine, running now into perpetual motion. He'd already asked Jeff who he was, asked it twice, then asked Jeff if he was here to stop him.

Then the Crest came; a ripple in everything at once, everything visible and everything heard. As if the entire farm were built on water, and that water was angry, storming below. Jeff saw the evergreens rise, one at a time, quick succession, saw the roof of the barn undulate, lift *up* off the barn; saw the grassy hill, the dirt path, the fences, the mud in the pigpen, the sky all *CREST* in a terrific, astonishing display of Pearl's terrible power. And as the wave washed over Bob Buck, the man repeated himself, but differently, as if the tape, the film of Bob, had been slowed down.

As the world swelled behind and beside him, Bob Buck asked Jeff:

"*Aaaaaaarrrrrreeee yooooooooouuuuuuu hhhhhhheeeeeeerrrrrreeeee tttttooooooo ssssssstttttoooppppppppppp mmmmmmmeeeeeee-eee??????*"

Then Bob fell to his knees and started grunting.

Oinking.

The axe handle between his teeth, he crawled through the Crest, toward the shed.

Then the Crest hit Jeff, and he was thrust to the ground, onto his back. The wave passed over his whole body, making it momentarily curl, like a dried worm on a sidewalk.

It passed.

And when Jeff brought his head up again, he saw the world had stabilized, and Bob Buck was crawling, yes, crawling toward the shed.

But something was crawling toward him, too.

A pig. Out of the shed.

Pearl.

From somewhere sweetly distant, Jeff heard the voice of his mother. But Jeff knew better this time. The relief he *wanted* to feel at hearing her voice, the relief he deserved, was tempered, mightily, by his experience in the farmhouse, in Mom's childhood bedroom upstairs.

Ahead, on the path, Bob rose to face Pearl. He raised the axe high.

Then Jeff saw movement to his left, something near the barn. He turned to see Mom, rushing toward him.

He wanted to holler, to tell her, *Oh my God, you're okay, oh my God, you aren't dead, oh my God, Mom, I came out here to help you and you're okay, let's go, let's go home, let's go!*

But no. He knew better. *Dammit.* He knew better!

And still, to make sure, he looked up to the farmhouse, to the bedroom window on the second floor of the farmhouse, Mom's room, the window that overlooked the pigpen.

Through the glass he saw the silhouette of a wigged father watching.

"Mom?" Jeff asked, no, didn't ask, *said*, as he looked back to the exhausted figure approaching on his left. "MOM?!"

She ran to him. He ran to her.

And when they were holding each other, when her physical form was there beneath his fingers, Jeff knew.

"MOM!"

"Where's Aaron?"

"I don't know!"

"We have to go, Jeff. We have to—"

But they were stopped by a sound. The axe striking the earth. And both saw Bob Buck swinging the tool, Pearl sitting on his ass below him.

"He's gonna kill him," Jeff said. "He's gonna kill Pearl."

Bob swung the axe again, and again it hit only the dirt beside the sitting pig.

SING FOR ME, BAWB BYUCK, SING FOR PEAAAAAAARL.

Jeff had to cover his ears.

Bob swung the axe once more, and this time he connected. This time the blade nicked the bottom corner of Pearl's bad eye, and the wrinkled skin split open, and the eye fell from the pig's face and rolled along the gravel path to the side of the shed.

Bob howled in triumph and lifted the tool again.

This is it, Jeff thought. *He's going to kill him!*

But Jeff couldn't take his own eyes off Pearl's one, plucked, lying in the darkness by the shed.

And a shadow there. Two ears emerging. A cocked head pressing itself to the ground, pressing its face to the dirt.

When the silhouette rose again, the moonlight showed Jeff that the eye was back where it belonged.

"Oh, God," Jeff said, looking back to Bob and whatever pig was with him on the path. Whatever pig Pearl had fooled Bob (and Jeff and Mom and everyone) into believing was himself.

Sherry screamed when Bob's head ballooned, became two heads, Grandpa and Bob, before morphing into the fatty shape of the pig Jeff met upstairs. And Pearl . . . Pearl on the path . . . that pig sat on its ass, limp-hooved and smiling like Mona Lisa, watching the man in pink stretch like taffy under the moon.

Jeff looked to Pearl by the shed again, saw the silhouette of the ears receding, fading like they had in the hall of his house.

"Jeff," Mom said, her voice shaking. "We have to go *now.*"

But neither started for the path, the driveway, Murdock Road, or downtown Chowder beyond. Instead, they watched as taffy Bob dropped the axe and fell forward, upon the pig, became one with the pig on the path, a singular sludge of bright pink, arms and hooves testing the skin, pressing, poking, trying to break free. Jeff and Mom watched the struggle as it moved, rolled, raging putty, pulled and reshaped, pink eyes in an old man's face, a pig with human hands, teeth, hair, snout, until it was all only a transference of colors, a blob, heading toward the pen.

Mom shrieked when she felt the other pigs, Pearl's pen mates, rush by her legs. She and Jeff held each other as the pack moved up the path and followed the elastic storm through the open gate of the pen.

Jeff looked back to the shed. Then he broke free from Mom and ran to it, ran to the shadows, ran to where he believed he saw Pearl jam his face into the dirt, forcing his eye back into his head.

But no pig.

No Pearl.

Not on the side of the shed or behind it. Not before, within, nor upon.

Jeff looked to the pigpen, to the bright war raging within. Pearl's mind unbound. Pearl's mind fired from a slingshot forged in Hell.

"Aaron?"

When Jeff looked up, he saw Mom was running to the road, running out into the road, reaching for a shape there, a silhouette.

Aaron.

Jeff turned back to face the pen (*Pearl is still loose, PEARL IS NOT IN THE PEN!*) to see if maybe he could tell how it ended, how it would end, how it could.

He looked to the shed. Back to the pen.

Then to the barn.

Mom was in the road crouched by Aaron, checking on him, hugging him, running her fingers through his hair.

Jeff picked up the axe Bob had let go.

He ran to the barn.

He ran past the shattered chicken coop, down the path so many people had taken today, more people than Grandpa ever had on the farm at one time before.

Through the splintered barn door he saw the flickering light within and he thought: *Life.*

Yes, something alive inside the barn.

Cautious, slow, gripping the axe with both hands, Jeff entered and saw Pearl sitting upon his throne, fires of hay on either side of him, blood like a moat surrounding him.

Then that blood rose, the bloodshed of the day, and hung suspended like flowing red curtains, obscuring the brilliant pig backstage.

And Jeff knew.

Knew Pearl was tired. Knew Pearl couldn't control what he was doing to Bob Buck and address the boy, Jeff, himself, at the same time. The curtain of blood (Susan's blood, Mitch's blood, Jerry's blood, the blood of the pigs) like the towel hanging to hide a person dressing, a person who needed a minute, just one minute, please, please, just one minute to finish getting dressed, can't get dressed and walk about at the same time, gotta take care of one then the other, one then the other, one—

"Your slip is showing," Jeff said.

The curtain split then, for only a breath, and Jeff saw Pearl behind it, both eyes open, both eyes upon Jeff.

Jeff felt cold hands upon his own. Spiderwebs spun in ice.

Then the curtain closed. The war raged outside in the pen.

And Jeff ran toward Pearl on his throne, breaking through the blood, covering himself from head to sneaker toe, choking on the bloodshed of the day, closing his eyes to it, feeling the entirety of it, all upon him at once, as he raised the axe high and brought it down.

44

Teach me.

No.

Teach me about the world.

You know too much. You know too much.

How big the world outside the farm? Bigger than the farm outside the pen?

You know too much.

Jeff held the axe only inches from Pearl's neck, a snapshot of a young baseball player, caught midswing, never to reach the ball he was watching.

How big the world? How many satellites the world?

But it wasn't Jeff who held the axe so close. It was Pearl.

Or, perhaps, Jeff crazily thought, nobody held anything at all, and he and Pearl were exchanging, conversing, all in the time it took to conclude one complete swing of death.

Teach me.

YOU KNOW TOO MUCH!

Pearl's head hung, exhausted, toward the dirt floor, toward the coming axe. Jeff saw the fire reflected in Pearl's open bad eye. Could feel the heat of it upon his own body. Saw his own fingers, painted red, the blood falling from the axe handle like too much paint in the pail.

He saw Pearl, too, as Pearl might have been. A farm animal. A pig. Only a pig and not a miscreation capable of controlling a town, a county, a world.

How big the world? How many more like you?

With Jeff's thought of the world and how big it truly was, Pearl turned toward him and the sky exploded pink outside, above the pen.

Pearl smiled. Truly. No suggestion, no partial, no maybe.

Jeff couldn't tell if the smile acknowledged defeat or declared victory.

But it was there.

Then, as Jeff felt the axe getting closer, closer to Pearl, Pearl's features began to pull apart, expand, like a pink balloon, until his snout was very far from his mouth, very far from his chin.

Jeff cried out as Pearl popped, like the farmer who had slaughtered Pearl's mother had popped so long ago.

"NO!" Jeff said, because he couldn't tell if that smile was acknowledging defeat or declaring victory.

He recalled the pink mist in his bedroom. The phony threats in the farmhouse.

The pieces of Pearl burst in every direction, striking the barn walls at once, striking Jeff's arms and legs like small bullets of bone.

Jeff finished his swing and was turned around for it, fell to the dirt, as the blood curtains fell down upon him, washing him clean of Pearl's guts, Pearl's bones, Pearl's mind.

When Jeff looked up, when he wiped the blood from his eyes, he saw the throne was empty.

Slowly, achingly, he got to one knee to right himself, to regroup, to breathe.

He closed his eyes, and when he opened them he saw he was facing the throne, as if Pearl still sat upon it. He recalled how Pearl exploded before the axe connected, and knew it was because Pearl had simply taken on too much too much too much.

Today.

Jeff pinched a piece of pink flesh from the barn floor and held it up to the empty space upon the throne, the place Pearl had just been sitting, limp-hooved, singing.

"You," Jeff said, lifting the piece higher. "This was you."

Teach me.

Then, quickly, Jeff dropped the piece, as if it were made of living spiders, as if it were made of heat.

He looked over his shoulder and saw Mom there, Aaron there, in the open barn door.

Mom didn't nod and Aaron didn't say come on, but Jeff rose, got to his feet, and walked through the bloodshed of the day, leaving his sneaker prints in the red, as if, no matter how fast he and Mom and Aaron got home, he would sort of still be here, in the blood, on the farm, proof of the bottom of his shoe in the barn.

45

Mitch limped through the hallways of Morgan High and nodded at the students who nodded at him first. There was no keeping a secret in a town this size, and everybody had heard about the incident out at Walter Kopple's farm. And yet the details were vague. And getting vaguer.

Mitch and Jerry and Susan Marx (of all people, how the hell did she end up with *those* two?) had gone out to the farm to fuck with the sleeping cows, and some madman had hurt them. Some deliveryman went nuts and tried to kill them, and somehow they'd escaped, but they were so stoned they thought the guy was one of the cows, exacting revenge. Mitch and Jerry got it bad; Mitch limped and Jerry had to be wheeled around for what they said would be four to six weeks. Somehow Susan had emerged as beautiful as she had been when she went out there, though the boys and girls of Morgan High could tell something was different about her. In class, she looked quickly to the door whenever it opened.

She jumped a little at the sound of the bell. She didn't raise her hand as often as she used to, and she stared out the classroom windows all the time, as if looking for someone, the deliveryman probably, worried that he was going to come after them again, come for her in the middle of the day in class. Nobody knew for sure what happened to the madman other than rumors about Officers Perry and Hahn shooting him dead in the pigpen right there on Kopple Farm. Some students were jealous. And not just the boys who wished they'd witnessed some wild action alongside Susan Marx; this was bona fide adventure for the first time ever in Chowder, boring Chowder. All sorts of people wished they'd gone with the trio out to the farm, where they would've become heroes, like these three, would've been cemented in Chowder lore as the three who saw the doors of Hell swing open, snuck a peek inside, and pulled their heads out of the way just in time, before those doors slammed closed again. None of them said much. Susan was asked out more times in the two weeks following the incident than she had been in her entire life put together, and she said no to them all. She understood that she'd acquired some kind of status out there on the farm. Had somehow, in the swirl of all that chaotic impossibility, been charmed with a more meaningful persona. People wanted to be near her, some to help, some to experience a taste of Hell through her words, her eyes, the heat that emanated off her body. Mitch was the only one of the three to embrace this. He enjoyed the attention until he really thought about why he was receiving it. If he let himself relive the moments in the barn with any clarity, he'd shut off and reach into his pocket for a joint. Once he did this in class, and the teacher actually saw him do it, saw him remove a joint from his pocket. But he didn't get in any trouble. The teacher only told him to put it away. Everybody understood, see, that Mitch and Jerry and Susan Marx deserved some kind of reprieve from the regular rules of the regular life because whatever they saw out there had to change a person, had to change their shape and size.

That's what happened when a madman deliveryman tried to kill you.

Jerry didn't talk about it at all, to nobody no how, except only for Mitch, whom he still joined out in the woods behind the school, even if they looked over their shoulders at every sound that was made.

"You ever dream about it?" Jerry asked Mitch, taking the joint from his friend's hand. Jerry was in his wheelchair.

"Dream about it?" Mitch was holding a stack of papers in his lap, leafing through them. "Fuck no. Do you?"

"I do. I don't want to, but I do."

Mitch laughed and socked his friend in the arm, but it didn't feel quite like it used to. *Plastic Satanic* wasn't as funny to them, now that they'd actually felt the flames of Hell. And there was a darkness to Jerry, as if he'd bottled some of the spirit from the barn and taken it home with him and wasn't really ready to give it up.

Sticks cracked, and both looked up to see a yellow T-shirt and jeans through the woods. A yellow shirt and blond hair. Susan. She'd come to talk to them, for the first time since the hospital.

"Hello, guys," she said, entering the clearing and joining them. She didn't sit down; she stood.

Mitch smiled up at her.

"How are you?" he asked.

Susan nodded.

"I'm okay. But I'm worried about something."

There was a tremor in her voice. She sounded like she might cry. Mitch didn't want her to cry. He was worried Jerry might join her if she started.

"What is it?" Mitch asked.

Susan breathed deeply.

"There are tons of rumors going around . . . you know . . . about a maniac . . . whatever."

"Yeah," Mitch said.

"Yeah . . ." Susan tucked her hair behind her ears. Swallowed hard. "But I read the actual police report. And you know, our parents say the cops said the pigs were dead. All of them."

"Yep. And thank God."

Susan nodded, but Mitch could tell she wasn't convinced.

"But that's *not* what the cops said."

"What did they say?" Jerry asked.

Movement deeper in the woods, and all three turned to look.

A bunny peeked around a tree. Jerry coughed, and the animal darted away.

"What did the report say?" Jerry repeated.

Susan crouched before them.

"Well, it said a lot of things. It said they found 'pieces of a pink suit' for starters."

"The guy you told us about," Mitch said.

Susan nodded.

"That's the man that was killed by the pigs. One of the men, anyway. But hang on," she said. She was obviously nervous. "The report didn't say the cops said 'all the pigs were dead.' It said the cops *believed* all the pigs were dead."

Mitch snorted laughter, but it was fool's humor. The three of them sat quietly for a long time.

"Believed," Jerry repeated. He tapped the wheels of his wheelchair with his fingertips.

They didn't have to say that this was insane. That anything anybody believed out at Kopple Farm couldn't be counted as true. The three of them had sipped from the fountain of obscurity, and if there was one thing they knew, belief wasn't belief anymore.

"So what do we do?" Mitch asked. "Go back out there?"

He didn't want to say it, and the second after he did he felt a fear as real as the one he'd felt when he was hanging by his feet, upside down, the ceiling stuffed full of snouts.

"No," Susan said. "Absolutely not. But is there someone we can . . . talk to? Someone who could check it out?"

She imagined Jerry rolling himself out there in his chair. Alone on the dirt road that nobody wanted to take anymore.

After a long silence, Mitch said, "I think we should go with it. We should believe all the pigs are dead, too."

Susan opened her mouth and stopped herself. Because rebutting what Mitch just said meant either going out there herself or fighting for someone to do it for her, and either way she wanted to get farther away from the farm, from the day, not closer.

"He wants us to return," Jerry said.

Mitch punched the ground hard.

"I just said we should believe, Jerry!" he yelled. "And that means the pig is *dead*! Nobody wants us to do *anything*! Get it?!"

Jerry nodded. He got it. So did Susan.

Mitch lifted the papers from his lap and held them out to Susan.

"What is this?' Susan asked. For a breath she was sure Mitch had written an account of what happened out there. She imagined every detail forever in ink on those flapping white pages. She didn't want to touch them, didn't want to know they existed, wanted them to burn like the hay burned in the barn. Burned in the very real center of Hell.

"The paper I promised to write for you," Mitch said.

Susan looked at him with real surprise. Even Jerry smiled. There was something so kind about the gesture. So much like their former lives.

Susan started to cry. Only a little bit.

"Pukin' good," she said. "Thank you."

The friends smiled at her use of the word. Then she took the pages from Mitch and set them at her feet. She placed a hand on each of their shoulders.

"We're going to be okay, guys," she said. "We just . . . we just experienced something really fucked up. But we're *going* to be okay. I know we are. I can feel it that we are. We've been through something, and that means we *got through* it. Do you know what I mean? Some people wouldn't have and some people couldn't have, and we *did*, and that means we're going to be okay."

Mitch nodded. Jerry nodded. They wanted her to keep talking like this. Keep talking like this forever.

"We got through it," Susan repeated. "And we're gonna have to get used to our new . . ." She searched for the words. She found them, somewhere, as if someone inside her head handed them to her. "We're gonna have to get used to our new shapes and sizes."

Mitch got up. He laughed. And it felt so good, felt so much like the truth that it had to be.

46

Sitting around the breakfast table, nobody wanted to be the first to have anything to say about the *Chowder Daily* headline that was facedown next to the orange juice pitcher. Mom had seen it first, though Aaron had been the one to bring the paper inside. And Jeff was the one to turn the paper over.

Eventually, it had to be Mom who spoke. That was part of being Mom.

"That settles that, then."

She got up and crossed the kitchen, carried the pan of eggs back to the table and doled some more out for Aaron. Aaron always wanted more. Jeff was a bit harder to read. Always had been.

"More?"

"No thanks."

After returning the pan to the stove, Mom put her palms flat on the counter and let her chin sink to her chest.

A headline should have been encouraging. Should have been good.

"'*Pig Parts Found in the Barn*,'" Jeff recited, though none of them needed to hear it again. And Aaron, who had seen the least out there, saw the most in the few lines under the headline, before the paper was turned facedown.

"Little pieces," he said. "So it had to be as you said it was, Jeff."

Jeff wanted to smile. Wanted to tell Aaron, *You're right, let's go ride our bikes without worry, without wondering, without fear.*

"They identified Bob Buck, too," Mom said.

"They found his mouth in the mud," Aaron said. Just like that. Flat. Emotionless.

"Just his mouth?" Jeff asked.

Aaron nodded. He looked to the paper like he wanted to flip it, wanted to read just a sentence or two more, anything that could shed a little more light on the events at Grandpa's farm.

Mom sat down at the table again. Looked Aaron in the eye, then Jeff.

"They left it so he could scream till the end," Jeff said.

Aaron opened his own mouth to say something. To say that's impossible, but that word didn't apply anymore.

"Like I just said," Mom said, attempting to sound stern. "That settles that. Pig parts in the barn. The story is over."

Jeff got up.

"Where you going, hon?" Mom sounded worried.

It'd been like that since they'd gotten home. Days now of where are you going, what's on your mind, you okay? Everything okay? Every little thing okay?

But Jeff just needed to pee.

"I'll be right back."

"Boys," Mom started, disregarding Jeff's declaration. "Have either of you considered becoming friends with those teenagers that were out there?"

Aaron blushed. Jeff nodded. He had thought of it. Talking to them was something he very much wanted to do.

It was silly, but it was impossible not to imagine the five of them forming a club. No, six. Mom deserved to be in that club, too.

"Go do what you have to do," she said, acknowledging the bathroom down the hall. "We'll talk more about this when you get back."

On his walk to the bathroom, Jeff let his mind wander; he daydreamed; the police report said something about "believing all the pigs were dead." Obviously this meant nothing. In every way; nothing. And there was no mention of a particular pig with a messed-up eye, but Jeff didn't know how there could be. He didn't expect them to put Pearl back together again. To place his good eye in one socket and his bad in the other.

And yet the vision felt real. Pearl whole. Pearl again.

It was as if Pearl had somehow avoided the inquest altogether. When Jeff, Aaron, and Mom told the police about what happened on Grandpa's farm, nobody took the "pig with the bad eye" part of the story very seriously.

Not even the two police officers who had been there that day.

Peeing now, Jeff daydreamed an image of Pearl trotting up Murdock Road, the opposite direction of downtown Chowder. He was alone and the sun was rising, and in a way he had been wounded, deeply, but in another, more important way, he was more powerful than ever.

A phrase, a question, came with the bad image:

How many like you?

Spoken in a voice that was not Jeff's own (that was Pearl's), the words were accompanied by a vague image of what could only be called . . . *the rest of the world.*

Or, perhaps, the world outside the farm.

As his urine splashed the toilet bowl below, Jeff realized he was trembling, suddenly, crazily, certain that this was no daydream after all.

This was a vision. This was happening.

This was something to believe.

Mom's and Aaron's voices came from the kitchen, they were talking to each other, and Jeff shook his head, no no, not a vision, a *fear*, and dammit, he didn't want to be the kind of boy who feared.

He was still shaking his head no as he reached out and swiped his arms in front of his face because he'd felt a spiderweb there, a cobweb maybe. He hated the invasive feeling, the sensation that a trap had been set for him, and he'd walked right into it.

It was a daydream, Jeff thought. Not a vision. Not real.

It was just a bad thought.

That's all.

A bad thought to have thought.

And then, another bad thought. A whole series of them. A *scene.*

Jeff tried to face it fearlessly, but it was hard. It played out dreamishly undefined, and yet . . . certain details were ice-cold real.

The bad scene went like this:

The brothers knelt in the dirt and taught the pig about *everybody else.* They did it because they felt like they wanted to, but both dreamed (awake, dreamed while awake) of themselves running from the farm, running from the barn that covered them. But the pig wanted to know about the rest of the world—how many people were out there, how many other pigs—and so the brothers taught him what they knew. They described a very big place where many men like the beast Bob Buck roamed and reaped. Where thousands of animals were kept slavelike in their pens, serving the stomachs of their masters.

The pig listened. The pig learned.

The brothers dreamed of fleeing, of running down the same road that took them to Grandpa's farm, of racing to Chowder, where they'd tell everybody about Pearl and how he . . . how he . . .

. . . how he what?

That was the thing they couldn't wrap their minds around. That was the thing that kept them there. They *wanted* to teach the pig, to tell him about foreign countries and countrysides and how there were so many farms and so many farmers and so many people like the beast, roaming and reaping. They *believed* that ultimately they wanted to be here, *here* in the barn, here with their knees in the dirt, teaching the pig who stared at them with a tilted head, a snout that shadowed a perpetual smile. They wanted to see what was under the flap, too, under the dead skin that hid the pig's other eye, but they didn't look because they knew the pig didn't want them to look, not yet, and that was good enough to stop them.

In the bad scene, Mom was upstairs in the farmhouse sitting up in bed. And that was good enough for the brothers, too. It didn't matter that she didn't look great, and it didn't matter that she smelled like a pigpen. All that mattered was that she was there to check up on, there to see, there to talk to and to tell about the pig's daily lessons and how far he was coming along. Yes, one brother would remain with the pig as the other entered the farmhouse alone, took the stairs, and visited Mom on the bed. One brother would continue to teach the pig as the other told Mom about the teaching. Never mind that sometimes Mom wasn't in the bed at all and in her place was mud from the pigpen. It just meant that Mom was somewhere else in the house. Stretching her legs.

Yes, the brothers taught the pig about the world, and the pig listened, and the pig learned. The pig thought, too, about the farmer, his first teacher, who taught him that you could make people do things as long as you made them want to do them, as long as you made them believe they were the ones who wanted to do them.

The boys wanted to teach the pig.

The pig learned.

He learned what they taught him and he learned that the lessons of his first teacher were masterful, were *right*, were truth, not just because they felt true but because the pig had seen them carried out, had seen what power a pig might have in making the characters (satellites) do what he wanted them to do, every single thing they did, from the start, from the beginning of the story to the end, not a word of it out of the pig's reach, not a word of it unwritten by the pig, touched by his web, never out of reach, not even as far as the place where the three teens walked the halls now, not even there out of reach, as the pig saw for himself the things he could make them do, all of them do, while making them believe they had decided to do these things for themselves.

The brothers knelt in the dirt, after one or the other had returned from the house, visiting the mother; they knelt before the pig and they taught him about everything else, about the size and shape of the world.

They did it for themselves. Despite the dreams of fleeing, they did it for themselves. Despite dreaming of eating breakfast and reading the daily paper with Mom, they *wanted* to be here in the barn with the pig.

After flushing the toilet, Jeff washed his hands in the sink and tried to shake the bad scene from his mind. But it was hard to move. As if it were made of hoof. As if it were real, and all this, breakfast and the paper, the bathroom and the bathroom sink, would be much easier to shake off if Jeff had half a mind to try it.

He closed his eyes and saw, clearly, himself and Aaron kneeling in the barn. He saw pieces of a pink suit on the gravel path and tire tracks where the police had come and gone, and he heard himself and his brother teaching the pig about Murdock Road, where it led, how many more like you, farmer, and the rest of the whole wide world.

And the pig listened. The pig learned.

On this, the Day of the Pig.

ACKNOWLEDGMENTS

First off, I gotta thank all the telepathic pigs I spent time with while researching this book. From Carla on Frigg's Farm in west Michigan to Simon up north, we spent hours talking without moving our mouths. It's really quite incredible how much you learn by just ... *seeing*. I took in as many visions and emotions as I could. None of them were as ghastly as Pearl's, but the pigs I (silently, telepathically) spoke with could sense the story I was going to write, and they all seemed happy with it. One even suggested I add a scene. I'll let you guess which scene that was.

Any mistakes I made regarding the mannerisms of telepathic pigs are my own. Don't blame them.

Also: Thanks must go to my immediate family, who all reacted real well to *Pearl*, giving me more pep than usual. My brother Ryan quotes lines when we talk on the phone. (When Ryan and I talk, we do use actual sound. But maybe ... one day ...)

Thank you to Cemetery Dance for first publishing the book as a limited edition. It was called *On This, the Day of the Pig* then and it meant and means the world to me.

Paul Miller at Earthling put out an incredible limited, lettered edition, as well. Thank you, Paul!

To the Del Rey team . . . eternal gratitude for bringing *Pearl* to a wider audience.

James Henry Hall . . . let's do another 5 in 5.

Allison Laakko . . . if ducks, dogs, cats, fish, snakes, rabbits, deer, turtles, skunks, raccoons, hawks, and owls . . . why not a pig?

Kristin Nelson, Ryan Lewis, Wayne Alexander . . . I love you guys.

And to Dave Simmer, as ever and always, thank you for opening the (barn) door.

ABOUT THE AUTHOR

JOSH MALERMAN is a *New York Times* bestselling author and one of two singer-songwriters for the rock band The High Strung. His debut novel, *Bird Box*, is the inspiration for the hit Netflix film of the same name. His other novels include *Unbury Carol*, *Inspection*, *A House at the Bottom of a Lake*, and *Malorie*, the sequel to *Bird Box*. Malerman lives in Michigan with his fiancée, the artist-musician Allison Laakko.

joshmalerman.com
Facebook.com/JoshMalerman
Twitter: @JoshMalerman
Instagram: @joshmalerman

ABOUT THE TYPE

This book was set in Caslon, a typeface first designed in 1722 by William Caslon (1692–1766). Its widespread use by most English printers in the early eighteenth century soon supplanted the Dutch typefaces that had formerly prevailed. The roman is considered a "workhorse" typeface due to its pleasant, open appearance, while the italic is exceedingly decorative.